Janice Steinberg's Margo Simon mysteries:
Death of a Postmodernist
and
Death Crosses the Border:

"A DELIGHTFUL DEBUT."—*San Diego Union-Tribune*

"A PROMISING DEBUT ... There's a wealth of fascinating information here on the avant-garde art world."
—*The Purloined Letter*

"WITTY AND MOVING ... An exciting debut novel."
—*Grounds for Murder*

"THE WRITING IS STRONG and Steinberg has launched a character with a resonance all her own."—*Mostly Murder*

"WELL-RESEARCHED AND HIGHLY READABLE ... Steinberg shows us a side of Tijuana that tourists never see." —*The Purloined Letter*

"A WELCOME ADDITION to the ranks of southwestern sleuths ... a good read that deals with real and complex issues." —Judith Van Gieson,
author of *The Lies That Bind*

MORE MYSTERIES FROM THE
BERKLEY PUBLISHING GROUP . . .

CHINA BAYLES MYSTERIES: She left the big city to run an herb shop in Pecan Springs, Texas. But murder can happen anywhere . . . "A wonderful character!"—*Mostly Murder*

by Susan Wittig Albert

THYME OF DEATH	WITCHES' BANE
HANGMAN'S ROOT	ROSEMARY REMEMBERED
RUEFUL DEATH	

KATE JASPER MYSTERIES: Even in sunny California, there are cold-blooded killers . . . "This series is a treasure!"—Carolyn G. Hart

by Jacqueline Girdner

ADJUSTED TO DEATH	MURDER MOST MELLOW
THE LAST RESORT	FAT-FREE AND FATAL
TEA-TOTALLY DEAD	A STIFF CRITIQUE
MOST LIKELY TO DIE	

LIZ WAREHAM MYSTERIES: In the world of public relations, crime can be a real career-killer . . . "Readers will enjoy feisty Liz!" —*Publishers Weekly*

by Carol Brennan

HEADHUNT	FULL COMMISSION
CHILL OF SUMMER	

Also by the author
IN THE DARK

BONNIE INDERMILL MYSTERIES: Temp work can be murder, but solving crime is a full-time job . . . "One of detective fiction's most appealing protagonists!"—*Publishers Weekly*

by Carole Berry

THE DEATH OF A DIFFICULT WOMAN	GOOD NIGHT, SWEET PRINCE
THE LETTER OF THE LAW	THE DEATH OF A DANCING FOOL
THE YEAR OF THE MONKEY	

MARGO SIMON MYSTERIES: She's a reporter for San Diego's public radio station. But her penchant for crime solving means she has to dig up the most private of secrets . . .

by Janice Steinberg

DEATH OF A POSTMODERNIST	DEATH CROSSES THE BORDER
DEATH-FIRES DANCE	

Death-Fires Dance

Janice Steinberg

BERKLEY PRIME CRIME, NEW YORK

DEATH-FIRES DANCE

A Berkley Prime Crime Book / published by arrangement with the author

PRINTING HISTORY
Berkley Prime Crime edition / November 1996

The Putnam Berkley World Wide Web site address is
http://www.berkley.com

ISBN: 0-425-15551-X

Berkley Prime Crime Books are published
by The Berkley Publishing Group,
200 Madison Avenue, New York, NY 10016.
The name BERKLEY PRIME CRIME and the BERKLEY PRIME CRIME
design are trademarks belonging to Berkley Publishing Corporation.

PRINTED IN THE UNITED STATES OF AMERICA

10 9 8 7 6 5 4 3 2 1

Dedication

For my mother, Harriet Steinberg, who introduced me to
Nancy Drew and led me into a life of crime

Acknowledgments

For generously sharing their professional expertise, I wish to thank Dave Cohen of the San Diego Police Department, forensic anthropologist Dr. Rodger Heglar, State of California Fire Captain Gary Eidsmoe, Jody Hammond of KFMB-TV, and Dr. John Eisele of the San Diego County Medical Examiner's office.

Thanks to Barb Sherman for giving Margo a Tarot reading that was uncannily on target; Blaize Mekinna; Dr. Michael Yapko; and Anne Herbert, who rarely receives the credit she deserves for creating the statement, "Practice random kindness and senseless acts of beauty."

Many thanks for their literary assistance to Teresa Chris, Karen Thomas, Kathi George, and the members of my writing group: Ann Elwood, Janet Kunert, Martha Lawrence, Mary Lou Locke, Abigail Padgett, and Lillian Roberts.

Thanks beyond number to Jack Cassidy.

About, about, in reel and rout
The death-fires danced at night.

Samuel Coleridge,
The Rime of the Ancient Mariner

Death-Fires
Dance

Prologue / Mama Said

Under a sky blindingly clear and cerulean from the hot, desert-born Santa Ana wind, Paula Chopin pulled over her Ford Taurus and parked on the residential street.

Camouflage jacket first. Awkwardly, crowded by the steering wheel, Paula wriggled out of her rose silk blazer. She reached for the grocery bag on the backseat, took out the Army surplus jacket, put it on. Next she pulled the red bandanna from the bag and draped it around her neck. Frowning—and cursing Donniger aloud—she jammed the hated green metal combat helmet over her natural helmet of black, Louise Brooks–bobbed hair.

She punched the start button on her timer, which was preset for three minutes. And looked around.

Though modest, all of the houses on this side of the street had canyon views, San Diego's many canyons playing no socioeconomic favorites. They sliced impersonally through wealthy La Jolla as well as this mixed-race, working-class neighborhood near primarily black Southeast San Diego. Through the gaps between houses, Paula glimpsed the usual chaparral vegetation: brittle grasses and brush, all bone-dry at summer's end. She saw no one around—anybody who was at home must be sheltering inside from the merciless mid-afternoon sun. The heat in the air was almost visible, radiating from the baked earth.

She had stopped the car but turned the motor back on for the air-conditioning. Environmentally irresponsible, yes, but it was brutally hot and the combat gear, as well as her nervousness, made her hotter. She checked the timer. Jesus, only thirty seconds had passed. She plucked her "toy," a sheathed knife, from the grocery bag, and occupied ten seconds watching the needle in the compass built into the knife handle. Paula liked the compass and rather liked the knife as well, with its wicked serrated edge. Not so the army canteen she'd bought, in which even the freshest water tasted like fifteen-year-old plastic. She'd tossed the canteen in the trash and stuck to a reused Evian bottle, from which she took a short drink . . . stopping as soon as she realized the water had gotten hot enough to brew tea.

Two minutes left.

Paula didn't know the name of this canyon, rarely came to this part of town. But she had finished early with her accounting client and had twenty minutes to spare. And she was religiously following the new regime; well, almost religiously, she thought, switching on the radio. Donniger had instructed her not to listen to the radio, not to read—to do nothing except sit. But the compass in the knife handle had limited entertainment value. The first radio station Paula turned on was broadcasting news, and she swiftly found another, playing sixties rock. She had sufficient anxiety in her life, thank you, without letting in the misery of the world. No newspapers nor radio or television news penetrated her consciousness if she could avoid it. Donniger intended to work on that with her eventually. Fine. For now, impersonating Rambo was enough.

"Mama said there'd be days like this," came from the radio. Paula thought of what her mother had said about the Rambo exercise: "Aren't you afraid someone will report you to the police if they see you sitting by the side of the road dressed like that?"

"No, Mom," she'd sighed. Thinking, *No wonder the daughter of this woman has an exaggerated fear of what people, even total strangers, will think of her. No wonder I've had panic attacks and agoraphobia for five years and haven't been able to drive a mile on the freeway without feeling like I'm going to pass out.* Her mother was the only person who had reacted with anything but curiosity and/or amusement to her psychologist's latest "assignment." *Thanks, Mom.*

She was supposed to drive five miles, pulling over every half-mile to put on the Rambo costume and sit for three minutes. Pattern interruption, Donniger called the technique. The idea was that instead of continuing to drive, getting more and more panicky, Paula had to stop and do something else, preferably something absurd. Donniger had a gift for the absurd. He also had a gift for breaking through the fear that Paula had built up during the past five years. In fact, this was the first time she'd gone alone to this afternoon's client, a teen drug diversion project; always before, she had taken along her bookkeeper . . . or more often, just sent the bookkeeper, since not only driving to the project but being in the unfamiliar office triggered her anxiety. After a month of therapy with Donniger, however, she'd felt ready to solo. And she'd done just fine, even driving two miles on the freeway!

"There'd be days like this, my mama said."

The infuriating thing was, she *did* experience the fear her mother had mentioned, the worry about "what people will think." Even going to the army surplus store to buy the outfit, she had felt compelled to say she was getting it for a dance performance, as if the opinion of the man at the checkout counter mattered. And sure enough, when she did the assignment, she often imagined someone alerting the police to this bizarrely attired woman sitting in her car. Then she'd have to try explaining that she wasn't about to go berserk and start slashing anyone with the knife; she was just doing an exercise prescribed by her psychologist. *That* ought to convince any cop that Paula Chopin was a solid citizen, a highly competent certified public accountant who upheld the tax codes as well as the rest of the laws of the United States of America and the State of California.

God, she was jittery today. She actually did feel as if someone were watching her. A full minute to go! Sweat trickled down her face. Under the oppressive metal helmet, her hair felt soaked. She turned up the air-conditioning. The Santa Ana was probably getting to her, it was supposed to do something weird to the ions in the air. Or maybe she was so jumpy because she'd missed her weekly massage two days ago. Leslie, her massage therapist, simply hadn't been there; hadn't even stuck up a note or responded to the two phone messages Paula had left since then.

Oh, no. She really did see a figure in her side mirror, pressed against the side of a canyon house. What was he— or she?—doing if not staring at Paula? *So what?* she chided herself. *It's not against the law to sit in your car dressed like Rambo* . . . unless the knife constituted a concealed weapon? She glanced back. The watcher hadn't moved.

Tough shit, Dr. Donniger. With thirty seconds left on her timer—and too upset to notice the plume of smoke rising above the canyon—Paula put the car in gear and stepped hard on the gas. Her heart was pounding and she felt lightheaded, symptoms of an advanced panic attack. She ripped off the helmet while she drove, but didn't pause to remove the stifling camouflage jacket (or turn off the timer, now insistently beeping) until she was a mile away.

Cursing and crying, she gutted through a drive back to her office—on surface streets exclusively, no freeway—that seemed to last an hour and surely undid several hundred dollars worth of therapy. She turned off the radio the second the deejay announced a "news flash," so she didn't hear that several teams of firefighters were rushing to Southeast San Diego, to the site of what threatened to be a major canyon fire.

1 / A Terrible Beauty

Every house on the block was in flames, and how the hell had Margo Simon ended up in this place completely alone?

"What's the temperature here?" she had called a few minutes ago, running up to a firefighter and aiming her cellular phone at his mouth.

"About a hundred and twenty," he'd replied, and Margo continued her live radio broadcast:

"There's no point, they say, in trying to save houses on blocks that are already burning. All they can do is water down the blocks that haven't caught fire yet."

"Thanks, Margo. We'll check back with you later," came the voice of Claire De Jong, the news director, who was anchoring the fire coverage. Disconnecting the phone, Margo monitored the station's broadcast over the portable radio she carried in her pocket, its plug in her ear. "That was Margo Simon, reporting live from the Encanto Hills fire for KSDR, San Diego Public Radio," she heard Claire say. Claire went on to recap that the fire had been spotted in a canyon six hours ago, at three p.m., and it had already destroyed at least thirty homes.

Margo had looked up then—and realized she was alone. Only moments before, the firefighters hadn't yet abandoned this block. Half a dozen residents remained, madly throwing things into their cars. A television crew was broadcasting, too. Suddenly, they had all vanished.

Damn, she'd better get out of here. The burning houses couldn't harm her, nor the blizzard of ash, but wind-whipped sparks flew everywhere. Although she had tied back her shoulder-length brown hair, Margo kept rubbing her hands over it, fearful that sparks would land there.

In spite of the danger, she paused, entranced by the beauty of the flames leaping against the night sky. She understood briefly what the arsonist might feel, the sense of power at having created this glorious disaster . . . if this *was* arson and not just a tragic accident, the result of a transient's unbanked campfire or a carelessly tossed cigarette. Investigators were already checking the fire's source point, where the blaze had consumed everything living hours ago. But they refused to offer even a hunch as to how the fire had started until they had gone over the scene in the light of day.

A flaming tree branch smacked into the road in front of her. She started walking fast, skirting the branch and glancing upward, on the lookout for more . . . and struck by the realization that, less than a year ago, she would have been terrified. What she felt now wasn't fear but excitement. During the past six months, she had been involved in two murder investigations and survived an attempt on her own life. She didn't know what had changed inside her, or whether the change was good, bad, or simply neutral. She only knew that for a moment, walking down the fire-reddened street, she was deeply aware that a change had occurred, as if she'd looked at her hand and discovered an extra finger.

Her cellular phone trilled and she pressed the Talk button. "Yeah?"

"You okay?" Kevin, KSDR's chief engineer, was coordinating the on-site and studio broadcasts. He continued without giving her a chance to answer, "Have you got anything to go on the air with?"

"Sure."

Margo heard Claire introduce her. Still walking quickly, she described the hellish but hypnotic scene.

"Margo, what's that noise I'm hearing?" said Claire. "The hissing?"

"Downed power lines."

"Sounds like you should get out of there."

Margo heartily agreed. Because of the hot day, she had worn sandals to work and she was starting to feel as if the pavement had burned through them and was searing the soles of her feet. She checked—the sandals were in one piece but they'd turned black on the bottom. She walked faster.

Reaching the end of the deserted street, she rejoined "civilization"—the clamor and intensity of the fire crews at work and residents frantically trying to drive out past the fire and the emergency vehicles. Many people had abandoned their cars and were proceeding on foot, refugees clutching children, suitcases, and assorted electronic equipment. One woman lugged a computer. Two teenagers stumbled under the weight of a wide-screen television. A man was trying to force his way back uphill, sobbing. A policewoman firmly turned him away, into the waiting cellular telephone of Howard Biele, Margo's colleague.

After Howard interviewed him, the man remained by the police blockade, pacing and crying.

"Hey, Margo." Howard's lean face was smudged and his dark hair whitened with ash. Margo figured she looked much the same. "Can you believe it?" Howard whispered. "The fool was going to go back for his cat."

"You don't have any pets," Margo responded, thinking of

a particular feline named Grimalkin. "Have you gotten an update from the PR people?" The fire department had set up a media information center down the hill.

"Twenty minutes ago."

"Any fatalities?"

"Thank God, not this time," said Howard.

He was clearly thinking of the same thing that had crossed Margo's mind. Four days earlier, a woman's body was found at another canyon fire, in San Diego's back country. A Jane Doe, probably a transient and possibly a prostitute since, according to the county medical examiner, the woman had had sex the night she died—a fact that could be established because even when the outside of a body is totally charred, the internal organs are often quite intact, the M.E. had explained. On a blanket, scraps of which survived beneath the woman's body, lay a brandy bottle. That was the one incongruity in Jane Doe's death—it was expensive brandy for a transient, Courvoisier. But no one had reported a connoisseur of fine spirits missing. And why would such a woman be sleeping in a canyon? So Jane Doe she remained. Her john had probably left as soon as the sexual part of their transaction ended and, according to the M.E., the woman had simply passed from sleep into death from smoke inhalation. There was no sign she had tried to escape, nor any conclusive evidence of how the fire had started. A charred abalone shell found near her body might have served as an ashtray, so maybe she had caused the fire herself, smoking a joint or a cigarette.

"Did you hear about the man who saved his house by cutting down every tree in his yard?" Howard said.

"Smart move. Why don't I check with the command people again," Margo suggested, "and you keep covering this area?"

"Sure."

She joined the downhill stream of refugees. The pavement

here couldn't be more than a hundred degrees, but she'd still love to plunge her feet, sandals and all, into a tub of ice water. Noticing two young Hispanic men carrying an elderly Asian woman, she walked alongside them and had Kevin put her on the air. The woman moaned about having lived in her house for forty years and not having enough insurance to rebuild. Next Margo interviewed a young couple, distraught because they'd loaded their car with jewelry, photographs, everything of value to them, and then couldn't find the car keys. The woman was clutching a photo album and a stuffed bear.

After ten minutes of slowly walking and collecting stories, Margo reached the command center, located in a trailer at the bottom of the hill (and, unless things got really bad, out of range of the fire). She phoned KSDR, went on air, and relayed the totals chalked on a board: forty-two houses burned, with the damage estimated at six to eight million dollars.

"Can you predict when it's going to be contained?" she asked Ernie Velez, the fire department spokesman.

"Nope. The winds are shifting too much. Every time one area dies down, another starts. Hang on a minute."

"Back to you, Claire," said Margo, watching Ernie pick up a crackling headset. "But Kev, don't hang up."

"Are you sure?" Margo heard Ernie say. "Oh shit."

"Get ready to put me back on," said Margo into the phone. Other reporters were gathering as Ernie jotted down notes. "Now," she said, seeing Ernie put down the headset. She moved in close with the phone.

"I just heard from the investigative team." Ernie appeared to grit his teeth. "A body's been found, close to the source point on Chaumont Drive."

"Could it be the person who set the fire?" said Margo.

"We don't know. And to keep the record straight, we don't know if this fire was arson."

"Is it a woman?" asked another reporter, obviously thinking of the Jane Doe.

"The body's unidentifiable at this time. That's all for now."

No one pushed Ernie to state the obvious, that this particular body couldn't be identified because it was charred beyond recognition: no facial features left, no fingerprints, probably not even any fingers.

Margo signed off, debating whether to go back to the area where the fire continued to rage or join the inevitable media throng at the site where the body had been discovered. The site would be cordoned off and she doubted there'd be anything to report until tomorrow at the earliest, after the medical examiners had done their work. And, unlike the well-staffed television stations and the big daily newspaper, KSDR had only herself and Howard on site. Better to return up the hill. She moved to leave the trailer, but found the doorway blocked by a lanky young black woman fighting to get inside.

"Authorized personnel only," insisted a department official several times, but the woman screamed over him:

"My grandmother's missing!"

"Let her in," intervened Ernie Velez and took the woman into a corner. Margo remained nearby. She had registered the terror in the woman's voice . . . that and the fact that the young woman, her long hair in cornrow braids, looked familiar.

"Did your grandmother's house burn down?" said Ernie gently.

"No!"

"Well, she's probably with friends or other relatives."

She grabbed Ernie's arm. "You don't understand. She gathers herbs, she's a healer. She goes walking in that canyon all the time."

"You're talking about Hannah," said Margo. The young

woman turned toward her. "I met you when I interviewed her for the radio." Margo pictured the tiny, eighty-year-old herbalist; dressed in a dashiki and gold Reeboks, Hannah had led her through the canyon, pointing out medicinal herbs. What was the name of the granddaughter, who had towered over Hannah . . . and projected the same intelligence? "Olivia, right?"

The young woman nodded. "I heard they found a body."

"Olivia," said Ernie, "they don't even know if it's a man or a woman. I'm sure it's not your grandma."

"I want to go there. Where the body is."

"The area will be roped off. You won't be able to see anything. Why don't you go home and wait? I bet you'll hear from your grandma any minute."

"No, dammit!" She was weeping.

"Look, Ernie," said Margo. "Why don't I go there with her?"

Margo's heart went out to Olivia—her heart and her gut feeling that the young woman was right about her grandmother. When Margo had interviewed Hannah last spring, the herbalist had taken her to the exact area where the fire had started.

2 / Vigil For a Corpse

Margo opened the passenger door of her silver Mazda Miata for Olivia, then grabbed a rag and dusted the ash off the windows.

"Don't do that! You'll scratch the paint!" exclaimed a passing man, apparently distracted from his own woes (he was carrying a suitcase and a toddler) when she started to brush the rag over the rest of the car.

Margo sighed. The Miata was one of the recent changes that had taken place in her life; she'd bought it, used, after someone sabotaged her car. And although she loved driving with the top down, she hadn't really aligned her self-image with being the owner of a sportscar.

Desisting from ruining her paint job, she stayed outside the car and called Kevin to tell him her plans. He transferred her to Claire, who was taking a breather from anchoring while KSDR aired the national news.

"We could use you at the station to put together the story for NPR tomorrow," said Claire. "But do you think you're onto something?"

Glancing at Olivia, in the car, Margo said softly, "I've got a feeling about this one."

"Then go for it."

Margo's friendship with Claire was another—a welcome—change, she reflected, as she got in and started the Miata. She'd initially seen Claire, a relative newcomer to KSDR, as not only a former colleague of the abrasive new station manager but his ally. This past summer, she'd discovered that Claire was very much her own woman . . . and a woman she liked and respected, feelings that Claire reciprocated.

For the first several blocks, Margo had to cope with the congestion of cars, foot traffic, and gawkers. Once she turned up the street toward where the fire had started, however, the only signs of life were the flickering lights of televisions in houses that had escaped harm—not, Margo understood, because of any special effort on the part of the firefighters or homeowners, but through sheer luck. The wind had shifted and one house would be untouched, while the next three were piles of rubble.

On the street at the top the hill, however, not a single house had been spared. Empty husks stinking of burned plastic, they still steamed from the firefighters' efforts to extinguish any sparks that could jump downhill. Finding the death site was no problem. Television as well as police spotlights illuminated the yellow tape at the top of the hill that cordoned off the scene.

Margo and Olivia got out of the car and stood on the edge of the canyon.

"Can you see anything?" asked Olivia in a small voice, and Margo realized how young she was—probably just a teenager.

"No." Margo doubted the TV crews were having much luck, either. Though their spotlights roamed down the hillside, she'd bet even the most sophisticated telephoto lens couldn't pick out a blackened body from among the blackened remnants of chaparral and the utterly black earth.

Strangely, no investigative activity was taking place. Four uniformed police officers stood at the top of the hill, but they were doing nothing except restraining the reporters. The hillside was empty.

Margo approached one of the officers and asked the obvious. "Is this where the body was found?"

"Yes, ma'am."

"Is the body still there?"

He nodded.

"Why isn't someone down there investigating?"

"Not our job."

"Whose job is it?"

He didn't answer. He didn't need to. Several nondescript cars pulled up and Margo recognized a man stepping from one of them—Donny Obayashi, a lieutenant with the San Diego Police Department. A homicide lieutenant.

She had broken her cellular connection with the station, but she hit Redial, got Kevin quickly, and dashed to Obayashi, beating her TV colleagues who were still scanning the hillside below.

"Lieutenant," she said, "is this death being considered a murder?"

She hadn't realized that Olivia had followed her. The girl let out a wail that drew the television reporters like sharks to a bleeding sea lion.

"Hey!" Obayashi held up a hand in a stop gesture. "We always come out for a death like this, it's routine."

"Was there anything to indicate foul play?" asked another reporter.

"Like I said, this is routine."

Obayashi turned away and the reporters left him alone. They had found a juicier story anyway: Olivia sitting on the ground, keening. The cameras zoomed in on her and Olivia shook her head, sending her long cornrows swinging. Her sobs quieted enough that she was able to speak; in fact, she spoke quite articulately. She announced that her grandmother, Hannah Jones, was missing, that Hannah was a respected healer who often collected herbs in this canyon, and that her family expected the city to put as much effort into investigating the death of an elderly woman of color as they would into investigating a white person's death. Margo revised her estimate of Olivia's age upwards. Hannah's granddaughter was at least twenty, and disconcertingly media-savvy.

"What makes you so certain that the body is your grandmother?" Margo asked her, once the television stations had captured their fifteen seconds and focused back on the charred hillside, where a yellow-garbed fire official was leading Obayashi and his team to a spot some thirty yards down. "Did she tell you she was going into the canyon this afternoon?"

"She didn't call me or anything like that." Media-savvy or not, Olivia was shaking. Margo put a hand on her shoulder. Olivia was silent for a moment, then said, "You interviewed her, so maybe you'll understand. I remember she said you seemed more open to her ideas than other reporters who talked to her."

Nothing like eight years spent in Santa Fe as a potter to make a person open to unconventional ideas. Margo said, "I liked your grandmother. I thought she had a lot of wisdom. May I tape you?" She indicated the recorder she was carrying over her shoulder.

"Not this. I'm going to UCSD, premed. Someday I'm going to combine my grandmother's knowledge with modern medicine. But right now, I don't want to do anything that would make my professors think I was some kind of flake."

"Okay, no tape. But tell me?"

"My grandma had . . . my psych professor would call it ESP, extrasensory perception. I don't know what I'd call it, but Grandma could communicate through her mind. Especially with me, from the time I was a little girl. That's why she chose me to train, to pass on her knowledge of herbs. She . . . she reached out to me today. It must have been about the time the fire started.'' Olivia's face, in the shadow of the television lights, was drawn in pain.

"I was in the middle of class, organic chemistry,'' she continued. "It's a tough class and I kind of mentally said, 'Not now, Gram.' Later, I heard about the fire. I tried to reach her with *my* mind then but I couldn't. I drove straight to her house. She wasn't home and no one in my family had heard from her.''

A woman was approaching them. Solidly built, she ascended the steep hill as if she spent two hours on a Stairmaster every day without breaking a sweat. The woman ducked nimbly under the police tape, introduced herself as Detective Gail Sands, and asked why Olivia believed the body in the canyon was that of her grandmother. Olivia gave the nonmetaphysical answer: that Hannah frequently came here for herbs and that her nearby house, although untouched by fire, stood empty. Why wasn't she home hosing down her roof and watching the fire news, just like her neighbors?

"Tell me what she looks like,'' said the detective.

Margo took a deep, ash-laden breath. Had the detectives arrived at some idea about the identity of the corpse, through general size or some features that hadn't burned away?

"An old woman of color.''

" 'Woman of color.' Does that mean black?'' said Sands, who was black herself.

Olivia nodded. "She's eighty years old, not even five feet tall, skinny. Can I see?'' She started toward the police tape. "I'm sure if I saw her, I'd know.''

Gail Sands grabbed her arm. "You wouldn't be able to tell anything. This person was badly burned. I'll tell you what you can do to help. Call me right away if you find out she's all right—probably she was just out shopping or visiting a friend, you know?'' Sands handed her a card. ''Like I said, I'm sure your grandmother's all right. But if she hasn't turned up by tomorrow, then let us know what dentist she went to.''

''Her dentist? I don't know, I think she went to Tijuana and saw someone there. It's cheaper. Why do you have to know who her dentist was?''

The detective said gently, ''Sometimes it's the only way to make a positive identification, through dental records. Thing is, you aren't doing your grandmother a bit of good sitting here. It'll take us another two or three hours to go over the scene, and even then, we won't be able to tell you anything. Until the medical examiner's had a look, we won't even know if this person is a male or female. Hon, go home. Your grandma's probably home herself now, and worried sick about you.'' Detective Sands turned and scrambled back down the slope.

Margo said, ''You want me to take you back to your car?''

''I can't. I have to stay here, her spirit's here. But you go ahead and leave.''

''At least call your mother and see if she's heard anything.''

Margo handed Olivia the cellular phone. But there was no word from Hannah. Next Margo called her own home. Her husband, Barry Dawes, was out of town at an oceanography conference and her stepkids, to her pleasure, had elected to stay with her even in their dad's absence. At fifteen and just-turned-twelve years of age, they were doing fine on their own; at least they were proceeding normally. Twelve-year-old David intimated that Margo was going to hear some news she wouldn't like when she got home, but it didn't sound urgent.

She could have left, since Olivia's attention clearly dwelt with her grandmother; Margo's few attempts at conversation went nowhere. And away from the fire, the night was chilly—the Santa Ana, a desert wind, brought the desert's cool nights as well as its scorching days. But just as Olivia couldn't abandon the body that might be Hannah's, Margo felt compelled to share her vigil. She stayed by Olivia's side until, shortly after midnight, the fire victim, shrouded in a plastic body bag, was carried up the hill on a stretcher and placed in a medical examiner's van. Two men conveyed the stretcher up the steep hill without even panting. Either the men were very strong or the victim was very light.

3 / We Are Family

Margo dropped Olivia at her car, then stopped by the fire department command center for the latest update. Sixty-four houses were now gone, but the fire crews were finally getting the upper hand. They expected to have the blaze contained within a few hours. She phoned in the news to KSDR . . . and sighed with relief to learn that they didn't need her to come in and finish producing the story. The adrenaline rush of covering the fire was abating, to be replaced by bone-deep weariness. At one a.m., she wanted nothing more than to go home.

Having witnessed the fire's devastation and the terror of people separated from their families, Margo felt a wave of tenderness as she drove up to her dark house with its sleeping children. Tenderness and gratitude, since her house, too, overlooked one of San Diego's canyons.

The house, although rented, had been her and Barry's home for the past five years; the only home they'd ever shared. A typical California Craftsman with wood paneling and cabinets, the house had a cozy feeling, as did the furniture Margo and Barry had assembled from garage sales and occasional splurges at "real" furniture stores.

As for the children . . . Despite all the hype about women's innate maternal drive, Margo at thirty-eight hadn't yet heard her personal biological clock ticking with any urgency. Still, she never—well, extremely rarely—regretted that Barry's two kids had tumbled into her life. Jenny embodied all of the contradictory yearnings for, yet fears of, independence that Margo hadn't entirely forgotten from her own teenage years; and she displayed a keen intelligence. The same intelligence sparkled in David, along with a passion for nature.

Margo entered the house quietly, greeted by a brush against her legs—Grimalkin, the cat. She would just go peek at Jenny and David, then take a long shower to try to cleanse herself of the stench of smoke.

"Margo?" came a voice when she looked into Jenny's room.

"Sorry, Jen. I didn't mean to wake you. Go back to sleep."

"I was up. Phew, you reek."

"I know."

"Was it awful?" said Jenny.

"Pretty bad. Thanks for asking." It occurred to Margo that Jenny hadn't used to inquire how her stepmom's day had gone. Of course, she had gotten a close look at a story Margo was doing the previous spring—a look far too close and too dangerous.

"Margo, can I talk to you about something?"

Not now, cried out Margo's weary body. But Jenny sounded as if this were one of those important stepdaughter/stepmom talks. Margo had a hunch that, since she'd met Jenny when the girl was on the verge of adolescence, she fairly easily accepted Jenny as a young woman; whereas neither Barry nor Jenny's mother, Rae, could look at their fifteen-year-old daughter without also seeing her as a baby and a young child.

Margo said, "Just let me just get out of these clothes. And

I've got to take out my contacts, my eyes are killing me.'' In a few minutes, she had changed to a robe, pried her contact lenses from her dry eyes, and dropped her smoky clothes outside on the patio. She returned to sit on the edge of Jenny's bed. ''What's up?''

''You know when I wanted to get my ears pierced the second time and Dad and Mom didn't like it, but you stood up for me?''

''Hmm.'' Actually, Jenny had somewhat exceeded the agreement they had negotiated, adding the permitted second hole in one ear but going for a grand total of three in the other and creating several weeks of friction between Margo and Rae. Sitting in the dark with Jenny, Margo grimaced. This must be the issue David had warned her about.

''Well, all I want to do,'' said Jenny, ''is get a tiny hole in my nose, not right through the middle or anything gross like that, just a tiny, tiny hole in one nostril. All I'd wear in it would be a very tasteful stud or maybe a small, thin gold hoop.''

That's barbaric, Margo thought, but recalled that that was precisely her own parents' reaction when she had come home from a slumber party with pierced ears. And *that* really had been barbaric, a painful ritual involving ice cubes, sewing needles, and bouts of nausea on the part of both piercers and piercees.

''Have you asked your mom about it?'' The stepmother's constant refrain.

''Not after the way she reacted last time. I thought I'd talk to you first. A lot of kids at school have pierced noses, you know.''

''Yeah, like Nick Costas.'' David was standing in the bedroom door. At twelve, his numerous endearing qualities were accompanied by a strain of self-righteousness that all four of his parents—step-and natural—mutually prayed he would outgrow.

"What's wrong with Nick Costas?" challenged Jenny.

Margo listened anxiously. This was the first time she had heard Nick Costas mentioned. Jenny went to school in University City, where her mother lived, and Margo didn't generally concern herself with Jenny's friends. But was she serious about this Costas boy? Oh, no, thought Margo, she *was* turning into her parents.

"David, back to bed," she said. She heard his feet padding a few steps down the hall. "Now!" This time he complied.

She turned to Jenny. "Personal opinion? Nose rings make me a little queasy. And if you decide later you don't want it, what kind of mark will it leave?"

"No mark at all." Jenny spoke with the kind of decisiveness that made Margo certain she hadn't considered the issue for even a moment. "The people who do it are really experts, just like the people who pierce ears."

Margo stifled a yawn. She was in no shape to deliver the kind of wisdom this situation required. "It's right in the middle of your face, not like your ears where your hair could cover it."

"It's my body!"

"That's true. The main thing is, you've got to talk this over with your dad and, especially, your mom."

"But you *do* think I have a right to do it?"

"Jen, I don't know. Go back to sleep."

"Promise you'll think about it?"

"Okay." Occasional fights with Rae were worth the trouble, but Margo had to choose the battles carefully. And hell, she didn't know if she'd support nose piercing. What would come next, a nipple ring?

Too tired to shower, she fell into bed, acutely aware of Barry's absence. After everything she had seen, how she wanted to be hugged! She slept fitfully, dreaming again and again of fire.

Margo awoke late and had to settle for a two-minute shower—while David hosed the ashes off the car—before she rushed the kids to school. She'd just made it to KSDR when a fax from the fire department arrived, announcing a news conference in forty-five minutes at the site of the now-dead fire.

"I'll cover the conference," said Claire.

"Do I look that bad?" said Margo, in response to the look of sympathy on Claire's face.

Claire said nothing, but Margo had her answer when she glanced in a mirror. She had left home with dripping hair, and the Santa Ana–dry air had transformed it into a tangled bush around her pale, sleep-starved face. Thank goodness she didn't do television.

She called Hannah Jones's number and felt a thrill of relief when someone picked up the phone. But it was Olivia, staying at her grandmother's house to prevent looting.

"Do you know anything?" Olivia implored.

"I'm sorry, no." The best Margo could do was tell Olivia to listen to the news conference.

Heart heavy, Margo located the reel-to-reel tape of the interview she'd done with Hannah last spring and made notes on what to use in an obituary, in case the body found in the canyon was that of the herbalist.

That possibility, that the woman was Hannah, appeared more and more likely, according to the news conference that Margo listened to. The medical examiner had made no individual identification of the victim nor would he for several days, pending a complete forensic exam. However, he had determined the victim's sex and approximate age: female, over seventy. The bad news didn't end there. The cause of the Encanto Hills fire was attributed to arson, and the elderly woman's death considered a homicide.

"Why homicide?" Margo heard a reporter call out. "Is there evidence of foul play?"

"Any death that appears to occur as the result of arson is treated as a homicide," said another voice, which Claire, reporting on site, identified as that of Lieutenant Donald Obayashi.

Another reporter asked if the victim was Hannah. But the authorities had said all they intended.

Feeling ghoulish—Margo would always, she hoped, lack the go-for-the-jugular instinct that distinguished born reporters—she phoned a weeping Olivia and arranged to meet her at Hannah's that afternoon.

"Walk through the orange trees in the front yard into Hannah Jones's house," Margo had introduced her earlier story, *"and it's like entering any tidy California bungalow. Except for the smell. Underlying the odor of furniture polish in the living room, you sniff something musky, earthy. It's not an unpleasant smell; in fact, it's inviting, and leads you into the next room, where dozens of Mason jars contain dried herbs."*

The interior of Hannah's house looked little changed in its owner's absence—still immaculate, the brown sofa flanked by a wicker rocking chair and the more modern version of comfort, a Barcalounger. Even the scent of herbs hadn't been entirely overpowered by the smell of the fire. The one obvious difference was the pile of textbooks scattered over the coffee table. Margo glimpsed a biology text and a tome on organic chemistry, as well as a pile of wadded, damp tissues.

"I've been trying to study," said Olivia, her face blotchy. "But I can't concentrate on anything." She sat on the couch and Margo took the rocking chair.

"Still no word from your grandmother?"

"I told you last night, she was in the canyon when the fire

started. Her spirit called out to me. But I thought she'd just gone into the canyon and gotten trapped there. I can't believe anyone would've killed her.''

''Wait a second,'' remonstrated Margo and repeated what Obayashi had said in the news conference. ''Any death that results from arson is considered a homicide.''

Olivia buried her face in her hands. Long-fingered, she wore three rings—an agate, a thick band of jade, and a snakelike silver design. Hannah had been a ring wearer, too. In fact, Margo remembered seeing the snakelike silver ring on the missing woman's hand.

Margo continued, speaking soothingly. ''The arsonist probably didn't know your grandmother was there. It was just bad luck that she was in the canyon.''

Olivia looked up. ''He knew.'' She hesitated, then said, ''I can't tell you how I found this out and you can't use it on the radio—not unless it looks like the police are dropping the investigation. Okay?''

''I won't use it unless I hear it from another source.'' Nor would she broadcast it just because Olivia later decided she wanted the information publicized, Margo added to herself.

''My grandmother was killed before the fire started.''

Margo planted her foot on the floor to stop the rocking chair. ''How do you know that? And how do you know for sure it's your grandmother? Did someone tell you?''

''Like I said, her spirit contacted me.''

''Olivia, is that how you know she was killed? Because her spirit told you?''

The young woman stood up and paced across the room, her back to Margo. ''You don't believe it, do you? That her spirit communicated with me?''

''I don't know,'' she said truthfully.

''Well, that's not how I know she was killed.''

''Then give me something concrete. Whatever I may think

of telepathy, I can hardly go on the air citing a dead woman's spirit as my source.''

Olivia came back, sat down. "Okay. You can't tell anyone, he'd lose his job. My boyfriend, Jamal, is a premed student, too. He has a job in the medical examiner's office. He won't give me any details unless the person is actually identified as my grandmother, but he's the one who told me.''

"He told you the woman died before the fire started? That someone killed her?''

"Yes.''

Over the years, Margo had talked to plenty of people whose hold on reality seemed tenuous at best. Olivia possessed none of their qualities. The young woman spoke calmly, her gaze steady.

"Your grandmother was a strong personality." Margo heard herself using the past tense and realized it felt right. "Was there anyone who intensely disliked her? An old boy-friend?'' During their interview last spring, Hannah had made some hearty comments about sex that had enlivened the story.

Olivia shook her head, smiled. "Her latest boyfriend was sixty-five years old. We teased her about robbing the cradle, going with a man fifteen years younger.''

"What about the neighbors?''

"There were no feuds, nothing like that.''

"They must have known she went into the canyon for herbs. What did they think of her healing?''

"What did they *think* of it? They came to her when they got sick.''

"All of them?''

"You mean, did somebody think she was a witch? Maybe in your neighborhood, where everyone has health insurance, they'd say that. Around here, people thought my grandma was a saint.''

4 / Paula Braves the Blue Cube

Paula had heard the downtown headquarters of the San Diego Police Department referred to as the Blue Cube. The name fit, she thought, sitting in her car parked on E Street, facing the southwest side of the seven-story building. The setting sun highlighted the blocky structure with its alternating stripes of bright blue stucco, dirty white stucco, and the smoky gray of the windows. What would you call that shade of blue, anyway? Peacock? Azure? The place looked like a failed Mondrian, with neither the sleek authority of modern architecture nor the whimsy of the postmodern buildings that had been springing up in the city lately. A dirty haze beyond the Cube served as a reminder of the big fire that had taken place two days ago—that was one piece of news even Paula hadn't been able to shut out, although she had stopped people before they revealed any of the gory details.

Teal? Turquoise?

Concentrating on trying to find a name for the blue diverted her for a moment from her purpose in coming here, allowed her to breathe a little more deeply and to feel her heart beating less wildly in her chest.

Why was she putting herself through this, anyway? She could just telephone rather than going herself. A police officer had told her that, when she'd phoned that morning and first tried to report Leslie, her massage therapist, missing. He'd said she could give him all the relevant information over the phone. Why not? It was so tempting to leave now, not to walk inside that forbidding building. And how could she walk, when her legs had turned to jelly? When she felt as if someone were watching her? She looked around, saw nothing, shook her head. The agoraphobic's constant bugaboo, the sense of being on display. Her mother's *Aren't you afraid someone will report you to the police?* Well, here she was, going to the police herself.

The point is, Paula argued with herself, she was sure she'd be taken more seriously if she told them about Leslie in person. She tried to shut out the frightening images that sprang into her mind, her own private horror movie: picturing herself talking to someone in the ugly building and feeling as if the floor were about to open up and swallow her—every cell of her body screaming, *Escape! Escape!* Fight-or-flight, it's programmed into everyone, except in agoraphobics the impulse occurs willy-nilly, when there's no modern equivalent of the tiger lurking in the bushes. All it takes is the high stimuli of bright lights, people, products, and noise in a grocery store, for instance, or the trapped situation of giving information to a police officer. At her absolute worst, Paula had been unable to force herself to walk to the corner to mail a letter. But that, she reminded herself, was several years ago. *Come on, you can gut through this, you've gutted through worse.* She reached for the door handle, but still paused . . .

The officer on the phone had said a woman in her midforties typically doesn't ''disappear,'' she goes off by choice.

Especially when her housemates, whom Paula had called again, showed no concern over her absence. In fact (though Paula hadn't told the officer this), the housemate claimed that sometimes "the Spirit" called, and Leslie had to spend a week alone in the mountains or the desert. What if Paula braved the police station and gave herself a major panic attack . . . and all the while Leslie and her Spirit were communing happily?

Bullshit! Paula didn't believe Leslie was on a spiritual quest. She knew Leslie was deeply involved in the New Age and might indeed go on a retreat. But Paula also did Leslie's accounting, and Leslie was a pragmatic businesswoman. It was now Wednesday, and Leslie had been gone since Saturday. If she were going to abandon her massage clients for several days, she would have let them know.

What did Dr. Donniger say? "Which one doesn't belong? Feeling good, feeling bad, feeling tired, driving a car?" In other words, no connection ought to exist between how Paula felt at a given moment and her ability to drive. She translated the example to her current dilemma: "Which one doesn't belong? Feeling good, feeling bad, feeling tired, reporting Leslie missing?"

She thought back over her day, hoping that would give her confidence. She had spent most of her time setting up an accounting system for a battered women's shelter and had also fielded some complex questions from an immigrants' rights organization. She really was a skilled accountant, a professional. She looked it, too, in her off-white linen suit, red and white designer scarf, and red silk shell (the damp marks under her armpits were invisible). Clearly, she was a woman who deserved to be heard.

Paula got out of the car and crossed the street to the Blue Cube.

Damn, there was no entrance on this side. She had to go

all the way around the block, working up a sweat that had nothing to do with exertion. Around the northwest corner of the building, the architect had tried (unsuccessfully) to break the building's monolithic impression by recessing some parts and painting a red stripe over the entrance door . . . on which a sign said that the lobby closed at five p.m.—over an hour ago!

Okay, she'd be lying not to admit she felt stronger walking back to her car than she had approaching the police department. But she wasn't going to forsake Leslie. She intended to return during business hours. In fact, she would bring a friend with her, someone whose job involved asking questions. Why hadn't she thought of that before?

She went to a nearby coffeehouse, a cozy place where she felt relatively comfortable, and ordered a salad for dinner and a pot of herb tea. At ten to seven, she drove to the downtown studio where her weekly improvisational dance class met.

The teacher and three of the six class members were already there. Paula chatted with them, enjoying the sense of comfort she always felt in the studio. She kept watching the door, however, until the person she was waiting for arrived.

"Margo!" She hastened to embrace one of her closest friends. "I need to go to the police about something. Can you help me?"

5 / Ladies Who Lunch . . . and Then Go to the Police

"Fabulous coffee!" said Margo, sitting in one of the comfortable chairs in Paula's office on Friday, shortly after noon.

"Organic decaf, it's the only kind my system can tolerate."

Margo had persuaded Paula to wait one more day before alerting the police. The day had passed and as of this morning, Leslie still hadn't returned. Though Margo was inclined to believe that Leslie had left of her own accord, a promise was a promise. As soon as she could get away from KSDR, she had headed for the cozy suite of offices Paula occupied in a converted house on Adams Avenue in Normal Heights. It was an older area known for antique stores and a growing number of coffeehouses, from one of which Paula had provided delicate chicken salad sandwiches for lunch and this outstanding coffee.

"You said Leslie's housemates still aren't worried about her," said Margo. "How many people does she live with?"

"Just two. Art and Cynara. Actually, they rent from her. Leslie owns the main house, where Art and Cynara live, and also a granny flat in back, where she lives and works."

"Art and who?"

"Cynara. It means 'daughter of the moon.'"

"Pretty. But probably not the name her parents gave her."

Paula grinned. "It's not. I don't do Cynara's taxes, but she taught some classes at the massage school that's my client, and I did her W-2. More coffee?"

"Please."

"Margo, would you talk to her?"

"You mean, ask her about Leslie?"

"Yes. According to Art, who's the only one I've talked to, he and Cynara both think Leslie felt a spiritual call and went off somewhere. But he's so absorbed in his divorce right now, he's not paying attention to anything else. Cynara knows Leslie better, but she won't return my calls. I thought you might get her to talk."

"Well, what about this idea of a spiritual call? Remember that book you lent me about a society where, if someone needed to be alone, they could go into a sort of cave and stay as long as they needed?" Margo still thought that was a terrific idea. Other members of the community brought food regularly, but the voluntary recluse didn't even have to say thank you.

Paula quickly finished a mouthful of chicken salad. "That was a utopia," she said impatiently.

Paula's bookkeeper, Elaine, stuck her head in the door. "Paula, got a minute?"

As the two of them discussed a bank reconciliation, Margo debated how to respond to Paula's request. She doubted she would get anywhere with Cynara, though it *was* strange that, with Leslie gone almost a full week, her housemates were so blasé. Were they hiding something? But when would Margo have the chance to question anyone? She was already using up work time to accompany Paula to the police station. And she had made a New Year's resolution (her sole observance of the Jewish New Year, last week) to say no more often.

Not that Paula was easy to say no to, she thought, observing the warm yet authoritative way her friend was dealing with the accounting question and the way Paula looked, her chic red suit enlivened by a paisley shawl. Paula had acquired much of her wardrobe during her tenure at a fast-track accounting firm, before she developed agoraphobia. Her illness may have turned routine trips to the supermarket into a nightmare, but it hadn't, Margo was certain, diminished her force of will.

"Tell me again," said Margo, resigned to the fact that she was about to break her resolution. "You went for your massage last Saturday, at Leslie's house, and Leslie wasn't there?"

"Right. And she didn't return my phone calls."

"Was her car gone?"

"Umm, I guess so. I didn't see it. But see, that's why I need your help! I didn't think of that. About Cynara, it's probably best to approach her indirectly. You know, talk to her about something else and then bring up Leslie. You could drop in at her store in Ocean Beach, near the organic grocery. Crystal Magic."

"Is that what Cynara does, crystal healing?"

"No, that's her partner's specialty—Richard Del Vecchio. I've had some sessions with him and he's great. Cynara does Tarot."

"You've had crystal healing?" interrupted Margo. "What happens?"

"I lie down and Richard surrounds me with crystals. I stay there for about an hour. And he helped me choose crystals to have around me, one for the car and one for home. You think it's hooey, don't you?''

Margo considered fudging, but nodded yes. She saw considerable merit in some kinds of alternative health care, like massage and acupuncture, but she tended to place crystal healing in the mumbo-jumbo category. Of course, unlike Paula, she hadn't been struggling with a chronic illness for five years. As Paula had put it in dance class one night, she would walk on her knees to Lourdes if she thought it would do any good.

"That's all right," said Paula. "Part of me thinks it's hooey, too. But there's something very comforting about Richard. You'll see when you go there."

"Are he and Cynara just business partners? Or a couple?"

"Just business now. I think they were living together at the time they started the store, but that was years ago."

Margo glanced at her watch. "We'd better go. I've still got to finish a story for the five o'clock news. What about Art?" she said as they walked to her car. "I suppose he's involved in the New Age, too?"

Art Smolin, Margo learned as she drove them downtown, was a fairly recent addition to Leslie's menage in the State College area. A successful chiropractor, Art owned an expensive home in Pacific Beach. With his recent separation, however, his wife and kids remained in the house, and she would surely get it in the settlement, Paula said.

"Art," she concluded, "is more or less camping out at Leslie's right now, keeping his expenses down until the dust of the divorce settles . . . and until he finds out if he's going to be sued, and for how much."

"Sued? For what?"

"Good question. Malpractice, maybe. There was a young man—his name was Teddy, I think—who went to Art and maybe half a dozen other alternative healers. Pretty typical in San Diego, except that Teddy got lots of opposition from his father, who's an M.D. But he was over twenty-one and his father couldn't force him to do anything. Unfortunately, it turned out he had cancer. By the time it was diagnosed, it was too advanced to be treated by Western medicine. About a year ago, he died. His father's been doing a lot of saber rattling since then, threatening to shut down every New Age healer in town.''

''Teddy's father doesn't happen to be Theodore Costas, Jr., does he?''

''Yeah. Do you know him?''

''I'm covering a news conference he's holding next week. Are you okay?'' she said, sensing Paula's tension as she pulled up outside the police department.

''I'll be fine. Just stick by me?''

''Sure.'' Margo squeezed her hand as they approached the door. ''Do you want me to do the talking?''

''Thanks, no. Not unless you think of some question I should be asking.''

Comfort had not been the guiding principle in designing the police department lobby, nor had aesthetics. On mushroomlike pods of low-backed vinyl-covered seats—it would be an exaggeration to call them chairs—eight or nine people had deposited their bottoms. A few of the people squirmed, whether from sheer discomfort or because of nerves. An older Latina was crying into a shredded tissue. Apart from a be-suited man whose briefcase marked him as an attorney, everyone looked beaten and scared.

They went up to the rounded reception desk, staffed by two uniformed officers, a man and a woman.

''We want to report a missing person,'' Paula said to the woman, who seemed to be the main receptionist.

''Over here.'' The woman cocked her head at the man.

Margo broke in, "Shouldn't we talk to someone in the Missing Persons division?"

"You make the report to him."

"Sorry," mouthed Margo, as she and Paula sidestepped down the counter to the man.

"Adult or juvenile?" he asked, pulling out a form.

"Adult," answered Paula.

"Name, last name first?"

"Getz, Leslie."

"Race?"

"Caucasian."

Margo knew that Paula might genuinely feel as calm as she sounded, or her heart might be pounding and her mind racing as she fought the terror that she was going to faint. Margo had been with Paula several times and later learned her friend had been having a severe panic attack. Paula had to be in very bad shape before it showed.

While Paula was answering questions, Margo recognized Donny Obayashi walking through the lobby. The lieutenant saw her as well and stopped to say hello.

"Do you have an ID yet on the body from the Encanto fire?" she asked him.

"Not yet. The only way we're going to get a positive ID is through dental, and it may take several more days."

"But you know it's an elderly black woman and Hannah is still missing, isn't she?"

Behind her, Margo heard a gasp. She turned. Paula had gone white.

"Sit down." Margo led Paula to a seat.

"Head between your knees," added Obayashi, kneeling beside Paula and placing a hand on her arm.

"I'm okay," said Paula in a moment. But she kept her head down and spoke in a near-whisper. "Did you say Hannah might have been burned in the fire? Hannah Jones, the herbalist?"

"Yes," Margo answered.

"I know her. And she's a good friend of Leslie's."

"Who's Leslie?" Obayashi's voice was gentle.

Paula looked up at him. "My massage therapist. She's been missing for a week."

"A week exactly?" said Obayashi. "Since last Friday?"

"Saturday." She stopped and considered for a moment. "I don't really know. I thought it was Saturday, but that's only when I realized she was gone."

Margo could virtually hear Obayashi thinking the same thing she was: *Jane Doe,* burned to death eight days ago.

6 / Is Leslie More?

"I'd like to ask you a few questions," Obayashi said to Paula.

Paula sat up straighter and color returned to her face. "That's why I came here, to report Leslie missing. I already started giving him information." She cocked her head toward the officer behind the desk, her hair swinging and revealing a silver and onyx earring. Margo would swear Obayashi's eyes never left Paula; if not for the seriousness of the situation, she would have grinned.

"I'll get the form and we can go upstairs." Obayashi snagged the piece of paper, along with a security clearance badge for Paula. "You okay to walk?"

"Isn't Margo coming?"

"We can't have a reporter there."

Paula went white again but remained upright. "I'm sorry, I have a disorder called agoraphobia. I get panic attacks. I'll feel more secure if Margo comes along."

Obayashi held up his hands in surrender, but said, "She's got to wait outside my office while you and I talk." He picked up a security badge for Margo, then led her and Paula through the locked door, into the elevator, and down the fourth-floor hallway to Homicide.

Jane Doe had had sex, then fell asleep in the canyon last Thursday night, thought Margo, sitting in a chair—a real chair at least, with a back and arms—in the narrow entrance to the homicide department. And from everything Margo had heard about Leslie, the massage therapist was just the kind of person who'd relish making love outdoors, especially in San Diego's rugged back country where the fire had occurred. Still, even if news-shy Paula had avoided hearing about the unidentified woman who had died in last week's canyon fire, what about Art or Cynara? If Leslie had disappeared the same night that Jane Doe died, wouldn't one of her housemates have been concerned?

Further, the Encanto Hills death was almost immediately declared an arson-homicide, whereas Jane Doe's death as well as the fire that caused it were considered accidents. Just because Hannah Jones and Leslie Getz were friends hardly meant that both of them had died in canyon fires. In fact, maybe neither woman was dead. Maybe Hannah and Leslie were together at some mountaintop sanctuary, milking rattlesnake venom or prostrating themselves before the goddess . . . not a road Margo desired for herself, but not one she dismissed as totally asinine, either.

Between living in Santa Fe and San Diego for almost two decades, she had known plenty of people who espoused one nontraditional belief or another. Many of them were intelligent people whom she saw as genuine spiritual seekers. As for Margo, her dance class sometimes chanted "om," a practice she found both soothing and energizing. And she would never turn down a chance to get a massage.

Still, she had always shied away from what she considered the fringier New Age practices. Living in New Mexico, for example, she'd had great respect for American Indian religions—she figured the Indians definitely had the right idea about living in harmony with nature, rather than constantly trying to subdue it—and she loved watching Indian dances at festivals. But she hadn't joined some of her friends who'd sought out Indian teachers or rituals. And she would be up in arms if Barry or one of the kids got sick and refused to see a doctor.

That's how Theodore Costas must have felt, she thought . . . and then experienced a *click!* Wasn't Costas the name of Jenny's friend, Nick, the boy with the pierced nose? If so, were the two Costases related? And just how close were Jenny and Nick Costas? Jenny had gotten the birth control/AIDS prevention talk from her mother; it had been further reinforced by discussions with Margo and Barry. Margo was sure the girl was smart enough not to have sex without a condom. But God! Margo winced, feeling every bit a parent. She hoped Jenny wasn't having sex yet . . . and helplessly knew that neither she nor Barry nor Rae nor Rae's new husband could eliminate that possibility completely.

The sex question aside, what about Nick? If he was Theodore Costas's son, he sounded like a wounded bird, and Jenny was just the kind of young woman to be attracted to a wounded bird. Hell, all teenage girls fell for wounded birds. Margo had nursed a few herself. It generally did no harm . . . except that this bird—if he *were* the survivor of a dead brother and son of a vengeful father—could be a lot more wounded than most.

Could Margo talk to Jenny about him? She decided to wait until after Theodore Costas's news conference. The doctor would probably have his family at his side, and she'd find out if Nick really was his son. That would provide a natural bridge to raising the subject with Jenny.

"Hey, Margo." Paula emerged from the lieutenant's office.

Margo glanced at her watch. She had passed nearly half an hour worrying about Jenny's love life. And Jenny was only fifteen! Margo felt as if she'd just aged twenty years herself.

Paula looked relaxed and shook Obayashi's hand warmly. He must have proven a kind interrogator. Paula didn't even act alarmed when he asked her to wait a few minutes while he talked to Margo.

He didn't speak until they had entered his office and he closed the door.

"Your friend," Obayashi said, sitting on the edge of his desk and gesturing Margo into a chair. "Does she have a screw loose?"

"Because of the agoraphobia? It doesn't affect her thinking ability. Paula's one of the most level-headed people I know. She's a CPA, didn't she tell you?"

"Yeah, but she only works for nonprofit organizations and old hippies. I wondered, you know, if maybe she's not a very good accountant."

Margo laughed. "Just like any good reporter would be bringing in the bucks on television instead of working for a public radio station?"

"I didn't mean . . ." Donny Obayashi actually blushed.

"Paula went straight from getting her CPA to the big time." Margo named one of the top firms in the city. "A few years later, she got agoraphobia. Except it wasn't diagnosed for a year. She kept on working, even though it was really tough. The thing is, getting sick made her reevaluate her life. She decided she could make plenty to live on working for little guys instead of fat cats." Margo had met Paula when Paula started doing the accounting for KSDR. Taking an immediate liking to one another, they'd discovered they lived only a few blocks apart. And Paula shared Margo's love of dance and had joined her weekly class.

"Okay, you've convinced me. Idealism lives." Obayashi

smiled, but he'd been tearing apart a foam cup and continued to demolish it. "What about this thing where she sits in her car, dressed up like Rambo? You know about that?"

Margo nodded. But why in the world had Paula told Obayashi? "It's unconventional," she acknowledged. "But this psychologist she's seeing is at the top of his field. He gives lectures all over the world. I've seen Paula improve more with his treatment than with anything else. The answer to all your questions is, Paula is an absolutely credible source of information."

Obayashi crushed what remained of the foam cup, and Margo voiced the fear she'd felt earlier. "Could Leslie be Jane Doe?"

He shrugged. "I had someone call one of the housemates, the chiropractor. He couldn't remember when he last saw Leslie. Maybe Friday, maybe earlier last week. She lived and worked in the back house on the property, so sometimes she didn't come to the main house for several days."

He leaned back and the light from the window picked up deep lines of fatigue in his face. Now that she'd started asking the questions, however, Margo wasn't going to let a little sympathy for a cop get in her way.

"What about the dental records?" she said.

"Good news, bad news. Paula knew the name of Leslie's dentist because she goes to the same woman. But hell, it's Friday afternoon. I called the M.E.'s office and they're trying to reach the dentist, but there's a good chance they won't get any records until next week. Actually, it's all good news, since I assume you want this Leslie to be alive. I'll ring the County Sheriff's homicide people, since Jane Doe died in their jurisdiction, but there just aren't a lot of similarities between that death and the woman in Encanto."

"For instance?" When she got no answer, Margo remarked, ''I heard the woman in Encanto didn't just die in the fire, she was killed first.''

Obayashi was probably a good poker player. With no expression except a slight lift of his eyebrows, he stood up.

''What about the autopsy report?'' Margo persisted. ''That's public record, isn't it?''

''While the investigation is going on, it's sealed. Have a good weekend, Margo.''

''How old do you think he is?'' asked Paula when they were back in the car.

''Obayashi? Late thirties, early forties? Interested?''

''In a cop? I just thought he was nice.''

''Is that why you told him about the Rambo exercise?''

''He thought I was loony tunes, didn't he?''

''No. Well, a little,'' Margo admitted. ''But I set him straight. Why *did* you tell him?''

''The afternoon that fire started, in Encanto, I guess I was right there. I was parked on a street just above the canyon, doing the Rambo thing. I noticed someone sort of hiding by the side of a house, staring at me. Donny thinks the person watching me might have been the arsonist.''

''Christ, why didn't you tell me?'' Maybe Obayashi had persuasive powers Margo only dreamed of, like letting Paula call him by his boyish nickname.

''I didn't know it was important. I didn't know that much about the fire—you know I don't listen to the news.''

''Did you see the person? Was it a man or a woman? Black? White?''

''I didn't notice any of that stuff. I was just so freaked by this person staring at me, I had a monster panic attack. All I could think about was getting out of there.''

''Damn!'' For a moment, Margo had hoped to have something to bring back to the station, to make up for the story she couldn't possibly finish in time.

"There *is* something I didn't tell him," offered Paula as they approached her office. "Ever since that day, when the fire started, I've felt—not like I was being watched exactly, but like someone's directing energy at me. When you were a kid, did you used to stare at someone's back in school and then they'd turn around? That's how I've felt, like someone is staring at my back. But when I look around, no one's there."

Pulling up in front of Paula's office, Margo turned and looked at her friend. For a moment, she saw what Donny Obayashi must have seen: a well-spoken, bright woman who might get some strange results on a psychological test. Margo gave her an extra-long good-bye hug.

Paula giggled. "Know what? Donny asked if I'd mind taking off my jacket so he could get a good look at my arms. He was interested in my ankles, too."

"That's not surprising," said Margo. She had parked behind Paula's Taurus and was admiring the bumper sticker: PRACTICE RANDOM KINDNESS AND SENSELESS ACTS OF BEAUTY.

"No, not like that. He left the room and had a policewoman come in to examine them. I had to take off my pantyhose."

Now, what was that about?

7 / Real Estate

Everyone in San Diego talked about real estate and Cynara (one name only) saw no reason why being a Tarot reader/psychic and operating a New Age store should make her any exception, especially when they had just opened on Saturday morning and had not a single customer.

"The interest rates are never going to be this good again," she said to Richard Del Vecchio, as she lit a stick of rose incense in an elephant-shaped holder on the bookshelf devoted to volumes on Tantric sex. She shook her head, sending masses of gray-streaked strawberry blond hair perilously close to the burning incense.

"Forget it," responded Richard.

"It's a buyer's market!"

Richard screwed up his face. Damn, thought Cynara, how had she ever found this man attractive? Now, whenever she looked at him, she thought the baker had taken Richard's face when it was still dough and pinched all the features together. Small brown eyes and a thin mouth both pushed toward what would only charitably be called a Roman nose. At least the years hadn't stolen his hairline, but he still wore the full brown Afro he had sported when she met him. Did the man ever look in a mirror? Richard's appearance did not radiate the combination of New Age harmony and contemporary sophistication Cynara hoped someone might experience when they walked into Crystal Magic. Rather, he looked as if he'd spent the last twenty years sleeping à la Rip Van Winkle, with regular wakeups for beer—Richard had gotten fat. Nevertheless, Cynara couldn't deny he had a genuine gift in working with crystals, a far greater gift than she'd ever shown with the cards. She had studied Tarot for years and sometimes even had flashes of psychic insight that surprised her. But Richard almost invariably selected the perfect crystal for balancing a person's energy and even for healing.

Richard hadn't responded, had simply continued dusting the glass shelves and the crystals on them. Cynara stomped her foot. She wore a flowing indigo robe in the style of a Moroccan burnoose and soft forest green suede boots. The boots had two-inch heels, however, and the stomp made a satisfying whap! that forced him to look up.

"It's not like I'm asking you for a palace in La Jolla," she said. "I've been pricing houses east of Balboa Park. You can get a really nice place there for under two hundred thousand dollars."

"Too much." Richard's terseness had been one of the "cons" Cynara had listed when she first got involved with him, but there were so many "pros" going against it . . . such as Del Vecchio Products, one of the biggest corporations in the country. Richard never wanted anyone to know he came from money, but at that time—fifteen years younger and twenty pounds lighter herself—Cynara possessed the skill to ferret out that particular secret. Even then, however, she'd had the feeling that Richard never showed her his deepest self.

"Two hundred thousand is *not* too much," she said as he kept going with the duster. For a man who had grown up with servants, he really knew how to clean. "It's lower than prices have been for years. It's a buyer's market," she repeated.

He stopped dusting, came over, and looked her in the eye; looked up, because he stood several inches shorter than she.

"I don't mean it's too much for a house in San Diego," he said. "It's too much for you to ask me."

"Oh no, it's not. Get him away from me," she added. Richard's lame golden retriever, which usually stayed, half-asleep, behind the crystal counter, had lumbered up, no doubt responding to some doggy urge to protect his master. Cynara had noticed and did not appreciate that the aging animal's mix of reddish-gold and graying hair resembled her own.

"Come on, Frodo." Richard led the dog back behind the counter.

Having gotten Richard to comply in one area, Cynara seized her advantage. "So far I've asked you for very little. A modest stipend each month, to supplement the pittance I earn here. Some help when I hurt my back last year and needed chiropractic. But look at me. I'm forty-five years old and I'm living like a twenty-year-old hippie. Renting a room in a house I don't own . . . and where, I might add, I may be evicted, since Leslie's made it known she won't tolerate having meat cooked in *her* kitchen anymore."

"I've been thinking."

"Not even chicken or fish! Christ, I hate vegetarian sanctimoniousness. You'd think they invented the carrot."

"I've been thinking," Richard said again. "You and I ought to clean the slate. Get a divorce. I'll give you a settlement, of course, a lump sum. But none of this extra money every month, plus ten or twenty or a hundred thousand more whenever you decide you need a house or a new car."

"A *new* car!" Cynara drove a Honda Civic, for which she had wheedled the money from Richard six years ago. You would have thought she'd demanded a Mercedes. Of course, Richard still drove his VW van. But back to the deeper subject at hand. "Cleaning the slate sounds fine with me. I'd love to get half your money from the Del Vecchios, since California's a community property state. I wouldn't mind ending this charade, either—pretending we just lived together for a few years when we actually got married."

"The trust fund doesn't exactly work like that." He was squirming.

Cynara wondered which he minded more, parting with the money or revealing their marriage. He had insisted on keeping it a secret because he considered marriage a violation of his innermost values. As for her, there was just one aspect of a potential divorce she cared about.

"How does the trust fund work, then?" she said.

"It's just more complicated than that."

Cynara recognized that evasive tone and felt as hurt by it as she used to feel, when she had loved this man. She wanted to hurt him back and almost did. But she was still reluctant to tell him what she knew would really get to him: that although they'd gotten married because she thought she was pregnant, she had actually gotten her period the day before the marriage ceremony—not a week after, as she had told Richard. She'd worn her diaphragm on their wedding night and said it hurt, when they made love, for him to go too deep; he hadn't had a clue. Cynara wanted to say the words so badly she had to bite her lip to keep silent. But she had a feeling that once she spoke, Richard would never give her another penny.

The tinkling of the small Tibetan bells hung on the door announced that somebody was entering the store.

8 / The Magician

Instead of a dusty, cluttered "head shop" reminiscent of the sixties, Margo found Crystal Magic bigger and brighter and cleaner than she'd expected. Well-lit displays offered massage implements, body oils, and other cruelty-free beauty products. There were five or six different varieties of incense, books, and environmentally conscious canvas and string shopping bags in a rainbow of colors. In what appeared to be a place of honor, just inside the door, stood a handsome polished wooden cabinet with glass shelves, where crystals were arrayed.

Margo was drawn to the sparkling crystals, especially a purple one on the top shelf.

"One of my best amethysts," said the pudgy, Vulcan-like man behind the counter—presumably Cynara's partner, Richard. "Amethyst is said to heal nightmares and insomnia. Have you been sleeping badly?"

"No, I just like the color." She gave a start, noticing a big dog lying behind the counter. But not even *her* fear of dogs could be triggered by the dozing animal with its graying hair. She wondered if the dog ever suffered from nightmares and if an amethyst could help.

"Would you like to hold it?" offered Richard.

"Okay." Margo took the crystal he held out to her and readied herself to be told that the amethyst balanced her entire aura and would cure some as-yet-unnamed but dreadful illness she had. Richard remained silent, however, while she held the crystal, which fit neatly in the palm of her hand. She decided she liked the rather ugly man. As for the amethyst crystal, it did its own sales job. Despite Margo's skepticism, she felt a sense of peace holding it and hated to relinquish it.

She made herself hand back the crystal, and wandered to the next counter, which was devoted to Tarot. The job she had taken on didn't involve the crystal seller.

"I had no idea there were so many Tarot decks," she remarked to the room in general. Cynara had stayed at the back of the store, barely visible behind the display shelves.

Margo recognized the traditional Rider Tarot, with which she and friends had played around just for fun. There were also, she discovered, a Mother Peace Tarot with round cards and a deck that used American Indian symbols. She picked up the next box, fascinated yet repelled by the image on the cover: a violet-faced man whose large, commanding eyes projected diagonal beams of yellow light. A yellow isosceles triangle in the middle of his forehead partially covered a yellow circle. Inside the circle rested an infinity symbol. Various objects lay on a table below the man. Margo barely glanced at them, however, drawn by the intensity of the man's eyes. Not someone she'd want to meet in a dark alley, or even in a sunlit park.

"That's the Cosmic Tarot."

Margo jumped, unaware that Cynara had come up behind her. God, the woman was tall! And one of her eyes was green, the other brown.

"The Magician, a very powerful card." Cynara indicated the image on the box. "Would you like a reading?"

"Sure, why not?" *Why not* was because, just as Margo had a friendly feeling toward Richard, Cynara gave her the creeps. But hell, they were just cards, and how better to establish rapport with a Tarot reader?

"I'll do a five-card reading for you," said Cynara. "Fifteen dollars."

"Fine." Margo followed her to a small round table at the back of the shop. "Do you happen to know Leslie Getz?" she asked, as they sat on chairs across the table from one another.

"Yeah." No mention that Cynara lived in Leslie's house.

"Do you know if she's out of town? I've tried calling for an appointment a couple times and she hasn't called back. She's usually really good about that."

"Leslie might be on a spirit quest." A catty tone, accompanied by a smirk.

"It doesn't sound like you think so."

Cynara gave a sharp laugh. "You know Leslie very well?"

"Not really."

"If Leslie's not around, she's probably with a lover. Someone unsavory, she goes for that. And either sex. You want a reading or not?"

Margo put great enthusiasm into her "Yes!"

Cynara reached into a woven basket and pulled out a small bundle tied in a green silk scarf. Slowly, ritualistically, she undid the scarf, revealing a Cosmic Tarot deck.

"If you have your own cards, always wrap them in some kind of natural fiber." It was as if Cynara's voice had gotten deeper, more authoritative. *A great trick of the trade,* Margo told herself, determined not to let this aging hippie get to her.

"Why natural fiber?" she asked.

Ignoring her, Cynara said, "What do you want to ask the cards today? Questions about your love life? Or something at your job?"

I want to know when Leslie disappeared and what lover she's been seeing most recently. But Margo sensed she had pushed her luck already with Cynara. Better to go ahead with the Tarot reading. Margo wished she didn't feel such a deep distrust of the woman. She also wished the damn incense weren't so close to the table. The odor was intoxicating.

"Could you move the incense a little? I'm allergic," she lied.

Cynara frowned but called out, "Richard? Could you move the incense to the other side of the store?" As he obliged, she told Margo, "I don't like to leave the cards once I've exposed them. Now, tell me your question."

Margo took a less heavily scented breath. She'd thought of making up a story, but the temptation to ask about her own life was too great.

"My daughter wants to get her nose pierced. My stepdaughter, that is. She's fifteen. I don't know how I feel about it in the first place—I don't like nose piercing—but she's at the age where it's important to assert her independence."

"Your stepdaughter, you said?"

"Yes, which means that the other issue is, how much should I get involved at all? She asked me to help convince her natural mother . . ."

"Perfect," Cynara interrupted her. "That's exactly enough information for me to proceed. Here. Shuffle the cards. Then cut the deck into three piles, focusing on your question as you do that."

After Margo had shuffled and cut, Cynara reassembled the deck and dealt out the top five cards: the first two cards next to each other; the third, centrally, below them; and the fourth and fifth, also centrally, above, forming a low-crossed "t."

"They're all upside down," observed Margo.

"That's very significant. I can see why you can't figure things out for yourself. A reversed card indicates an area where you're blocked in your perceptions, and to have them all reversed . . .''

Cynara reached across the table and took Margo's hands in her cold, dry grip. It was like being held by a lizard.

"Have you ever been told you have psychic power?'' Cynara asked.

"No.'' As soon as she could without seeming grossly rude, Margo extricated her hands from Cynara's.

"This is an incredible spread. Just incredible.''

Superstition, Margo told herself. She felt a chill nonetheless.

Cynara placed her hands on the first two cards she'd dealt. "These,'' she said, "represent the heart of the matter.''

The first card, the Nine of Wands, showed the head and upper body of a strong-looking young man, hair brushed up from his wide brow—a cosmic James Dean, with a lion standing in the background. The card beside it was the beautiful, bejeweled young Empress, who wore a crown covered with stars.

"This fifteen-year-old acts like a princess at home, doesn't she?'' said Cynara, indicating the Empress. "Independent, she has a mind of her own, she won't do a thing you ask her to do. But—'' her hand moved to the James Dean figure— "she's not really as independent as she appears. She has a boyfriend and he's a very strong character—see the lion? He has a great deal of influence over her.''

Margo gulped. She hadn't uttered a word about Nick Costas.

"The card below them, the Queen of Cups, represents the past,'' Cynara continued, pointing to the figure of a lovely, dark-haired woman. "Her natural mother. A teenage girl who wants to pierce her nose is trying to establish who she is. But it's also an act of rebellion. She knows her mother won't like it and her boyfriend will. That's where you come in. The present." Cynara picked up the fourth card, the High Priestess, whose face contained images of the sun, the ocean, and a male-female symbol. Below her was a sickle moon.

"See the small Roman numeral two on the Priestess's forehead? That means being torn in two ways. You want to do the right thing, but the two represents paradox—this or that, night or day, sun or moon. You can get in your head a lot with the number two and not know what to do. Should you give her the freedom to pierce her nose or let her rebel in other ways instead? Should you just keep quiet? What you're really asking is, what is your role as a mother?"

Had someone moved the incense close to them again? Margo felt a bit giddy.

"The answer is," announced Cynara, "you don't have a role as a mother."

"But . . ."

"It's very clear. This last card, the Ten of Cups, represents the future." The card showed a seated woman, nude except for a veil that covered only her hair. "You need to *strip away* your role. You love your stepdaughter, but she doesn't need you to take so much control."

Margo had run out of cynical inner responses. The cards were uncannily apt—the young, headstrong Empress and the attractive rebel in her life; and the two women, in the past and present, both of whom were concerned about her. Even the nude, wistful Ten of Cups. Cynara's interpretations made sense as well, although she could have delivered them with greater sensitivity. Had she never raised a child herself?

Her interpretations were one thing, however, and her advice another. No matter what Cynara said, Margo intended to have a talk with Jenny—not to warn her against Nick Costas, but to emphasize the importance of establishing her own independence, which included independence from men.

"I'm sorry?" she said, realizing Cynara had spoken to her.

"There's something else, isn't there? Something on your mind. I'm not always psychic, but I really sense you have another important question to ask me. I can do a three-card reading, as long as you pose a yes-no question. It's usually ten dollars, but I'll only charge you five."

What a scam! Margo's instinct told her to get away from Cynara. The woman did possess a kind of power, but it was a power that felt unhealthy. Still, Margo had figured out a way to ask about Leslie's disappearance without mentioning Leslie's name. And Cynara's first reading had so hit the mark, maybe the cards would give Margo information that Cynara was unwilling to provide directly.

"I have a friend." Margo felt her way into the question. "She has this illness and sometimes it makes her exaggerate her fears." Paula would forgive her; actually, Paula would agree. She'd said that "catastrophizing" was a major symptom of agoraphobia. "My friend is very worried about something, and she's asked me to help her. Should I help, or should I try to convince her that she's blowing her fears out of proportion?"

"So let's say the yes-no question is, 'Should you help your friend?'" Was Cynara really hissing her s's?

Following the Tarot reader's instructions, Margo shuffled the cards and cut again, this time only once. Cynara dealt three cards next to one another: the Ace of Pentacles, the Three of Pentacles (upside down), and the menacing Magician.

As she turned over the Magician, Cynara gasped. Her eyes—the green one and the brown—met Margo's, and Margo could have sworn she looked genuinely afraid. *Another parlor trick,* she told herself, trying to ignore the sweat trickling down her sides.

Cynara rushed through the interpretation, as if she were

suddenly as anxious to get rid of Margo as Margo was to leave.

"The first card, the Ace of Pentacles, means your friend was very solid in the past, a star shining brightly. The Three of Pentacles, in the middle, represents the present. Three men are building something. But the card is reversed, the men are falling. Your friend is very overwhelmed. She does need your help. The simple way I know that is that two cards are up and one down, which means 'yes.' But it's obvious that something very dark is happening. See how dark the Magician's eyes are. Symbols of all four of the suits—Cups, Wands, Swords, Pentacles—are on the table in front of him. That means he has the ability to use all dimensions. Someone very dark is involved, very powerful. Your friend is really losing her balance. She's in danger."

9 / The Zucchini Thief

The woman's a phony, insisted an inner voice that Margo identified as her rational self as she paid Cynara and left the table. *A phony and a jerk. She wanted to tell me things that upset me. If she had any skill at all, it was in figuring out what would shake me up. Being told I had no role as a mother anymore, and that Paula was in great danger!*

But I cut the cards! countered her intuitive self. *How could Cynara have made them fit the situation so perfectly? The Empress representing Jenny, the young man Nick Costas, the Queen Rae, and the last two cards, both women—me?*

Although Margo was eager to leave the New Age shop, on her way out she found herself drawn to the amethyst crystal again.

"You know, even though the lore says that amethyst is specific to sleep, I figure every relationship between a crystal and a person is individual," said Richard. "That one calls to you, doesn't it? Would you like to hold it again?"

Walking out of Crystal Magic—the amethyst in a paper bag and fifty dollars less in her wallet—Margo's rational and intuitive selves continued their debate.

Some of the cards fit, sure, Rational Margo argued. *But what about the young man? I don't know if Jenny is seeing Nick Costas, or anyone else. And the idea that I should "strip away" my maternal role? Jenny's only fifteen, she still needs guidance.*

Her intuition jumped in. *She needs independence, too! And look at Cynara's second reading. Didn't she hit the bullseye with Paula, describing her as a former star whose life is now in disarray?*

Forget it! Rational Margo drove herself to the nearest automatic teller to get some cash, having spent almost everything in her wallet at Crystal Magic, and then picked up a takeout salad at a deli. She realized she had eaten nothing but a bagel that morning. She'd probably feel a lot more solid with food in her stomach. She took the salad to the beach to eat. The Santa Ana winds having retreated, it was a glorious early autumn day, warm enough that a few sun addicts were lying out in swimsuits, but with enough of a breeze that Margo was glad she'd brought a light jacket along.

Her intuitive self didn't give up easily, continuing to whisper that if Leslie really was the burned Jane Doe and if Paula "witnessed" the person who started the Encanto fire and killed Hannah, then Paula had indeed encountered something evil. Fortunately, Margo's salad required plenty of attention. Half of its ingredients were sprouts at least two inches long, difficult to get into the mouth under any circumstances—and especially using a flimsy plastic fork and trying to avoid the gritty sand that kept threatening to dust the top of her meal like an unwanted sprinkling of black pepper. Beaches, she knew from one of Barry's colleagues who studied them, were among the most inhospitable environments for small animals because of the mercilessness of the sand that got inside shells and clogged digestive systems. After she had finished her salad (holding her amethyst crystal, which was embarrassingly comforting, in her lap), she hadn't completely silenced the scared voice, but she felt strong enough to let her rational self take the reins. She found a phone, called the police, and asked if either the Encanto victim or the Jane Doe had been identified. Not yet, she was told.

Now what? She put another twenty cents in the phone. According to Art Smolin's answering machine, Art was conducting an all-day chiropractic workshop. And Cynara was tending her store. That meant that, unless Leslie had suddenly reappeared, there was no one to stop Margo from going there and poking around. The address was in the State College area, some twelve miles inland from the beach and a good fifteen degrees hotter. Margo didn't mind the warmer temperature while she was driving her convertible Miata, but she shed her jacket the moment she arrived.

Someone in the household was a gardener, or else Leslie considered it worth the money to hire one. A profusion of flowers bloomed in the front yard, in an untamed country style. Margo, no green thumb herself, could identify only the roses, but she admired the vivid reds and blues that brightened up the house, a nondescript Spanish-style dwelling whose mint-green stucco needed a touchup. Actually, she realized, the flowers could use some care as well; there were numerous drooping blossoms.

Leslie, she recalled, occupied the granny flat. She walked around and down a flight of steps to the rear of the house, which was built on another of San Diego's canyons. The absent Leslie must surely be the gardener, thought Margo, coming upon a vegetable patch where tomatoes and zucchini were rotting on the vine. Further on, a stand of corn looked equally in need of tending. Below the vegetable garden, down an inviting path, Margo spied a cottage that must be Leslie's. She followed the path and knocked; as she'd expected, she got no answer.

She came back through the vegetable garden to her car, thought a moment, then grabbed one of her canvas shopping bags. She hated to see so much good food going to waste . . . and Leslie's tenants were clearly ignoring the bounty growing in their yard. Returning to the vegetable garden, she started to fill her bag.

Odd, she had a feeling someone was watching her. She looked around, saw no one. Maybe Paula's jitters were catching. But a moment later, when she was bending to pick a zucchini, she noticed a definite movement in the corn. She stood slowly, reaching into the purse over her shoulder. She didn't turn directly toward the figure in the corn until, inside the purse, her fingers found the can of Mace she had taken to carrying.

"Who's there?" she said.

"Sorry, didn't mean to scare you." It was a low, intimate male voice that, given the circumstances, made Margo grip the Mace, although she kept it out of sight inside her purse.

The man emerged from the corn stalks. Freckled and twenty-something, he wore beige chinos and a short-sleeved polo shirt that showed the kind of muscles you get from pumping iron for hours. Thank heaven, he had the sense not to come any closer.

"I'm Scott Nelson, an old friend of Leslie and Cynara," he said. "Are you a new housemate?"

"Just a friend, too." She was beginning to feel silly holding the Mace; but instinct told her not to let go.

"Did you have a massage appointment with Leslie?"

"No, I came by to look for her. I've tried calling a few times this week and she hasn't called back." Might as well brazen out the zucchini theft. "What about you?"

"No appointment. I just hadn't seen Les for a long time. I was in the area, and I wanted to talk to her. But I don't know, maybe it was a bad idea." The smile was boyish but strained—that of an unloved kid desperate for approval. Under other circumstances, Margo might have found something touching, even appealing, in that raw need. Isolated with Scott behind an empty house, she continued to feel uneasy. Just how long had he been standing in the corn watching her?

"Actually, Leslie's not home. I was just leaving," she said, backing out of the garden as they talked.

"How's Les doing?" He followed her but continued to maintain some distance, as if sensing her distrust. "Like I said, I haven't seen her in a while. She was one of my teachers at massage school."

"Oh, you do massage?"

"Not anymore. I gave it a try instead of med school, but I decided to stick with traditional medicine after all." Something about the way he puffed out his chest made her doubt that he was actually a medical student.

She was probably an idiot to let this overgrown adolescent scare her. Still, she continued making small talk as she regained the relative safety of the street, and she didn't let go of the Mace.

"Seems like you could combine them," she said. "Traditional and alternative healing." That was Olivia's goal.

"Oh, no! No!"

What had she said to provoke that cry of distress? No matter. Having made it back to the street, she climbed quickly into her Miata without opening the door—an advantage of long legs and years of dance training. Brown-eyed Scott made her think of a puppy, and she couldn't help thinking that puppies bite.

"Bye, Scott. Nice meeting you."

God, she'd gotten easily spooked, she thought, speeding away from Leslie's. Most likely there was nothing to the unbalanced feeling she got from Scott, nothing but fallout from the spooky Tarot reading earlier in the day. She'd probably find Barry and the kids threatening when she got home. The cat, too!

Margo got a call from KSDR shortly after she arrived home. The police had sent a fax confirming that the body found in the Encanto fire was that of Hannah Jones.

"Go ahead and broadcast it," she told the weekend reporter, a student intern. "I'll come in and do a longer story for tomorrow morning."

She almost called Olivia but feared intruding; and Olivia would certainly have heard the bad news. There was one person she did have to call, however—Paula. Margo told her about Hannah and filled her in, sketchily, on her visit to Crystal Magic, omitting the part about Paula being in danger. What would it do except add to Paula's already bulging basket of anxiety?

"What about Leslie?" asked Paula. "Do the police know yet if she was the person burned in the other fire?"

"Not yet."

"But what if she was?" Margo had to consciously resist being infected by her friend's fear, as Paula continued, "Margo, what if somebody is burning witches?"

10 / Sweet Bird of Prey

Sitting on the floor in the corner of the living room, Nick Costas reflected that there were three reasons he'd agreed to attend the meeting his father had called for late that Saturday afternoon. The first was that his mom had begged him. "You don't have to stay for the whole thing," she'd said; and Nick didn't intend to. Reason Number Two was that he'd gotten such a laugh from the word his father used for the meeting—a powwow. Glancing through the dirty blond hair that fell over his face, Nick shot a look at his father, Theodore (Ted) Costas Jr., M.D., and imagined him wearing a feather headdress and beating a drum. That'd be a kick! Especially since Theodore Jr. had the kind of looks political parties liked to put on their campaign posters—silvery hair, clear blue eyes, none of those paunchy Teddy Kennedy jowls suggesting too much gin or any other kind of debauchery.

The mouth was moving now, as it had during about half the meeting. Most of the other mouth moving came from the public relations advisor, along with occasional comments by Nick's sister, Georgianna Costas, M.D.—comments that Theodore Jr. mostly acted as if he hadn't heard. Poor Georgie, wouldn't she ever stop trying? Nick's mom sat quietly; Nick knew why she was saying nothing, but would never tell. And there was the typical reverential silence from the half-dozen hangers-on. *Get a life!* he wanted to tell them.

Nick himself wasn't actually taking in a whole lot because of the third reason he'd been willing to be here—the joint he'd smoked about an hour ago. At a real powwow, they all ought to be smoking, shouldn't they? The late Ted the Third used to dope, even though you wouldn't know it from the way Ted Jr. talked about him these days. The Sainted Third, he had become. The Sainted Turd, thought the sixteen-year-old brother who still had the misfortune to be alive. Nick had chosen his seat carefully—"positioning," the public relations advisor called this technique. Well, he had positioned himself near the hall to the bathroom. Now, without needing to stand, he did a neat, unobtrusive roll into the hall. Once out of sight, he got up and kept going . . . out the side door, where he couldn't be seen from the living room, and down the hill into Rose Canyon.

Freedom!

Nick followed the trail he'd made over the years, the narrow line through the chaparral where he used to go exploring when he was a kid, playing cowboys and Indians, earthmen and aliens, watching the Amtrak trains that came through the wide canyon on their way between San Diego and Del Mar. Lately he had discovered the canyon offered another kind of exploration. The way the game worked, all you had to do was walk to a part of the canyon all the kids knew about, and most avoided. Head down, but alert, the way a small animal might alertly skitter through these dry grasses, all its senses attuned to hunt.

Nick hunted by pretending he was the prey. The innocent kid who would look like a surfer if his hair were just cleaner; if his face weren't a relief map of acne. At least he wore the right baggy cutoffs and big T-shirts, clean, thanks to his mom; the laundry was one thing she had kept doing after The Sainted Turd died a year ago. She'd pretty much given up on cooking, though. Too bad. Nick used to love his mom's cooking. And she hardly drove anymore either, a secret she and Nick kept between themselves. He didn't think his dad even realized he'd gotten his license eight months ago. He didn't mind driving his mom places. That way, he got to use her car whenever he wanted. And there were other benefits, like her giving permission for him to get his nose pierced.

The late afternoon sun was still warm but the breeze refreshing. Nick didn't even know if he wanted to play the game today. Maybe he'd just take a walk. They used to walk in the canyon a lot, Nick and his dad. His dad told him interesting things, like the fact that five million years ago, all of San Diego was relatively flat; the canyons had been formed by the action of the uprising Pacific plate and erosion from flash floods.

He would only play, he decided, if the game chose him. It did. He had grown up in this canyon, and he could almost smell the man before he saw him. Propped on his elbow, the guy looked like he was just catching a few rays. But the tilt of his hips, the way he displayed his crotch, gave him away. He didn't even look at Nick right away, which gave Nick the chance to check him out: thirty-something, clean—that was good—wearing shorts and a Hawaiian shirt with yellow and lavender flowers.

He kept walking slowly, reacted as if he'd just seen the man, and looked up as if shyly, eyes as blue as his father's. "Hi," he said.

"Hi," said the man. "Just another day in paradise, huh?" Nick was amazed how often they said that. Had they all gone to the same training class, How to Pick Up Boys in Rose Canyon?

"Yeah," said Nick. Time to act the hunter. "There's this beautiful place near here, it's really secluded. You want to see?"

"Sure." The man scanned the area, saw no one around (Nick had already checked that), and got up.

"Nice shirt," said Nick, as he led the man behind some bushes.

The guy had come partially prepared, with a tube of K-Y jelly in his pocket, but—stupid shithead!—no condom. Nick always carried condoms with him, top of the line, so that was okay. His shrink, Dr. Morgenthal, would say that bringing the condoms meant Nick didn't want to die after all, he wanted to live. Not that Dr. M. knew about Nick's little canyon jaunts. Not that Nick told the shrink much of anything. He only went to Dr. M. because the school had insisted after what happened last year.

Dr. M. probably wouldn't care if he was gay, but he would ask why Nick played the game at all, and he'd keep asking until Nick gave him some kind of answer . . . which would be hard to do, since Nick didn't know why he felt compelled to do this and he didn't want to know. As a matter of fact, he didn't really know if he was gay or not. Half the time when he had a man inside him, he didn't even get a hard-on, whereas he always got hard just kissing Jenny Dawes. With Jenny, it was like his body took on a separate existence from his mind, his tongue pushing between her lips as if her sweet mouth were a magnet, his hands acting like they'd jump off his wrists if one of them didn't reach under her shirt and the other slide into her panties, go for the wet place between her legs . . . Just thinking about Jenny now, with the man grunting away behind him, Nick came.

Afterward, he and the man watched the sunset together. Nick shivered in the growing cold, and the man gave him the Hawaiian shirt to put on . . . but took it back before he left.

Nick had learned that the game had certain rules, and although they might change a bit from man to man, one rule was inviolable: *Never give a kid anything that could be traced to you.*

Hurrying back, Nick spotted his father coming toward him. He almost dove into the bushes to hide, but it was too late.

"Nick!" Theodore Costas sounded surprised; he mustn't have even noticed that Nick had left the powwow. And if his father smelled the sex Nick surely reeked of, he didn't show it.

"Hi, Dad."

"Just taking a walk," the elder Costas said.

"Me, too."

For a moment, Nick thought his father was going to ask him to come along, like in the old days. And just for a moment, he wanted that as keenly as a little kid wanting a chocolate ice-cream cone. But his dad just said, "See you," and kept going; and whatever dumb impulse had made Nick want to go along with his father burned to ashes.

Nick only had one more thing to do before he left the canyon. Once he'd rounded a corner where no one could see him, he took an amber pill bottle from his pants pocket and shagged it into a clump of bushes.

11 / Culture Clash

The things Paula got her to do! thought Margo, sitting in the passenger seat of Paula's car on Sunday morning. At least Paula was doing the driving this time, and on the freeway. The latest psychologist really was making a difference.

Nevertheless.

"Are you sure we shouldn't just wait and go to the funeral?" Margo said . . . as she had said yesterday when Paula suggested attending Hannah's church.

"I'll go to the funeral, too," said Paula. "But hearing about Hannah last night, I felt a need to be around other people who cared about her."

"You've never been to her church before, have you?"

"No, but there'll be a whole group of us. People from the New Age community who knew Hannah and appreciated her wisdom."

In other words, white people . . . who might or might not be welcome at Hannah's black church.

The church parking lot was full, and Paula found a place on the street. A van pulled up behind her. "Art!" Paula called to the man who emerged from the driver's side of the van.

Art Smolin, Leslie's second housemate, Margo presumed.

Art came over and enfolded Paula in a bear hug. Chubby-cheeked and bald, the chiropractor nevertheless looked powerful. Margo had had several sessions of chiropractic when she had thrown out her back. The man had used his entire body weight to adjust her spine and had twisted her neck so forcefully she'd thought her head would come off; it was no profession for wimps.

With Art's arm around her, Paula introduced him. Margo, struck by the sadness in his furry-browed brown eyes, remembered that Art was recently separated, living apart from his wife and children. Certainly his minivan looked as if it were meant to transport youth soccer teams, not merely Art and the rangy, ponytailed man who accompanied him.

"Dylan Lightwing," Art introduced the man.

Paula, extending her hand, looked starstruck. "I've heard of you. Are you here in San Diego for long?"

From Dylan Lightwing's reddened face, Margo would bet he spent a lot of time seeking enlightenment in extremely dry environments—mountaintops, deserts—without the benefit of sunscreen.

"A while. Great bumper sticker." Lightwing gestured toward PRACTICE RANDOM KINDNESS AND SENSELESS ACTS OF BEAUTY. "Yours?" he asked Paula.

She nodded, beaming, then asked Art, "Has Leslie come back yet?"

"No, but I wouldn't worry."

"It doesn't seem like Leslie to take off and not inform her clients," replied Paula. "By the way, who was she seeing lately?" Margo had told her Cynara's theory, that Leslie was off with a lover.

"Romantically?" Art laughed. "Mystery to me. There's a house rule, adopted long before I moved in. Leslie can't bring lovers to the main house. Apparently she's had some strange ones. She could be dating little green men, and I wouldn't know it.''

Margo listened, but as they walked from their cars, her eyes followed Dylan Lightwing, whose name fit him better than she would have expected. In contrast to his dessicated face, which made him look fifty, he moved with the grace of a much younger man. Margo wondered if he had ever studied dance; or more likely, T'ai Chi or some other Eastern movement discipline.

Inside the church, she and Paula found seats at the end of a row.

''Wow! Dylan Lightwing!'' breathed Paula. Dylan was sitting a few rows behind them.

''What's the big deal?''

''He's a legend. He spends part of each year traveling all over the country, leading workshops, things like that. The rest of the time he studies with a Navajo shaman in Arizona. He's part Navajo himself.''

Their conversation ended when the choir burst into song, the voices sending shivers through Margo. She had always loved listening to the cantor at temple when she was growing up, but that was like hearing an operatic performance. The gospel singers at Hannah's church made her feel she was being lifted to heaven itself.

She crashed back to Earth fast when the minister started in with a Bible reading, and fought boredom by looking around. Further down the row, Cynara, the Tarot reader, was also scanning the crowd. For a moment their eyes met. Cynara's (brown and green) flashed a brief but uncaring ''Where do I know you from?'' The Tarot reader glanced past her to Paula, and Margo would swear Cynara got the same terrified look as the day before. Why would Paula scare her—Paula, who was scared of everything?

Looking toward the center of the church, near the front,

Margo spotted the proud, cornrowed head of Olivia. Hannah's granddaughter was surrounded by people of varied ages, no doubt her family. At that moment, Olivia turned and fixed her gaze on the corner of the church where, somehow, all the white New Agers had clustered together. The young woman's face filled with such rage that Margo wasn't surprised by what happened later.

After the service, everyone was going over to console Hannah's family, who stood beside the church door with the minister. The New Age contingent moved over in a group— Margo tried to escape, but Paula was gripping her hand. Someone (a painter, mentioned Paula) knew one of Hannah's daughters and expressed her sympathy. As if in chorus, the other New Agers murmured their assent. Hannah's daughter thanked them graciously. The younger members of the family appeared less friendly, however. Olivia in particular glowered. *Get me out of here,* Margo thought, somehow stuck at the center of the little group of white sheep and hoping they would quickly trot away. No such luck.

"We'll feel her loss so much in the community," said one of the New Age men.

It was the trigger Olivia had been waiting for. "What community?" she demanded, striding forward, thrusting her face at his.

"Our healing community." The man gave a vapid smile.

"Olivia!" hissed one of the older women and grabbed her arm.

Olivia took a step back, but it was as if she couldn't halt the fury she'd been bottling up all morning.

"You people were never my grandmother's community. *This* is her community, people of color. She was mixing up cures for the people in her community for years before you 'discovered' her. Everyone here knew she was a healer. Of course they did, most of them couldn't afford to go to a doctor. I used to ask her why she even bothered with you all.''

"Olivia, your gram would help anybody who needed help," said the older woman. "Now, why don't you show a little of that charity?"

"You don't know. She had her own joke on white people. Know what she did? She charged them four times, five times what she charged her real community." Olivia again addressed the whites; apparently transfixed, they hadn't moved, despite Margo's attempts to nudge Paula away. "She always thought it was real funny that none of you ever questioned her charges. Now, people in *her* community sure would've thought twice before they paid twenty or thirty dollars for one of her medicines. But not you. Or maybe one of you did. Maybe that's why one of you took her into the canyon and set her on fire, because you didn't like being overcharged. Did you know what happens to a body that burns up? Did you know that all the water in the brain boils into steam and because the steam has no place to go, the top of the person's head blows off?"

"Olivia! Enough!" The admonition—from a twentyish, well-dressed black man—was quiet, but Olivia heeded it. She half-fell into the man's arms, weeping.

"We're sorry," said one of the older women. "Olivia is just so upset by what happened to her grandma. I hope you understand."

"Of course we do," replied one of the New Agers. They were finally drifting away, saying, "She's just really hurting. . . . She's young, she hardly knew what she was saying."

"Margo! Margo!" Olivia was running after her. Was Margo going to come in for special excoriation as a reporter? Still, she stopped and let Olivia catch up. "I didn't mean you," Olivia said. "You did a nice story on my grandmother on the radio this morning, and I appreciated the way you sat with me the night of the fire. Can I talk to you for a few minutes? Alone?"

"I'll wait in the car," offered Paula, moving away.

"Let's walk." Olivia led Margo down a side street of modest stucco houses. Once they were out of earshot of anyone leaving the church, she said, "I think you cared about my grandmother. I want to tell you what I found out about her death. Maybe you'll do more than the police, because I figure they don't really give a flying fuck about an old woman of color."

"What can you tell me?"

"I told you about my boyfriend who works as a technician in the medical examiner's office. Once my grandma was positively identified, he filled me in."

"Is that how you found out about her head blowing off?" Margo knew a private investigator with a touchy stomach, who constantly popped antacids. Right now, she wished she had his supply of Tums.

"Actually that didn't happen, the fire wasn't hot enough. I learned about it in school, and I just wanted to gross people out."

They stepped aside, out of the way of a kid caroming down the street on a tricycle.

"What *did* happen?"

"You can't tell anyone. Jamal'd lose his job."

"Agreed." Jamal must have been the young man who jumped in quickly when Olivia threatened to reveal the details of her grandmother's death.

"I guess I'm glad about this, because it meant Gram suffered less. She didn't die on account of the fire. Someone gagged her first. They stuffed a handkerchief down her throat. That was the actual cause of death, asphyxiation from the gag, not smoke inhalation or anything else associated with the fire. I guess they thought the gag would burn away. But it didn't.

See, when a person burns, their tongue swells up like a sponge and fills their mouth. That kept the gag intact."

Antacids weren't going to do it. Bile filled Margo's throat. She bent beside a graffiti-covered wall and spat it out.

Olivia patted Margo's shoulder. "Sorry," she said. "You get used to talking about things like this in premed. You okay? Can you take a few deep breaths?"

"Yeah." They started to walk back.

The child on the trike raced by again, and Olivia bent down and stopped him. "You watch how fast you go on this sidewalk, there's a lot of holes in it," she cautioned. Standing up, she said, "How about you? What do you know that you haven't put on the news?"

"The only thing I can tell you is, remember the fire in Deerhorn Valley, the week before the fire over here? A woman was found there, but the police couldn't make an identification. Another healer, someone who knew Hannah, went missing at about the same time."

"A white woman?" Everyone's death might diminish John Donne, but Olivia sounded as if only black people's deaths meant anything to her.

"Leslie Getz."

"Oh, no." Olivia sounded genuinely distressed. "I knew Leslie. Gram really respected her. They used to trade, you know, Leslie would give Gram massages and Gram gave her herbs. In fact, Gram sent me to Leslie when I hurt my shoulder in a car accident. She helped me a lot. Are you saying Leslie got burned, too?"

"I don't know. They just started looking into it on Friday, Leslie wasn't reported missing till then. Jamal might have some information on that. Did he say anything else about your grandmother?"

"Yeah. They put her on a kind of pyre, piled-up branches, things like that, but they didn't light the pyre. They started the fire a hundred yards upwind of her. Did you know that meant the fire would be burning hotter when it got to her? This person—this animal—knew enough about fire to know that.''

For all Olivia's patina of clinical detachment, Margo realized that the young woman was shaking. "God, Olivia, I'm sorry," she said, putting an arm around her. They must have formed some kind of bond, because Olivia accepted the hug for a moment, before shrugging it off.

"Well, I'm not sorry," she said. "I don't have any room for sorry. I'm just mad. I want to find the animal who did this and, the same way he killed my grandmother, I want to kill him. I want to stand there and watch him burn, except I'm not going to give him any gag. I don't want him to go fast. I want it to take a long time. I want to hear him scream.''

12 / Hot Spots

"One more thing." Acid could have dropped from Olivia's smile. "This creep has got to have one hell of an itch."

"Why?"

"The pyre he put my gram on? A lot of it was poison oak."

Was that why Obayashi had checked Paula's arms and ankles? thought Margo, parting from Olivia at the church. *He couldn't suspect Paula!* But why not, since Paula had freely admitted to being at the Encanto fire at the time it started? Oh God, and since he figured Paula was unbalanced. To think that Paula considered Donny Obayashi a nice guy! He was just doing his job, Margo reminded herself. Routine police work. Still, she couldn't help being outraged on Paula's behalf, as she hurried toward the car.

Heading down the street, she heard loud rock music. The music, not Paula's usual choice, was in fact coming from her car radio.

"Guess what?" exclaimed Paula, half dancing in her seat.

"Just a sec. Do you have some water?"

"Sure." Paula handed her a plastic bottle.

Margo took a large mouthful of water, swished it around to cleanse the sour taste from the bile that had risen to her mouth, and spat the water into the street. Then she took a long drink.

"Guess what?" Paula repeated as she started the car, too wrapped up in her own excitement to register Margo's distress. Thank goodness. Margo had no wish to relate Olivia's story. But neither did she feel strong enough to fend off questions, if Paula demanded to know.

"What?" Margo tried to sound enthusiastic.

"I talked to Dylan while I was waiting for you. He just got back yesterday from spending the summer studying and leading workshops in Arizona, and he invited me—he invited *us!*—to the sweat he's doing next weekend."

"Sweat, as in sweat lodge?"

"Yes!" Paula was so jazzed, she barely seemed to notice she was accelerating onto the freeway.

"No way." There was a limit to what Paula could drag her to. A sweat lodge sounded like a form of torture that combined intense heat, claustrophobia, and coed nudity.

"Margo, you don't understand. Dylan's a real shaman. You don't just go to his sweats if you feel like it, they're by invitation only. I'm amazed he asked us."

"I'm not amazed. He wants to get a look at you without any clothes on."

Margo considered her own looks satisfactory: wavy, shoulder-length if haphazardly styled dark brown hair, a slender body, cheekbones she'd been told were Slavic, and warm brown eyes that invited confidences, the latter an asset in her job. Paula, on the other hand, had the kind of figure—plus the dramatic black bob and bright lipstick she favored—that really did make heads turn. Margo always marveled when she walked into a room with Paula and *it* happened.

"Cynic!" chided Paula. "I've talked to people who have done Dylan's sweats. Leslie went to one, maybe six months ago. Everyone says it's an incredibly healing experience. It's at a beautiful site in Julian, too," she added, naming a mountain community some sixty miles inland. "Think about it," Paula urged when she dropped Margo off at home. "Then decide."

Margo had already decided that she had no desire to prance around nude in front of any man except Barry. Speaking of which, Barry had returned from his conference, and the kids were at their mother's today. Prancing around nude struck both her and Barry as a swell idea, and they did, followed by eating cheese and apples and reading novels in bed (in Barry's case, John D. MacDonald, and in Margo's, Alice Hoffman). Margo told him the horrors she had heard from Olivia and, finally, took a long nap she hadn't known she needed. She awoke with two ideas nagging at her—Olivia's mention of the pyre built under her grandmother and Paula's comment yesterday: "What if someone is burning witches?"

She reached for the bedside phone and called the sheriff's department. Still no identification on the Jane Doe. She realized she wanted to see the spot where the woman had been found . . . and that she couldn't bear the thought of going alone.

"Barry, will you come somewhere with me?"

"Planning some cat burgling?" he said, eyeing the black jeans and sweatshirt she'd put on.

"Going someplace ashy. The Deerhorn Valley fire."

"What for?"

She put a finger across his lips. "I'm not sure. No arguments yet."

Lovely man, he put on similar clothes without pointing out that the Deerhorn fire wasn't considered arson, nor was Jane Doe's death considered murder. Margo found Barry's scientifically trained mind extraordinarily helpful, when she was ready to listen to his observations. She wasn't ready yet, however, and as he drove them to the site of the fire, southeast of the city, she directed the conversation to his daughter's wish to pierce her nose. Had Jenny talked to him about it?

"She mentioned it." Characteristically, Barry had asked Jenny to do some research and find out what would happen if she decided to stop wearing a stud—would she have a noticeable scar?

"You mean you wouldn't be opposed to the idea, on a gut level?"

"A lot of the kids I teach have nose studs and, for all I know, worse. I've gotten used to it."

"Has she discussed it with Rae yet?"

"No. Of course, I told her she had to. Where do I turn?"

This was really the back country, an area of sparse population and rough hewn hills, marked by eight-and ten-foot-tall rock outcroppings that looked like a giant's pebbles, flung so hard they had embedded themselves at weird angles in the earth.

"Look for Deerhorn Valley Road," Margo said.

Almost immediately after they turned, the earth they passed was denuded and black; two thousand acres had burned. Margo remembered a particularly dramatic grouping of rocks near the fire's source point and directed Barry to keep driving until she spotted them. They parked, got out of the car, and trudged up the barren hill.

Fires are a natural part of the southern California ecosystem, a state forestry department investigator had told Margo for a report she'd done after the blaze. Some plants only release their seeds upon exposure to intense heat. And a fire clears out the dead brush underlying new growth. Even with rain last year, several years of drought had left a fifty percent dead fuel load under the new greenery.

Give it two years, he'd said, and the land would look as if nothing had happened.

Only ten days later, however, the area looked like the victim of a crazed general's scorched earth policy. Dead, brittle sticks, somehow still rooted in the blackened ground, were all that remained of a rich chaparral vegetation that typically included sage, oaks, prickly pear, broom, California holly, and countless other species. The plants were all gone now . . . as was most of the evidence of Jane Doe's death.

Scraps of yellow police tape and Margo's own memory took her to the spot where the victim had been discovered, close to a startlingly vertical rock that was nearly flat on top.

"Reminds you of Stonehenge, doesn't it?" said Barry.

"Maybe that's why Leslie would have come here. Maybe she thought it was a sacred place."

Margo stood where Jane/Leslie had died, but she received no enlightenment. Was that why she had wanted to come here? Did she think she would somehow *know* what had happened, that she'd get emanations from the dead woman? She did feel something, but only a vague unease that made her move a few feet away from the death site . . . and focus on the hard facts.

"They think the fire started there, about five feet from her," she said and repeated what she had learned: The investigators had identified the source point by looking for the "V" the fire made as it fanned outward.

"Didn't they said she was nude? How did they know her clothes just didn't burn off?"

"She was lying on her back on a blanket. Some of the blanket, that was underneath her body, was still intact. But there was just the blanket and then her skin, nothing in between." The authorities had wanted reporters to know the details of the woman's death, once they'd decided she had died by accident. They'd hoped the publicity would lead to her identification.

"Where the fire starts isn't where it burns the hottest, it picks up heat as it goes," Margo continued the lesson she'd been given. A lesson the arsonist had also learned, before killing Hannah? Olivia had said the Encanto fire was started upwind of Hannah's body. "They even found some of her clothes. They looked like they'd been folded neatly at the edge of the blanket. Poor Leslie."

"You don't know it was Leslie. The circumstances of this woman's death sound pretty different from Hannah's."

"Right," she responded, finding that—because she had stood where the woman died?—she now welcomed rational argument, both Barry's and her own. "And I didn't hear anything about her lying on a pyre, like Hannah was. She couldn't have been gagged, either, or the investigators wouldn't have ruled out murder." Margo walked back to Jane's last resting place and paced in a circle there. "So dammit, why do I have this gut feeling that Jane Doe was Leslie and that she was killed, too?"

She glanced at Barry, who had far less respect for gut feelings than she. But he was listening, as he picked the blackened outer layer from a stem of chamise, revealing a beautiful mahogany color under it.

"Why do you?" he said.

"Think it's Leslie? Because she's still missing. And she knew Hannah. What if some zealot decided New Age healers are the latest scourge from hell and they should all be condemned to flames?"

"It's not impossible."

"What?" Margo had expected the voice of science, telling her she'd been hanging out with Paula too much. It turned out she *was* hearing the voice of science.

Barry said, "This city recently spent millions of dollars,

fortunately unsuccessfully, to prosecute a deformed man for Satanic abuse at a church day care center. The local spiritual beliefs range from paganism to a Christianity so far right and so full of hate that, even being brought up as a good Catholic, I can't comprehend it. Why not have a witch burner on the loose?''

He peeled more black from the chamise. "Is this alive?" he asked. "The red wood underneath?"

"No, it's dead." Margo had asked the arson inspector the same question, had hoped for some sign of survival amid the devastation.

"What a shame, it's so beautiful."

13 / Breath

It had been a very long Monday, what with meeting two new clients and preparing for the audit to which a third client, a small theater company, was subjected annually by its major funder. When Paula finally got home, after eight, she noticed the light on the answering machine was blinking wildly, at least five calls. She ignored the machine and headed straight for the kitchen, where she popped a Lean Cuisine into the microwave and rinsed lettuce and a tomato for salad. She didn't even kick off her shoes—usually her first action when she entered the condo—until she had poured a glass of white wine.

She sat back in a chair, enjoying the wine, a Napa Valley Fumé Blanc. Good California wine was something that she—she and Eric—had developed a taste for when they'd first met, working together at the big accounting firm. Post-Eric, Paula had learned that focusing on nonprofit clients didn't obliterate the wine budget, as long as you cut a few other corners, such as dining out, a fancy car, the newest clothes. And housing: She had let Eric buy her out of their splashy condo at a time when real estate prices were still high and waited to buy another, less posh but comfortable, when the prices and interest rates had fallen.

She roused herself enough to get up and turn on the radio—the jazz station, in spite of a vow she'd recently made to work on her phobia about listening to news. But it was clearly a jazz night, if she was thinking about her ex-husband . . . who had just honeymooned with his new wife in Bali. He could afford it. Eric had risen in the ranks of the accounting firm, as he'd anticipated, as they had both expected to do at the time they got married, seven years ago.

How tidy their life plan had been. And how it had been shattered by her agoraphobia. She felt a familiar twinge of anger. In some ways, the reason for their breakup—for Eric's leaving her—was ridiculously simple and trite: he just couldn't handle her illness. Though to be truly fair, Paula had to admit that their separation came after months of her own questioning, since once she'd gotten sick, nothing was the same anymore, none of the goals she had believed were so important, and none of the people—including Eric—whom she'd once tried so hard to impress. Yes, Eric had done the actual walking out. But hadn't she already left in spirit? She had just been too afraid of being alone with the agoraphobia to do it for real. But she'd survived.

She hadn't merely survived, she'd done damn well, she thought, surveying the condo whose clean, modern lines she had purposely decorated against, buying cushy used furniture and Art Deco vases and draping the stark white walls with bright, sensuous fabrics: a crimson Japanese kimono, a silk hanging of a nude, enormous woman painted by an artist friend, a paisley thrift store shawl. Thrift store shawls also played a key role in her wardrobe, giving a gypsy air to the expensive suits she had acquired during the fat years. She knew her clothes would look dated, were she to walk into her old firm. Among *her* clients, however, she received plenty of compliments for her stylishness.

"Dinner!" the microwave beeped, at the same time that the phone rang. Paula waited a couple of rings—it was undoubtedly a sales pitch—but she could never ignore a ringing telephone. Maybe that was something else to work on with Dr. Donniger.

"Hello? . . . Hello?" she said.

She was aware of breathing, but the person didn't speak.

"Hello, can you hear me?" she tried again. "This must be a bad connection, you'd better call back."

She hung up, but the phone remained silent. A crank call, she told herself, assembling her dinner on a tray. She ate curled up on the couch in front of the television, watching a Barbara Stanwyck movie on the classics cable channel. Cable, like wine, was another luxury she'd been unwilling to relinquish on her relatively gentle slide to a lower standard of living.

The movie was only a two-star film, however, not one of Stanwyck's greats, and she didn't mind getting up to answer when the phone rang again an hour later. Again, she heard only soft breathing. This time she felt nervous, her heartbeat quickening. She talked herself out of it, reminding herself that (a) agoraphobics are notorious for catastrophizing, (b) she lived in a gated security building, and (c) although her number was listed in the telephone book, her address wasn't. Even if the jerk knew her name, it didn't mean he could get anywhere near her.

Since she was next to the phone, she played back the six messages that had been waiting when she came in. Two were from friends, one from a client to whom she had unwisely given her home number, one hangup. And two calls appeared to be the breather—ten seconds of silence, too long for someone who just hadn't wanted to leave a message on the machine. She would call the phone company tomorrow and get her number changed. No, that was overreacting. She might as well wait a few days and see if the breather kept it up. Probably some kid who was subjecting a dozen women to the same little joke tonight and would amuse himself by watching an Arnold Schwarzenegger movie tomorrow.

The next call came at eleven, just before she went to bed. The last woke her at two a.m. Even though she unplugged both phones in the condo then, she was so rattled she lay awake the rest of the night. She couldn't stop thinking of the feeling she'd had last week, of energy being directed at her. Did the energy and the creepy phone calls emanate from the same source—someone who wished her harm?

Dammit, Paula! she chided herself. *Cut it out!* She didn't just turn her anger inward, however, she had gone through enough therapy to know better. She was furious at "the Breather," too. She'd heard you should never succumb to the desire to scream at a crank caller, it only turned them on. But she had no objection whatsoever to inflicting pain. Maybe that nice Lieutenant Obayashi could tell her where to get a police whistle.

14 / Holy War

The Costas entourage, Margo dubbed the three people whose chairs flanked a lectern at one end of the red-tiled courtyard behind Dr. Theodore Costas's home in University City, a well-to-do suburb near the University of California–San Diego. The chairs and lectern stood on a riser, the kind that people rent for backyard weddings. Behind the riser, a rage of pink bougainvillea climbed a stone wall. The bougainvillea was interrupted, however, by a professionally printed banner hanging on the wall: PHYSICIANS FOR RESPONSIBLE MEDICINE.

On the right of the handsome wooden lectern, Margo recognized the local state senator, Harlan Eberhard, chatting with a woman sitting next to him. The woman, perhaps in her late twenties, looked not so much attractive as expensive. Her light brown hair, cut close to her head, was expertly styled and kissed with blond. Over a fawn silk dress, she wore a loose linen jacket in a weave of coffee-brown and rose, the kind of garment designed to conceal a multitude of figure flaws. Margo got a closer look when she went to secure her microphone to the lectern. The woman's patrician features would have said money even without the finishing touch of perfect makeup. In fact, the makeup was too perfect, the obvious lipliner and thick mascara reminding Margo of her own occasional department store "makeovers"; she always wanted to scrub her face for an hour when she got home.

Seated on the other side of the lectern, a woman with short white hair was, Margo assumed, Costas's wife. Although well-dressed—and looking as if she too had just visited a makeup artist—Mrs. Costas had a lost, unfocused air that Margo associated with women living on the street. Theodore Costas may have submerged his grief over his son's death by masterminding a crusade against New Age healers, but Margo doubted that his wife had transformed her sorrow into any kind of constructive endeavor. She turned several times to the empty chair next to her—where Nick Costas was supposed to be? Margo was avid to set eyes on the young man who might be Jenny's boyfriend.

Off stage, the entourage was augmented by two public relations people, an older man and a perky young blonde woman, who greeted the media representatives at the entrance to the courtyard. They handed out press packets in glossy white folders, with Physicians for Responsible Medicine embossed in gold on the front. There were also several exceptionally clean-cut young people, the women in dresses and men in dress shirts and ties, whom Margo thought of as dogsbodies. The dogsbodies kept (pointlessly, as far as Margo could tell) moving around the chairs set up for the media, and generally hovered as if waiting for the call, whatever the call might be.

"Hey!" she said, noticing that one of the dogsbodies was the man she had encountered in Leslie's garden. What was a friend of Leslie's doing assisting a sworn foe of the New Age?

"Can I get you anything?" he said smoothly—not as if

he'd never met her but as if there were nothing odd about his having gone to visit Leslie and now being here. He stopped himself, however, and turned toward the riser, his eyes shining, the way he might have faced his guru back in his massage days.

A white-haired man, with the same aristocratic features as the expensive younger woman, stepped energetically onto the riser and approached the lectern. Margo was even more interested in the teenage boy slipping into the fourth chair, next to Mrs. Costas. No kid who had a nose stud and rampant acne could look as squeaky clean as the dogsbodies, but Nick, if that was he, had taken the trouble to put on well-pressed chinos and a sport jacket. And his hair, though grazing his collar, looked freshly washed and combed.

"Thank you very much for coming," said the white-haired man. "I'm Dr. Ted Costas. I'm honored to be joined this afternoon by our esteemed state senator, Harlan Eberhard, for whose support we are deeply grateful." Costas gestured toward Eberhard, then presented the rest of the onstage entourage. "Allow me to introduce my daughter, Georgianna, my wife, Anne, and my son, Nicholas." Merely glancing at his family, Costas missed the expression on his wife's face: the look of a woman drowning.

The physician had a commanding voice, a baritone that surely prevented anyone from arguing when he broke the news that they needed . . . what kind of doctor was he, anyway? Flipping through the press kit, Margo located his bio: Theodore Costas Jr. was an ophthalmologist. She also came across a bio for another doctor in the family—Georgianna, although her father hadn't mentioned her professional status when he introduced her. Georgianna was the Dr. Costas with truly tragic information to impart to her patients. She specialized in oncology.

Ted Costas was telling the story Margo had heard a few

days ago, but with greater medical detail. His older son, Theodore III, began experiencing lethargy and a general sense of malaise about two and a half years ago. The young man was then twenty-four years old. Refusing to consult an M.D., "Teddy" had instead made the rounds of various New Age healers, very much against his father's wishes. While Margo could sympathize with the frustration Ted Costas must have felt, he struck her as the kind of father whose wishes you'd want to oppose.

"Finally," said Costas, "after a year of consulting—and handing over hundreds of dollars to—these greedy New Age charlatans, Teddy became so ill he agreed to see a qualified physician. The diagnosis was lymphatic cancer. Although aggressive chemotherapy was initiated immediately, it was too late. One year ago, on this date exactly, my son died."

Margo, scanning the stage, thought Anne Costas was going to faint. Nick reached for his mother's hand. A point for the kid, she thought.

She glanced at the notes she had made. Even though she was getting everything on tape, she liked to jot references to statements she could use as actualities. Ted Costas hadn't given her much. The doctor had spoken coherently, but, with the exception of his remark about greedy New Age charlatans, he'd sounded more the clinician than the grief-stricken parent, saying little that Margo couldn't just paraphrase. The next speaker, however, possessed the passion her father lacked.

"I'm an oncologist," said Dr. Georgianna Costas. "As you probably know, that means I treat people who have cancer. What you may not know is that a diagnosis of cancer is by no means a death sentence. With the advances being made in treatment, cancer that's detected early, particularly in young people, can often be treated successfully. You might be thinking that since my brother had cancer, he was going to die anyway, so what difference did it make if he saw a physician or he went to a voodoo ceremony and had chicken blood poured over his head? Well, I'm here to tell you it would have made a big difference, literally the difference between life and death. My brother had a type of cancer that could have been treated, had it been discovered when he first manifested symptoms. If it weren't for the irresponsible people who took an ill, vulnerable young man and convinced him that they knew more than legitimate physicians, Teddy Costas would be alive today. These so-called healers killed my brother.''

It wasn't just what Georgianna said, but the fire with which she spoke. Margo saw that she wasn't the only callous reporter dabbing at her eyes. On the platform, Anne Costas had silent tears dripping down her cheeks, and Harlan Eberhard appeared a tad wet-eyed as well. Nick, perhaps overcome, had left the stage. Even Theodore Costas, who had introduced Georgianna as if he'd reluctantly indulged her desire for a moment in the spotlight, seemed to feel her power to move the crowd. He stared at his daughter as if she had just emerged full-grown from his forehead, Athena spawned by Zeus.

He paused a moment before returning to the microphone, then said, ''Dr. Georgianna Costas, thank you. And now I'd like to welcome my friend Hal Eberhard, the distinguished state senator for this district.''

It turned out Eberhard wasn't just there for window dressing. He announced that he was introducing a bill that would require anyone seeking nontraditional medical care to receive a checkup from a physician first; the person would then receive a certificate good for two years.

''That's like trying to tell Californians what they can and can't watch on TV,'' commented a reporter.

''Not at all,'' said Eberhard. ''We're just asking people to get a doctor's certificate before trying some of these unproven treatments. The so-called healer must have a certificate from each patient or be fined.''

Margo doubted the senate bill would get far, in a state that not only contained more than its share of New Agers but also thousands of immigrants for whom a visit to the *curandero* or the acupuncturist *was* traditional care. Hell, half the state senate probably went to alternative healers as well as to regular M.D.'s. Eberhard, a fourth-term senator, didn't seem surprised to receive only a few questions.

Ted Costas wasn't finished, however, and his final announcement sounded as if it could put a genuine chill on New Age practitioners.

''Today my attorney has filed suit against Richard Del Vecchio and Hannah Jones for two hundred million dollars each, for practicing medicine without a license.''

''Are you aware that Hannah Jones died last week?'' asked Margo.

''Yes, I am. The suit will be against Hannah Jones's estate.''

''What kind of healing did she and Del Vecchio do?'' asked Bob Kolchek from Channel 9.

''Ms. Jones used herbal remedies. Del Vecchio claimed to be healing my son with crystals.''

Richard, Margo realized, was the man at Crystal Magic. She was carrying the amethyst crystal in the spacious Guatemalan bag she used for a purse, reaching for it, like worry beads, when she felt rattled.

Kolchek followed up. ''So this has nothing to do with the fact that Richard Del Vecchio is an heir to the family that started the Del Vecchio Corporation?''

Margo could have applauded. Kolchek, one of the most respected reporters in town, had really done his homework. Del Vecchio Brands had started with canned spaghetti in the 1950s and had gradually acquired enough other companies that probably everyone standing in the Costas's courtyard had had some encounter with a Del Vecchio product in the past twenty-four hours.

"Aren't you just going after the deepest pockets?" came the inevitable question . . . and the inevitable answer:

"Absolutely not. And you'll notice I'm not just suing Del Vecchio, but Ms. Jones as well."

Margo might be soft enough to shed a tear at Georgianna Costas's expression of grief, but she didn't for a second believe Costas and his attorney had thrown Hannah into the lawsuit as anything but a smokescreen for their obvious target, the Del Vecchio fortune. They wouldn't care that legal fees alone could wipe out anything Hannah's family might inherit.

Returning to KSDR, Margo quickly put together her story for the five o'clock news. She focused on Georgianna Costas's statement and telephoned to get a sound bite from an attorney—who was characteristically vague—as to whether there was any precedent for a lawsuit of this kind. Off the record, the attorney felt that with powerful legal representation, Costas had a chance.

She was still in her office, lining up interviewees for a piece on cars stolen in San Diego and sold across the border in Tijuana, when her story on the Costas news conference aired. Her phone rang. She innocently answered it.

"Margo, I loved it!" The voice was that of Alex Silva. In the ten months during which Alex had been KSDR's general manager, Margo had discovered she cringed more when Alex was enthusiastic than when he was raking her over the coals. "The Costas story," Alex went on. "Let's put them, the father and the daughter, on *Air San Diego*—how about this Thursday?"

"Have you checked with Dan?" Margo didn't host *Air San*

Diego, the station's hour-long morning call-in program. That duty belonged to her officemate, Dan Lewis, who had gone home for the day. "He's probably already got someone lined up for Thursday," she said, glancing at the disaster area that habitually constituted Dan's half of the office. Could she possibly locate his schedule of this week's guests?

"He can reschedule," said Alex. "And I want you to host that day. You've done all the background on the story. So Thursday's okay?"

"But . . ."

"All right!" Alex hung up.

Margo almost rushed to Alex's office but held back. Why, she asked herself, did Alex's idea make her so uncomfortable? The Costases *would* make good call-in show guests, wouldn't they? Margo considered the possibility that she was just experiencing her usual knee-jerk opposition to her abrasive boss. She had to admit that the answer was, partly, yes. But only partly. Having clarified her own motives, Margo went to see Alex.

"We ought to have someone representing the other side," she said.

"What other side? In San Diego, there'll be plenty of callers defending rubbing sage into their belly buttons." An easterner, Alex made no effort to hide his belief that the majority of Californians—Margo included—lacked several essential chromosomes related to higher mental functions. "The Costases are qualified M.D.'s. KSDR isn't in the business of giving official air time to quacks."

"What about an acupuncturist? They're not quacks. They have a centuries-old medical tradition. Or someone like the doctor from India who advocates Ayurvedic medicine?"

"That guy, sure," said Alex, knowing—as she did—that she didn't have a prayer of landing him for a minor local radio program. "Or if you can find, say, an acupuncturist who's also an M.D. But we're not inviting some local crazy to come on and claim to know more than a medical doctor.''

Margo reached into her purse for her crystal, but she felt no better able to deal with Alex. Holding the hard object simply gave her the idea of hurling it at her boss's head . . . an urge that she fortunately resisted.

15 / Playing With Fire

Crouched so he could just see over the window sill in his parents' bedroom, Nick observed the news conference, the amplified words coming in clearly through the glass. He had sneaked out when Georgie came up to speak. He hated the way his sister acted like she personally could have saved Teddy's life. But she sure got the crowd going.

Poor Georgie. Nick had discussed his sister with Dr. Morgenthal and understood that all Georgie wanted was their father's approval. Even at twenty-nine, she hadn't figured out that there was nothing she could do, she had just been born the wrong sex. So what if she had aced her way through premed and then med school? Teddy was the one Dad had wanted to follow in his footsteps . . . Teddy the Sainted Turd, who had wanted nothing to do with medicine; who had taken six years just to get through college, not because he'd done anything noble like taking time off to go work with Mother Teresa, but because he was a goddamn fuckup. Like Nick.

In a class at school, Nick had learned the stages of dying or losing a loved one: denial, anger, bargaining, depression, acceptance. His dad, he figured, was stuck in anger. Nick's mother, on the other hand, was simply stuck, as well as doped out of her mind, not that either of the two doctors in the family noticed.

Speaking of which, Nick checked under his parents' bed. Sure enough, Mom had let one of her empty pill bottles roll underneath. That asshole Senator Eberhard was speaking, and Nick didn't give a shit what he had to say. Nick took the amber plastic pill bottle into his own bathroom to peel off the label. Except the fucking label on this one must've been put on with Super Glue. He could only get it off in little bits that, once he stripped them from the bottle, clung to his fingers. Some of the white paper still adhered to the bottle when he finished, but at least he'd removed all of the identifying information: his mother's name, the name of the drug—Xanax, which Nick knew was a tranquilizer—and the names of the doctor and pharmacy that had supplied this particular bottle. His mom got the prescriptions from three different doctors that he knew of and went to a different pharmacy for each one. She was clever about that, but not so clever when it came to getting rid of the empty bottles. Nick looked out for the bottles, as well as taking his mom to the appointments and pharmacies since she'd stopped driving. The way he saw it, his mom's reaction to Teddy's death was the most honest of anyone's in the family.

Standing over the sink, Nick clumped together the strips of paper he had peeled off the bottle, lit a match, and set the paper on fire. Wow! Some of the paper was still sticking to him. He watched as the orange flame danced around his fingers. He stood a few seconds, experiencing the pain, before he blew out the flame. More carefully this time, he peeled the rest of the paper from his skin and lit it again. What a stink, between the plastic stuck over the paper and the glue! Not that anyone would notice except Lupe, the maid. No one else came into his room these days. In fact, although he felt guilty even thinking it, that was one excellent benefit he'd gotten from his brother's death. No one gave a flying fuck what he did any more.

After he'd burned all the paper, he turned on the tap and washed the remains down the sink, then kept his burned fingers under the cold water for several minutes. One thing about growing up in a doctor's family, you learned basic first aid. He hadn't burned himself badly, the skin didn't even look very red, but one finger sure smarted. He dried his hands and put the now-denuded pill bottle into his pocket. He would ditch it the next time he went to the canyon.

Even in his room, at the other side of the house, he could still hear the yakking from the courtyard, his father's voice now. He picked up the phone, dialed Jenny Dawes's number, and got the answering machine at her house. Dumb idea, of course Jenny was in school this morning; right this minute she was in the second-year Spanish class where he'd met her. Dumb idea, anyway, imagining anything could happen with Jenny. Nick was gay, wasn't he? Wasn't that why he went into the canyon and let men fuck him in the ass? So what if he got a hard-on when he held Jenny? Sixteen-year-old boys got hard-ons just sitting in history class. It was a biological reaction, a reflex like the way your leg kicked when the doctor hit you with that little hammer right below your knee.

It sounded like the news conference was ending. Nick ran downstairs and loaded a plate with some of the spread Lupe had put out for his family and the people helping them, whom Nick thought of as "the cretins." Made it! He had a plateful of food (and a beer) back to his room before anyone came inside the house.

"Nicky?" came a voice fifteen minutes later. "Nick, are you there?"

Damn, his mother had noticed his absence after all. He opened the door and came into the hall, so she wouldn't notice the burned smell. At least with his mom, he had a can't-miss strategy.

"I felt really sad after everyone talked about Teddy," he said. "I just need to be alone."

"I understand," said Anne Costas, her eyes filling up.

Nick gave his mom a big hug.

16 / Tea and Sadism

"Paula! Paula! What's wrong?" begged Margo, embracing her friend, who had walked into their Wednesday night dance class and burst into tears.

The other women gathered round, one reaching for Paula's hand and another stroking her arm.

After a few minutes, Paula stopped crying enough to talk. "It's stupid, really. Just crank calls. It wouldn't be so bad if I were sleeping. I just haven't slept for the past two nights."

Encircled by the half-dozen women in the class, Paula explained that "the Breather" had phoned her some half-dozen times on Monday night, the last time at two a.m.—after which she had unplugged her phones but been too upset to sleep. Last night, she'd unplugged the phones after a single call, but just thinking about him out there, knowing her number, had again kept her up all night.

"You said it started on Monday?" said Tess, one of the class members.

Paula nodded.

"Was there some client you saw that day, someone a little odd who might think this is a way to, um, court you?"

"I can barely remember who I saw on Monday. Sleep deprivation is rotten for the mind. I saw a couple new clients—a mental patients' rights organization and an acupuncture clinic. And the Theater of the Abjured, but I've been doing their accounting for two years."

"The mental patients' organization?" suggested Fay, their teacher.

"I think the people there struggle a lot more with inner demons than spend time bothering anyone else. I can relate to that."

"Well, it's no wonder you can't sleep," said Margo. "Jenny and David are with their mom tonight. Come stay at our house."

Paula shook her head with surprising fierceness. "I am so goddamn afraid of so many goddamn things. I'm not going to be afraid to stay in my own house. I had the phone company change my number today, and the new number's unlisted. I'm sleeping at home."

"It's just some creep," Tess reassured her. "One time a man called and asked for me by name. He sounded really upset. He said a good friend of mine had been beaten up and taken to the hospital, and she'd asked him to call me. Of course, I got really involved in the conversation. It wasn't until I asked him my friend's name, which he didn't know, and then I asked him to describe her, which he couldn't, that I realized he was making it all up . . . no doubt whacking off every second he managed to keep me on the phone."

"What a jerk. There was a performance art piece," commented Sharon, a painter, "where women placed anonymous calls to other women and wished them well. Why don't we do something like that for Paula tonight? A dance where we physically support her and make her feel safe?"

*　　*　　*

"I feel a lot better," Paula told Margo after class. "In fact, I haven't been eating well. Let's go out for something fattening."

"Sounds good."

They got in their cars and Margo followed her to a coffee-house not far from where they lived. Owned by a theatrical designer, the place stood out with bold red paint on one wall and high-tech metal shelves holding newspapers and games. Yet for all the trendy design touches, it had the warm, inviting atmosphere of a place where you could chat for hours.

Over slices of lemon poppyseed cake, decaf cappuccino (Margo), and chamomile tea (Paula), Margo recounted the news conference Ted Costas had held the day before.

"I already know," Paula said proudly. "I heard your report. I decided to start listening to the news."

"Now I *really* know why you're not sleeping. By the way, have you ever met . . . damn, he told me his name but I've forgotten. He's very muscular, say in his late twenties, and he studied massage with Leslie?"

"A lot of people have studied massage with Leslie."

Margo recalled the intimate voice that had scared her, taking her by surprise in Leslie's garden. Under other circumstances, she supposed she might have found the voice attractive. "A bedroom voice," she said.

Paula laughed. "Scott Nelson."

"That's it. You know him?"

"I dated him for a while. So did Leslie. That voice never failed."

"But the relationships didn't last?"

"No, but was that my fault or Scott's? Or just because we live in anxious times when everyone's afraid to commit? You and Barry are an anomaly. How do you know Scott?"

Margo explained about meeting him at Leslie's on Saturday and then finding him among Ted Costas's dogsbodies.

"He's a lost soul," murmured Paula sympathetically, taking a forkful of cake and loading it with the whipped cream mounded on the side. Margo, avoiding her own whipped cream, could never figure out whether Paula skipped meals on the sly or her panic attacks kept her metabolism unnaturally high.

"Why 'a lost soul'? He's turned against his friends, if he's hanging out with Ted Costas."

"Scott has turned against himself." Paula sighed. "He started out in premed in college, but it seemed so cold and unconnected from real human beings. Then he tried a few massage classes and, the way he described it to me a few years later, he felt like he'd found his true calling. So he dropped out of college and went through a massage training program. He was good."

"You're speaking from experience, I gather."

"Yes." Paula smiled as she took a sip of tea.

"But Scott doesn't do massage any more?"

"No. He stopped during the time he and I were dating, about a year ago. In fact, that's why we stopped seeing each other. I think he wanted to put anything connected to the New Age behind him. Aren't you going to eat your whipped cream?"

"It's all yours."

Scooping up more fat and calories, Paula gazed at her cake as if to avoid Margo's eyes. "I know you're going to ask why he stopped doing massage, and I happen know the answer. But I . . . I didn't exactly promise never to tell, but I knew Scott was talking to me in the strictest confidence."

"Paula, this could be important. Remember what you said the other day, about someone killing New Age healers?"

"Not Scott! I doubt that he's happy. He's probably as screwed up as anybody else, including me. But he has a good heart. Really, Margo. If I thought it mattered, I'd tell you."

Paula licked the last of the whipped cream off her fork and put on her jacket. "Damn! Thinking about going home, I'm nervous again."

"You really *can* come stay with us," offered Margo.

"Nope. But I wouldn't mind if you followed me home."

"Sure. I'll get out and walk inside with you."

"You don't have . . . Well, thanks," said Paula, as they walked to their cars.

Margo followed her home and accompanied her into the condo complex.

"By the way," said Paula, "I got a map on how to get to the sweat lodge this weekend."

"Paula, I really don't want to go," said Margo and added when Paula didn't respond, "You didn't need me to give you a ride there, did you?"

"No, it's fine."

Damn! thought Margo. She had never expressed the slightest inclination to attend the sweat. So why did she feel guilty? Maybe *she* ought to be seeing Paula's therapist.

"What is it?" she asked. Paula had stopped, and Margo realized a man and woman were standing at the door of Paula's condominium.

"Paula Chopin? I'm from the sheriff's department," said the man, approaching them and displaying a badge.

"How do I know that badge is genuine?" demanded Paula, a true urbanite.

"It's okay," said Margo, recognizing the woman. "That's Gail Sands, she works with Donny Obayashi. Do you want me to stay?" she added.

"Not, it's all right," Paula said and walked through her door with the law.

The officers' presence at Paula's suggested only one thing to Margo. She called the police department the moment she got home and had the luck to get Donny Obayashi—did the man have any life outside of work?

"Has the Jane Doe been identified?" she asked.

"There's no reason to keep it from you; the PR guys are drafting a news release now," said Obayashi. "I'm sorry. It was your friend Leslie Getz."

"Oh, no."

"How well did you know her?"

"I didn't, not personally. But Paula went to her for quite a while and talked to me about her."

"What did she say?"

"I don't know if Paula actually said this or I just created my own image. I got the impression of Leslie being soft, calm, the opposite of Type A. Does that tell you anything?"

"Hell, I don't know. Was Leslie the kind of person who'd think it was fun—or holy, or whatever—to sleep out in a canyon in the nude?"

"I guess so. But," said Margo, realizing what was wrong with this picture, "isn't this a County case? Why was Gail Sands at Paula's house, along with the man from the sheriff's department? Do you think Leslie and Hannah were killed by the same person?"

There was a slurp, as if Obayashi was drinking a cup of coffee. "First of all, there's no evidence that Leslie was killed," he said carefully. "Could be she was sleeping outside, the fire started, and she couldn't rouse herself and get out of there. She had a lot of alcohol in her body."

"What about the man who was with her? The one who had sex with her the night she died?"

"What about him?" Obayashi sounded exhausted. "He's probably meditating on the experience. Man, I hate investigating these New Age types. Half the time you can't even run a simple background check to see if someone has a record because they've all given themselves new names. Cynara—what kind of name is that?''

"It means . . ." Margo searched her memory. "It means 'daughter of the moon.' ''

"What about your friend?''

"Paula?''

"Yeah. Does she call herself Chopin because she's musical?''

"No, it's her real name. Actually, her ex-husband's real name.''

"She doesn't seem like the type to keep the name of a man she's divorced, unless she's got kids.''

"No kids. But she was already known as Chopin professionally, and it's not the kind of name you forget. Which is useful when you're in business for yourself.''

After talking to Obayashi, Margo called KSDR to report the identification of Jane Doe.

Typical of late September in California, the day had been summer-hot, but the night was nippy (although no one would dream of turning on the heat for another month). Margo felt chilled through by the time she completed her phone calls . . . and she didn't think it was just because of the temperature. She put on a flannel nightgown and wool socks, got into bed, and snuggled against the heat generator she had the good fortune to have married. Slightly bulky—though less so after a summer diet—Barry always warmed up within minutes of getting under the covers; it was a trick Margo's body had never mastered.

Barry's arms around her, she told him about Leslie . . . and about her gut feeling that Ted Costas might take justice into his own hands.

"I don't buy it," responded Barry. "Why take an extremely public posture against New Age healers and at the very same time, start killing them?''

"True. And say he could have been watching Hannah's house and grabbed her when she went out to pick herbs . . . How would he get Leslie to go to Deerhorn Valley with him in the middle of the night? Unless he was her latest weird lover? I can't believe I'm laughing. It's just imagining Ted Costas Jr., M.D., making love in a canyon, no doubt under a full moon."

Barry let out a wolf howl.

"Exactly. Oh, I'm finally getting warm. Thank you, thank you. Um, especially warm there," she murmured, as Barry's hand moved between her thighs.

The phone rang.

"Answering machine," they said together, continuing their foreplay.

"Margo! I've got to talk to you." It was Paula's voice.

Grumbling, Margo pulled away from Barry and reached for the bedside phone.

"What time is it?" she said, lifting the phone. Without her contact lenses, she couldn't read the lighted clock dial.

"Just eleven," said Paula. "Sorry, did I wake you?"

"No, it's okay. Talk to me." As long as she didn't have to get out of bed and get cold again.

"The police were here because they identified that Jane Doe as Leslie." A sob in Paula's voice that continued for a moment.

"I know. I'm really sorry."

Paula took an audible breath. "I've been thinking again, about the idea that someone is burning witches. I don't for a minute believe Scott could do anything like that. I really don't, but he *is* involved with that Costas group. Maybe someone else in the group . . . Anyway, I decided to tell you why Scott stopped doing massage."

Paula paused, and Margo restrained the urge to throw questions at her. Paula had to break this secret in her own time.

"You know, don't you, that there are all different types of massage, different intensities?" said Paula. "Well, Scott specialized in very deep bodywork. I'm sure you've heard of Rolfing?"

"Yes." What Margo had heard had convinced her never to get within ten feet of a Rolfer. The technique, as she understood it, involved separating muscle from bone, thereby getting at early emotional traumas that were buried in the body. Margo agreed that emotions could be stored physically; that was a basic tenet of her dance class. But she questioned any technique reputed to cause as much pain as it was supposed to heal.

Paula continued, "The kind of massage Scott did was similar to Rolfing. Where if the person you're working on says it hurts, you don't ease up, because you're getting to the root of the problem. Scott was working on a woman's shoulder one day, someone really tight, and the woman was screaming."

"Screaming?"

"It's not the way it sounds. That's part of the process, the emotional release."

Definitely, Margo would avoid a Rolfer if one ever came her way.

Paula's voice dropped so low that Margo had to strain to hear her. "That time, Scott pushed too hard. He broke something in the woman's shoulder."

"Holy shit."

"You've seen how strong he is. He was like that then, too. He's always worked out with weights."

"Is that why he stopped doing massage? Because he was scared he'd hurt someone again?" Margo almost found herself feeling sorry for Scott Nelson—trained to use all his strength in giving a massage and to regard a client's screams as a sign of growth, then devastated when he did just that and caused real harm. Her sympathy died when Paula continued.

"Sort of. Not really. Scott and I were dating then and he was very sweet, very open emotionally. He told me everything, the kinds of things anyone might feel but not tell a soul. He said . . . Margo, he said there was just an instant when he knew he was pushing too hard and he didn't stop. He was crying like a baby when he told me. He really does have a good heart." She sounded, thought Margo, as if she were trying to convince herself. "The reason Scott stopped doing bodywork and completely broke his connections with the New Age community, it wasn't just that he made a mistake and injured someone. He could've learned to control that."

Paula paused again, before saying, "What freaked him out so much was that for just that instant, when he kept pushing and felt the bone break . . . for the tiniest nanosecond, he enjoyed it."

17 / In the Cards

Cynara hated the way the two cops had looked around the house while they questioned her. She didn't have to be much of a psychic to pick up what they were thinking: *What a dump.* And it was. Leslie remained (well, Leslie *had* remained) in the junk store furniture and dozens of potted plants school of decorating; and *Leave the spider webs alone, Spider is our friend.* Yecch! The place was a damn time warp.

She really did feel bad about Leslie, okay? Nobody ought to die that way. And she and Les had had some good talks over the years, they had been friends. Even if Leslie had occasionally called her Cyndy, and in spite, too, of the recent tension over Cynara's spiritually incorrect taste for meat.

The point was, Leslie was gone and Cynara had to think about her own future. Which brought her back to her desire for a little piece of the American dream, her own house that she could fix any way she wanted to. She might leave the walls completely bare, just paint them colors associated with the chakras—yellow (the solar plexus) for a room in which she wanted to feel confident; blue for doing Tarot readings, the Third Eye's powers of intuition and imagination; and of course red for the bedroom. No plants. No housemates! And a better part of town. Actually, a condo would be all right. She had always asked Richard for a house, but maybe he'd spring for a condo. Surely he wouldn't stand by and let her be thrown onto the street. And there was no telling what was going to happen now.

Leslie had two kids, both grown up and on their own. Cynara supposed they inherited the place. They didn't live in San Diego, and she doubted that either would want to move here. Maybe they'd just keep renting the house out and wait to put it on the market, hoping the housing prices would go back up. But that would mean bringing in another housemate, since Cynara couldn't possibly afford half the rent on her own. She hadn't even liked having a roommate during the two years she'd spent at college. At forty-five, she had a lot less tolerance for other people's little idiosyncrasies. At least she'd only had to deal with Art lately. In the past Leslie had often taken in strays, destitute artists and other free spirits (too free to work) whom she would let crash in the attic or the basement, virtually rent-free. The last stray had apparently cured her of the habit, when he vanished along with the television set. (Les, being Les, had interpreted it as a cosmic message that television was polluting their minds.)

But even Art was too much. Tonight, for instance, after the cops left, he had tried to interest her in lighting a smudge stick and meditating on Leslie's soul. Cynara, pleading a headache, had retreated instead to her room, after a brief stop in the bathroom to pee and remove her contact lenses (leaving her with two matching hazel eyes).

She didn't really need her contacts to see the Tarot cards she was using, the Mother Peace deck. She sat at her little table by the window and laid out the cards. Should she put more pressure on Richard for a house right away or wait until Leslie's kids actually threatened to force her out? Even though Richard always came around in a crisis, he disliked crises, and he especially disliked what he saw as Cynara's habit of getting into them. He would do something to keep her from landing on the street, but he might do something a lot bigger—such as buying the condo—if she hit him up long before any crisis developed.

Nearsighted, she glanced out the window ... and experienced a zing! of insight that had nothing to do with the Tarot. The brainstorm came from looking out the window, from which she could view the path leading to Leslie's little house in back. Cynara usually tuned out anyone she saw there, part of the house policy of having nothing to do with Les's lovers ... but now she had a sudden image of a figure going down that path the night the police said Leslie was killed. The image was out of focus, her nearsightedness being extreme.

Cynara reshuffled and dealt the cards, concentrating on her new questions: Who had gone to see Leslie that night? And, once she had answered the first question, what should she do next?

18 / Very Hot Air

"It's not that I don't think the Costases have a strong case." Margo felt far more eloquent talking to Barry over breakfast Thursday morning than she'd managed to be in Alex's office two days ago. "It's that they're mounting a well-orchestrated, well-financed campaign. I object to giving them a free soapbox." She poured a second cup of coffee, desperate for clear-mindedness. In two hours, she had to go mike-to-mike with Drs. Theodore and Georgianna Costas—LIVE!

"You can ask them tough questions, can't you? Like questioning their financial motivation in suing Richard Del Vecchio?" Barry took an English muffin from the toaster and spread it with sugar-free preserves.

"Yes and no. *Air San Diego* isn't exactly *Sixty Minutes*. We don't do super-adversarial journalism."

"This sugar-free stuff has no taste." Barry made a face and put down the muffin. No wonder he had lost weight.

"Even if we did," continued Margo, "I've had only one day to prepare for this thing. I talked to a few alternative practitioners who gave me some ideas about questions to ask, but I'm no medical expert. And none of them would agree to go on the air.'' She had actually tracked down an M.D.-acupuncturist, who had ardently declined her request to come on the program and carry the flag for alternative medicine. There were too many unqualified people out there claiming to be healers, he'd said, and he wasn't willing to be grouped with them.

"At any rate, in San Diego you're sure to get a lot of callers defending alternative healing.''

She winced. As the M.D.-acupuncturist had euphemistically put it, there were plenty of oddballs out there. All she needed was someone breaking into Tibetan chants the second he or she got on the air.

Driving to work, she kept repeating one of the precepts she'd learned in broadcasting classes: *Never relinquish control of the interview.*

She arrived at the station at nine, giving her nearly an hour to review her questions and psych herself up—plans thrown into disarray by the call she got from the front desk at nine-fifteen:

"The Costases' advance man is here.''

"Their what?'' Did they think they were running for office?

"Their advance man. Scott Nelson.''

Great. Mr. Bonebreak.

"I'll be right out.'' She poured herself a cup of coffee on the way, but didn't offer Scott any. Boy, was she tough.

Scott was wearing his dogsbody uniform, a blue dress shirt, and a navy tie with tiny, conservative gold polka dots, plus neat gray slacks. As for his advance man duties, they consisted of such salient tasks as fussing over the back support provided by "Ted" 's and "Georgie" 's chairs and meticulously depositing a pad of yellow legal paper, a pen, and an oblong package of throat lozenges at each place, honey flavored for Ted and cherry for Georgie. He fiddled awhile with the position of the packs of lozenges, finally turning them perpendicular to the table edge. Scott *didn't,* Margo noticed, quiz her on the questions she planned to ask in the interview; Costas's PR firm had done that already. It occurred to her that Ted and Georgie probably had no idea Scott had appointed himself their advance man.

She considered asking him to wait in the lobby, freeing her to go back to her office and prepare. But she couldn't pass up the temptation to ask him a question.

"Did you hear the news about Leslie?"

"Leslie Getz? What news?"

Margo told him, not gently, about Leslie being the woman burned to death in the Deerhorn Valley fire . . . thinking that this was a man who, no matter how much it might distress him later, derived pleasure from inflicting pain.

Absorbed by her own anger, she didn't notice for a moment that Scott was crying. "How awful for Leslie," he said, sitting down. Under his tan, his skin looked gray.

Margo thought of Paula's words last night, when Margo had pressed her to tell Scott's secret to the police and Paula had forcefully declined: *Margo, he did one bad thing, for which he'll never forgive himself. That doesn't make him a murderer.*

"Can I get you a cup of coffee?" she said.

"Yeah, please. With sugar? . . . I hadn't seen Leslie for months," he said, when she returned with the coffee. "She and I used to be good friends, but . . . The day I met you at her house, I was there because Dr. Costas was getting ready to hold his press conference. I wanted to explain why I was helping him. I knew some of my old friends would condemn me, but Les was the kind of person, she wouldn't like what I was doing, but that wouldn't make her dislike *me.* Oh!" He stood up. Margo wouldn't have been surprised if he'd saluted. "Good morning, Dr. Costas."

With only a nod in his direction, his mentor entered the room. Mentor and Daughter.

"Dr. Costas. Dr. Costas," Margo greeted them.

"Ted and Georgie," said Ted, shaking her hand. His was the warm, firm kind of hand you'd want doing delicate things to your eyes, in the event your eyes needed things done to them. She still felt a gut dislike for the man.

Georgie, however, elicited her instinctive sympathy. The oncologist's handshake was nervously cold, her appearance far less polished than at the news conference. She had done her own makeup this morning, a touch of pink blush and rose lipstick—no lipliner, no eye makeup. Her white linen suit was the kind of outfit on which Margo would spill coffee in record time . . . and in fact Georgie *had* spilled something on the suit, evidenced by a stain on one sleeve.

"You'll be surprised how fast the hour goes." Margo smiled at Georgie. "Georgie, why don't you sit here? And Ted here. Let me just tell you a few things about the technology."

While a student intern brought in glasses of water, she ran through the basics: Stay four to five inches from the microphone so you don't pop your "p's." If you need to clear your throat, lean back from the mike. Wear your headsets—she handed one to each doctor—to hear the phoned-in questions. And there'd be a five-minute news broadcast right at nine.

Taking on her professional role, Margo's own nervousness abated. She felt quite calm when she glanced through the window into the control room and saw the show's director, Bailey Kamens, holding up two fingers: two minutes to air time.

"Scott, you'll have to leave," she said. "You can sit in the control room if you want."

"Sure."

"Ted and Georgie," she went on, "we'll just talk for a

while and then we'll invite the listeners to join in.''

"I want to start with the story of what happened to my son," said Ted.

"Of course. We're about to start," she said, hearing Bailey count down—"Five, four, three, two, one." Margo saw he'd been joined in the control room by the news director, Claire De Jong. Claire, to whom she had confided how much she was dreading this interview, flashed a victory sign. Maybe this would go all right after all.

Maybe pigs would fly.

As soon as Margo introduced her guests, Ted Costas launched into the story he had told at the news conference the other day. As she had said to Barry that morning, Costas had a case. She just hated feeling used by someone who'd so obviously rehearsed with a PR coach.

"Two and a half years ago," said Costas, "my elder son, Theodore Costas the Third, began experiencing what a lay person might call 'the blahs.' Fatigue, a general sense of feeling less well than he had in the past. At that time, Teddy was twenty-four years old. He didn't mention the problem to me immediately. When he did, I urged him to see a physician. Instead, I learned that he'd been going to at least half a dozen so-called healers: an herbalist, a massage therapist, a psychic, even a nincompoop who claimed to be healing Teddy by laying crystals around his body. He continued seeing these people, in spite of my efforts to convince him to get proper medical care. A year later, he became so ill that he finally saw a physician. His symptoms at that time were weight loss and night sweats, as well as fatigue. He had lymphatic cancer. By then, it was too late to save him."

"I'm sorry," murmured Margo and paused a moment, having heard the genuine pain in Teddy's father's voice. Then she proceeded to do her job. "Isn't it true," she said, consulting the notes from her research the day before, "that because of the vagueness of your son's initial symptoms—you used the term 'the blahs'—the type of cancer he had is often not detected, even when a person does see a doctor early in the disease?''

"Of course, but had a qualified physician been involved and followed Teddy as his symptoms developed, his cancer would have been detected at the earliest possible time." Costas sounded testy.

Georgie reached over and touched her father's arm, saying, "No one can know how soon my brother's cancer would have been diagnosed. What we can say with certainty is that the earlier he was diagnosed, the better Teddy's chances for survival would have been. The point is that for a year, Teddy was strung along by these so-called healers. He had one appointment every week, often two each week, and these people's services are not cheap. Many of them charged fifty dollars or more for a session.''

"Are you saying that these healers misled him purposely for financial gain?" said Margo, admiring Georgie's ability to adapt her script . . . and cautioning herself that although Georgie lacked her father's surface assurance, she was probably better able to run away with the interview.

"I'm sure that to a large extent," responded Georgie, "these people believed in the value of their methods and truly thought they were helping him. There is that element, of course, that they happened to profit by convincing Teddy he needed to see them regularly for a year.''

Margo took a moment to give out the talk show phone number, then continued, "Even though it sounds like Teddy saw a great many different healers, you're only filing suit against two of them, is that right?"

"Yes." Georgie continued to take the lead. "Hannah Jones and Richard Del Vecchio were the main people my brother talked about. Any time we tried to get him to see a physician,

he always said he had absolute trust in Del Vecchio and Ms
Jones.''

Alex, Margo noticed, had joined the group in the contro
room. Margo tried to ignore the station manager, who wasn'
going to appreciate her next question any more than the Cos
tases would.

"Dr. Ted Costas, you said your son should have seen ;
physician much sooner. I'm sure many of our listeners woul
feel the same way. But you also said Teddy was twenty-four
an adult. You and your daughter tried to persuade him to se
a physician. He wouldn't do it. Doesn't that raise the issu
of allowing adults to make their own choices about thei
health care, even if they make bad choices?''

Georgie answered, heatedly, "That particular choice killed
him.''

"You must understand that any person who is ill and i
pain is in the worst possible state, psychologically, to mak
an informed choice,'' said Ted Costas. "That's the purpos
of the bill Senator Eberhard is introducing in the state legis-
lature. It would require people who wish to consult these alternative, um, practitioners to obtain a physician's certificate
first.''

Margo would have loved to get into a discussion of the
bill's realistic chances of passage, but Bailey had told he
earlier that there were two callers on the line. Now the number had risen to three.

"Let's go to our first caller,'' she said.

Bailey said into her headset, "Ruth from Tierrasanta.''

"Ruth from Tierrasanta,'' repeated Margo. "Hi, Ruth
You're on the air.''

In a well-modulated voice, Ruth from the Tierrasant:
neighborhood of San Diego said, "All of these New Ag
healers, as they call themselves, are agents of Satan. Many
even refer to themselves, proudly, as witches. It's not enough

just to ask people to get a doctor's certificate before seeing them. These devils and witches should not be allowed to practice their evil ways.''

''I'm only looking at this from the medical point of view.'' Addressing the rabid Ruth, Ted Costas had the opportunity to sound broad-minded. ''Some people will always choose to go to these practitioners. Senator Eberhard and I simply want to ensure that people use physicians as their first line of health care.''

''Well, bless you,'' said Ruth. Bailey signaled he had shut her off. Praise the lord.

''Thanks for your comments, Ruth,'' said Margo. ''Our next caller is Jeff from Del Mar.''

Jeff, taking the opposite side of the question, lacked Ruth's clarity of expression. He launched into a jargon-laden explanation of a homeopathic treatment called Bach Flowers (which Margo remembered Paula having tried). At least she could sit back for a few minutes, while both of the Drs. Costas attacked homeopathy.

After some forty minutes, Margo was wondering whether everyone in San Diego either felt that alternative health care cured all of the illnesses in the world or, as several callers besides Ruth had stated, considered it the work of the devil. Did moderates never call radio talk shows? Not even on public radio? She tried prompting the listeners again.

''Have any of you had personal experience with alternative health care? Did it help you? Call us at five six two-KSDR. Our next caller is Pat from City Heights. Hi, Pat.''

''I want to know—'' Pat's voice boomed; Bailey quickly lowered the sound level—''why you doctors haven't said anything about the lawsuit you're filing against a dead woman.''

''I assume you're talking about Hannah Jones, the herbalist who died recently?'' Margo found the caller's voice familiar.

"I'm talking about the woman who was killed in the Encanto Hills fire last week. Why are they pursuing a lawsuit against an eighty-year-old woman who was murdered? As a matter of fact, I'd like to know where Dr. Ted Costas and Dr. Georgianna Costas were when that fire started."

"That's preposterous!" said Ted Costas.

"Slow down, Pat," said Margo—who had identified "Pat" as Olivia. "You seem to be making some very serious charges."

"You bet I am. This man believes Hannah Jones killed his son, and he's suing her for practicing medicine without a license. But he's not going to get anything by suing her estate. Hannah Jones had no money. So I'm wondering if he took justice into his own hands."

Bailey signaled that he was turning off the caller's microphone.

"Pat, I won't ask our guests to respond to your allegations," said Margo. Still, Olivia's comments had opened a door. "Pat did raise a question we might want to consider. Doctors, you have in essence launched a campaign against alternative or New Age healers. As you've heard from our callers today, this is a subject that brings up extremely strong feelings. Hannah Jones, one of the people you're suing, burned to death last week. The police consider her death a homicide. And yesterday, the medical examiner identified the woman found dead in the Deerhorn Valley fire as a massage therapist named Leslie Getz."

Both Costases had hardened their faces when she'd begun her question. It was impossible to tell how they felt about either death. (Alex's reaction was easier to read. "What the hell are you doing?" he mouthed through the soundproof glass.)

"You're surely not saying we had anything to do with the deaths of those poor women," said Georgie stiffly.

"Absolutely not. But have you had any second thoughts about raising public hostility toward alternative healers in general?"

Ted Costas neatly held an immaculate white handkerchief to his mouth and deposited his throat lozenge in the handkerchief, before speaking. "Naturally, my sympathy goes out to these unfortunate women's families. I don't know a great deal about it, but I'm not aware that there is any evidence indicating the death of Ms. . . . the masseuse . . . was anything but a tragic accident. As for raising public hostility, that is in no way our aim. Our aim is to save lives, by keeping people from being victimized."

"We have time for two more calls," said Margo, responding to Bailey's direction.

What the hell? The door opposite her was opening, and Scott Nelson was entering the room. She waved at him to leave, saying, "Peter from Hillcrest is on the line." It was a losing battle.

"Just a moment," said Ted Costas. Scott had come up next to him. "I'd like to introduce Scott Nelson, a fine young man who is helping with our campaign. Scott has a unique background in that he's been trained in both traditional and nontraditional medicine."

Costas shifted his chair to let Scott lean into his microphone.

"That's right," said Scott. "I spent two years studying premed. Then I completed a massage therapy program and practiced massage for two years. I agree with Dr. Georgianna Costas that most New Age practitioners are well-intentioned. But they just don't have the knowledge of an M.D. And during the time I was involved in massage, I discovered something very disturbing. Even though the New Age people always say they'll refer someone to a physician if they feel the person needs conventional medical care, I almost never saw that happen. I'm afraid I came to the conclusion that these people can be very dangerous.''

"Thanks for your views, Scott," said Margo, as she raged internally. "Peter from Hillcrest, are you still on the line?"

She had badly underestimated Scott Nelson, seeing him as a not-very-bright groupie whom Costas would never take into his confidence. Staring at the muscular biceps evident even under Scott's dress shirt, she thought how easily he could have grabbed frail Hannah and stuffed a handkerchief down her throat. As for Leslie, Scott had once dated her. What if she'd willingly accompanied him to Deerhorn Valley in the middle of the night? Margo assumed the police were considering Ted Costas's people in their investigation of Hannah's murder. Still, it wouldn't hurt to call Obayashi and encourage him to look especially hard at Scott.

Margo barely heard "Peter from Hillcrest," but apparently she dealt with him coherently. And she signed off smoothly when Bailey gave the word.

She shook hands with the Costases but didn't need to show them out. Alex rushed in to do that, thanking them obsequiously as he escorted them down the hall. Alex was apparently glad to overlook Scott's little intrusion into the interview.

Mr. Bonebreak, Margo thought again and wondered how far Scott might go to fulfill whatever he perceived as his mentor's wishes—or to exorcise the demon he had found within himself.

19 / Calling Cards

It was a perfect San Diego day, clear but not brutally bright, even so close to noon. A slight crispness in the air made Paula think of a favorite poem—*There is something in the autumn that is native to my blood*—though surely the poet hadn't been thinking of autumn in this semitropical clime.

> *Touch of manner, hint of mood,*
> *And my heart is like a rhyme,*
> *With the yellow and the purple and the crimson keeping*
> *time.*

More like palm fronds, thought Paula, clutching the audit she had just finished under her arm and walking to her car, parked on the street outside her office. As usual, something had been stuck under one of the windshield wipers. A flyer for a pizza place? An inducement to lose fifteen pounds in a week? But this didn't look like an advertisement.

Lifting the windshield wiper, she picked up two cards—like playing cards—that had been placed face-to-face. She slid off the top card without turning it over, so first saw the

Queen of Pentacles from the most common, Rider Tarot deck. She had never done much with Tarot, but she knew the Queen of Pentacles represented a dark woman—herself? She flipped over the other card and her legs turned to jelly. It was a black armored knight with a grinning yellow skull for a face: Death.

20 / A (Senseless?) Act of Malice

"Yum. Yum yum!" Margo didn't know which was more heavenly, the pasta with salmon and fresh dill, the California Chardonnay, or the view of the Pacific.

"You deserve it." Claire poured more wine.

Claire had grabbed Margo's hand and rushed her out the back door of the station, before Alex could upbraid her for badgering their distinguished guests. "Don't worry about Alex," Claire had said; having gained Alex's respect while working with him at National Public Radio, she was a whiz at "managing" the manager. "Give him a couple hours, and he'll have to admit that was terrific radio. Meanwhile, let me take you to lunch." Jumping into Claire's car, they had fled to a restaurant on the beach in La Jolla.

The breathless, giggling getaway—and the lunch—had cooled Margo's anger, but only temporarily.

"Damn, I was set up!" she said, tearing off a piece of sourdough bread from a steaming chunk. "Scott really was the 'advance man' . . . since he and the Costases planned that little trick in advance."

"Not 'the Costases,' plural."

"What do you mean?"

Claire's hand, bearing a swordfish-laden fork, stopped half way to her mouth. "I guess you didn't notice—you were a bit preoccupied at the time—but Georgie didn't have a clue that her dad had arranged that little scene with his buddy Scott. I thought she was going to punch him out."

"Her dad or Scott?"

"Scott, I think. When you're jealous, who are you more angry at, the person you love or the person they seem to prefer to you?"

"Isn't she a little old to still be trying to get Daddy's attention? Never mind," said Margo, considering her own life long competition with her younger sister. "Didn't Tolstoy or some Russian writer say something about unhappy families?"

" 'Happy families are all alike,' " contributed their waiter, who had placed a fresh chunk of bread on the table and was refilling their wine glasses. " 'Every unhappy family is unhappy in its own way.' *Anna Karenina*."

"Thanks." Margo toasted him with her wineglass. Claire followed suit.

"Do you think the Costases are that unhappy?" said Claire after the waiter had retreated. "I mean, beyond the fact that they lost a son—in Georgie's case, a brother—a year ago?"

"I think so." Margo pictured the lost-looking wife and the son who had made an appearance at the news conference but then disappeared.

"Well." Claire shook her head, gestured toward the ocean. "It's a gorgeous day. Forget about unhappy families. How are Barry and the kids?" she said, pouring the last of the wine.

"Good. That is . . ." Margo grinned, and marveled that she had once seen Claire—who *had*, it was true, landed a job she wanted—as an enemy. *Blond Ambition*, Margo used to call the younger woman; Claire had roared with laughter when Margo finally admitted it to her. "They're great, except Jenny's bugging us to let her pierce her nose. Also, I think she's involved with Nick Costas."

"Costas?"

"The living brother."

"You make it sound like a burden, to be the brother who didn't die."

"Yeah. I think it is."

Their conversation ceased for an awe-filled moment when the waiter wheeled over a pastry tray. Margo picked a fruit tart and Claire a huge piece of chocolate mousse cake. They sat back and appreciated the view until the waiter brought the desserts and coffee, which he poured from a silver pot that Margo realized she was staring at in a sort of admiring haze. Oops, she'd gotten rather sozzled. Better have seconds on the coffee. Claire, for a tiny person, was exhibiting a surprising capacity for alcohol, but even she looked a tad disheveled, her cheeks flushed and short blond hair awry.

After lunch, they walked on the beach for twenty minutes, letting the coffee jolt them into relative alertness before they drove back to the station.

True to Claire's prediction, Alex had calmed down, especially given the volume of calls, both during and after the show. As Claire had said, it was terrific radio. Alex *didn't* invite Margo to host the call-in regularly, but neither did he give her more than superficial flak, almost a reflex reaction, for the way she had questioned the Costases.

Among the postshow calls, Margo found some twenty messages in her box. Most, bearing no last names and no return numbers, repeated the polarized sentiments of many of the on-air callers: New Agers—and, according to a few callers, Margo as well—were satanists; or else, M.D.'s were the quacks and alternative practitioners the real healers.

The caller Margo found the most intriguing was Dylan Lightwing, the ponytailed sweat lodge leader whom Paula had called a "real shaman." Margo didn't know what a shaman was. She *did* believe there were people with genuine spiritual gifts, though she had no idea whether Lightwing happened to be one of them. Curious, she returned his call.

"That was a good show." Dylan Lightwing spoke the slightest bit more slowly than most people. "I wish you could have had someone on from the healing community, someone with real credentials."

"Me, too. I wanted to, but my station manager didn't agree."

"So you took the position of defending the New Age. You did it well."

"Umm, not necessarily because I believe in it." She sensed Dylan had misinterpreted her views, just like the anonymous note leavers who'd accused her of being a satanist. "It's my job to question what people say."

"But you could have cut off Olivia, or refused to deal with the issue she brought up." So he, too, had recognized Hannah's granddaughter's voice. "She's coming to the sweat this weekend. So is Scott."

"Scott Nelson?" It was hard enough to imagine Olivia wanting to hang out with a bunch of white folks pretending to be Native Americans; but Scott had repudiated the New Age.

"He used to be one of us. I'm hoping I can help him remember why." Dylan chuckled. "Of course, that's not what I told *him.* I offered him a chance to get to know the enemy better. I hope you can make it, too. I should have invited you personally, not just through Paula. Can you come?"

"I haven't decided." *You have no intention of going to that sweat lodge!* her inner voice protested.

"A lot of people have misconceptions about sweat lodges," Dylan said. "For instance, they think you have to be nude. Actually, I wear a pair of cotton shorts. The women often like to wear loose cotton dresses." He had clearly talked to Paula. "Even if you're not into the sweat, it's a beautiful camping site."

"Well, maybe," she heard herself saying.

Automatically, she jotted down the instructions Dylan gave her and only murmured "Okay" when he told her the cost was seventy dollars, even though Dylan himself hemmed and hawed, saying that in the tribe you'd never charge for a sweat, but "in the world" this was his livelihood. By that time, however, she wasn't going to quibble over price; she'd been hooked.

Paula would get a kick out of that, she thought, returning a call from her friend next.

"Is that offer to stay at your house still open?" asked Paula.

"Sure. More phone calls?"

"No, I'll tell you later. I'm right in the middle of things now. But Donny thinks it might be a good idea not to stay at my own place for a day or two. And could you pick me up, say in an hour? The police are going over my car."

"Donny Obayashi? As in homicide? Paula! Give me some idea of what's going on."

"Later. I've really got to go."

"For a woman who tends to catastrophize," said Margo, "you are remarkably calm. Are you sure you're not in shock?" She had picked up Paula as requested and, after a stop at Paula's condo for a few night things, they were sitting on Margo's patio, Paula drinking wine and Margo, who'd imbibed plenty at lunch, sticking to mineral water.

"I might be. Although I usually do better than you'd expect—better than *I'd* ever expect—if I'm in real danger. For instance, if someone makes a bad move on the freeway, for a few moments I completely focus on that and I'm not panicky at all."

"So tell me again," said Margo. "You went out to your car and found the two Tarot cards under the windshield wiper."

"The Queen of Pentacles and the Death card. Do you have a deck? I could show you." The police had bagged the two cards to test for fingerprints.

Margo shook her head. She had owned a Tarot deck at one time, but it was among many things she'd left behind, fleeing a disastrous relationship in New Mexico.

"Anyway," said Paula, "my first reaction *was* panic. I went straight back into the office; into *my* office, my personal space. Actually, that turned out to be the smartest thing to do. Donny said a lot of people would have just gotten into their cars and turned on the engine."

"Do they really think the car could be booby-trapped? A bomb or something like that?"

"Probably not, but he wants them to check."

"Are you sure you're not in shock?"

Paula laughed. "The thing is, the cards were less upsetting than the phone calls. Because it's obvious who put them there—which means she probably made the phone calls, too."

"Cynara?"

"The police don't have any witnesses, but Cynara can't prove where she was before she opened Crystal Magic at ten, and my car was parked on the street from about eight. I'd been bugging her about Leslie. I must have left four phone messages. Then you came into her shop on Saturday, asking about Leslie. And on Sunday she saw us together at the church, and she must have figured I'd put you up to going to see her. The next day, I started getting the phone calls. From what I know of Cynara, that's exactly her style.''

''Why escalate things with the Tarot cards?''

''Because last night the police came to her house about Leslie, and they probably gave her a hard time for not reporting Leslie missing. Not logical, is it? But Cynara isn't real logical. The good news is that while she seems capable of slimy, creepy things like the phone calls and the Tarot cards, I don't see her harming me or anyone else. So actually, I feel better about the whole thing.''

Lying awake that night, Margo wished she shared Paula's relief. She kept remembering Cynara's expression when she had seen Margo at the church, sitting next to Paula. Cynara hadn't appeared irked to realize that Margo knew Paula; the look that had crossed her face came closer to horror. And Margo hadn't told Paula about the Tarot reading the day before, when Margo had asked about her ''friend'' and Cynara, seeming genuinely rattled, had said her friend was in great danger.

Margo also thought about the person who had watched Paula at the time of the Encanto Hills fire. Paula, caught in the maelstrom of her own panic, hadn't observed enough to identify the person, but the watcher—the arsonist/murderer?—wouldn't know that. The next week Paula had felt someone was ''directing energy'' at her; that was a phenomenon that went beyond Margo's sphere of knowledge. But wasn't it possible that, a week later when the phone calls started, the watcher had found out who Paula was? Margo wondered whether the watcher had been standing in front of Paula's car or behind, where he—or she—could have noted not only the car's make and color but the distinctive bumper sticker, PRACTICE RANDOM KINDNESS AND SENSELESS ACTS OF BEAUTY.

21 / Going With the Flow

"Behind the car," said Paula, turning onto the freeway on Saturday afternoon. Her car released with a clean bill of health from the police bomb squad, Paula had insisted driving the sixty miles to the sweat lodge outside Julian. She couldn't have managed the drive alone, she'd explained, but with Margo as a passenger she would be fine. "He was on the canyon side of the street, behind the car. I saw him in my rearview mirror."

" 'He'?" Margo queried. "I thought you weren't able to tell what sex the person was."

"Not really. I guess I just said 'he' automatically."

"What if there were signs you picked up unconsciously? Height or size? Something that really did tell you it was a man?"

Paula thought for a moment, then shook her head. "I wish I could say. Donny wants to know, too. Let's see. I'd say the person was adult height, rather than a child, but shoot, it could have even been a tall teenager. Check the map, would you?"

Margo looked at the neatly hand-drawn map that had been sent to all the sweat lodge participants. "You stay on the freeway until five or six miles east of Alpine. Then turn north onto seventy-nine.''

They drove without talking for a while, to the accompaniment of a New Age instrumental tape on Paula's cassette deck. Despite her recent resolution to listen to news, Paula hadn't wanted to expose herself to the world's chaos on the way to the sweat.

"Margo, I wanted to ask you a question." Paula's tone implied that whatever she was about to say, Margo wouldn't want to hear it.

"Go for it."

"When I talked to Donny this morning—when he called to say the car was okay—he asked me about Scott Nelson. I didn't know . . . that is, I wondered . . ." Definitely a touchy subject, the way she was stumbling. "I could see why he'd be interested in Scott, or anyone connected to Ted Costas. I just didn't know why he was asking *me*." Paula, who generally kept her eyes riveted to the road when she drove, turned her head and gave Margo a probing—a reproachful—look.

"I . . ." Now Margo stumbled, took a breath. "I didn't tell Obayashi anything you told me the other night, about Scott breaking that woman's shoulder. Actually, I didn't say much more than Scott said himself on the radio. That he used to be very involved with the New Age and since then he's strongly turned against it. And that I ran into him at Leslie's last Saturday, and he acted strange."

"If that's all you said, why did Donny ask me about him?" Paula's accounting mind bore a lot of similarities to Barry's scientific thinking. But Paula took offense more quickly than Barry, and Margo had a feeling she was about to give it.

"He asked me who Scott used to be friends with in the New Age community. I mentioned you."

"Margo!"

"Obayashi's not the enemy."

"I know that," declared Paula. "In fact, I've helped him. He said how frustrated he was because he didn't know people's real names, and when he asked them for their names, they were really evasive. First of all, I explained that it wasn't that they've done anything wrong, but that they've consciously left their old identities behind. Their real names *are* the names they've chosen for themselves. Just saying their old names might feel like a violation. Anyway, I happen to know a few people's legal names, because of my work. So I told him."

"For instance?"

"Cynara used to be Jane Hoffman. Socrates Plato—have you met him, he was a good friend of Les?—was Dennis Chesniak."

"Socrates Plato? I bet Obayashi got a hoot out of that."

"He didn't laugh at all," said Paula sternly. "You said turn on seventy-nine, right?" The exit was marked just ahead.

"Right."

Paula concentrated on the road for the next few minutes, taking the exit to a stop sign and turning left onto the two-lane highway that led into the mountains.

"Back to Scott . . ." she said.

"I swear I didn't say a word about Scott injuring the woman he was massaging," Margo said, but added, "Paula, I think you should."

"Tell that to the police? Margo, you really don't get it. Scott does have a good heart. You *know* something like that about a person who was your lover. You didn't tell that to Donny, did you?"

"That you and Scott used to be lovers? Of course not. I'm ravenous," Margo grumbled, anxious to change the subject . . . and truly hungry. One of Dylan's instructions had been to skip lunch, as part of the preparations for the sweat in the evening.

"You promised no kvetching."

"*That's* not kvetching. Wait till I'm dying of heat and claustrophobia. Then I'll kvetch."

Margo took a drink from the one of the plastic bottles of water they were carrying. She offered it to Paula, who drank, too. They were supposed to drink plenty of water beforehand, Dylan had said, and to each bring two towels, one to take into the sweat lodge with them, another for afterward. They also needed fresh clothes to change into. Dylan's final instruction had been that Margo should not be on her moon. "My *what?*" "Um, your period." He'd sounded embarrassed at using such a nonspiritual term.

The sun was warm and if Margo weren't already drowsy, the tape Paula was playing, a formless flute and harp duet, would have induced sleep in the most confirmed insomniac. She closed her eyes.

When she woke up, they were parked on a narrow turn-off from the two-lane mountain road, and Paula was crying. At least, Margo thought she had awakened. But then, why was polka music filling the car?

"What is it?" she asked.

Paula struck the steering wheel angrily. "I can't do it. I thought I could drive all the way, but I can't."

"Hey, this is really a tough road. Plus," Margo added, eyeing the tight line of cars inching uphill to their left, "half the population of San Diego is going to Julian this weekend because it's apple season, and they want their apple pie." Just saying the words *apple pie* made her salivate. Would it really ruin her experience of the sweat lodge if she had a piece of pie in her stomach? Of course, maybe you had to fast not for any spiritual reason but because the heat would make you throw up.

"You made it this far and that's great," she reassured Paula. "I'll take it the rest of the way. Um, Paula," she added delicately, as Myron Floren—or whoever—launched into "It's a Small World." "I didn't know you liked polka."

"I hate it." Paula ejected the cassette and dropped it out the window. "It's Donniger's latest exercise. Any time I'm driving, if I feel anxious, I have to pull over and listen to polka music for two minutes." She indicated the timer propped on the dashboard.

"You know, there are some New Wave polka bands you might enjoy. Brave Combo, for instance. They're from Texas and they mix in a lot of salsa . . ."

"No, I'm supposed to hate it. The idea is to make driving preferable to listening to the music. Actually, it works pretty well," she said, retrieving the cassette when she got out to change places with Margo. "I guess I didn't pull over soon enough this time. I was in a hurry to get to the sweat lodge, and I thought with you in the car I'd be okay."

"Hey, you made it this far and that's great."

Still, Paula hung her head as Margo started the car and edged into the traffic.

"Isn't it beautiful here?" Margo said. A Connecticut native, she had never fully adapted to San Diego's semiarid landscape. She always felt starved for green, like the trees surrounding them. "What other tapes do you have? I like to drive to jazz or how about Bonnie Raitt? You like Bonnie Raitt." But other than the polka tape, Paula carried only New Age music. Margo settled for a very bad country station she was able to pick up on the radio.

"I ought to be like Dylan," Paula murmured. "He doesn't drive, as a spiritual practice. He mostly rides a bicycle or walks."

"I bet he's not walking all the way to Julian."

"Of course not. But he only takes rides when he has to."

Margo stopped talking and concentrated on the traffic, which was brutal. One time she tried to pass but cut it so close that she decided against any future attempts. Instead, she prayed for the drivers of crawling RVs to pull over and let a few dozen cars get ahead.

By the time they arrived at the site of the sweat lodge—on someone's private land just southeast of Julian—she was in a rotten mood.

At least the place is wooded and serene, she told herself, trying not to start with a chip on her shoulder.

Yeah, came her cynical voice, *and aren't those people up ahead through the trees stark naked, after Dylan said everyone would wear clothes in the sweat lodge?*

Her calm, accepting voice responded, *Look, there's a big pond. They're just skinny dipping. What are you so afraid of, anyway?* she challenged herself. *Your body is fine.*

No dice, I am not going skinny dipping.

But the water *did* feel lovely, after the hot drive and the sweaty work of pitching her tent—as well as witnessing a brief but angry discussion between Paula and Cynara. Cynara denied having anything to do with either Paula's anonymous phone calls or the Tarot cards on her car. "I don't believe her," Paula told Margo afterward, but she and Cynara had made at least a surface peace.

Floating now, eyes closed, Margo felt as if years were draining from her body. Years and something else. Hadn't she once been a person who would have easily—gleefully—stripped off her clothes and jumped nude into this pond? What had changed? Her body, a little, but not that much. She felt like an insect shedding a carapace, the flinty product of returning to college at thirty after a decade as a free (at least a freer) spirit; becoming a stepmother; and most recently, enduring the severe competition, inflamed by Alex, for her full-time job at KSDR. She had beaten out the other part-timers, knowing then that the victory tasted bitter, a triumph at the cost of friends' defeat. Now she wondered how much had rigidified inside her.

Around her, she heard low conversation and laughter. Paula's laugh, as she treaded water with Dylan Lightwing. Margo's skeptical voice, which had not entirely dribbled through her toes into the pond, broke in to confirm her hunch that Dylan *had* wanted to see Paula with no clothes on. *So what?* her tolerant voice lazily replied. Paula was beautiful, clothed or un-. And Renoir could have painted the scene. Among the people swimming, Margo spotted Art, the chiropractor, and several people she'd just met—Laura and William, who were graphic designers, and Victor, an attorney. Olivia and Cynara sat in gauzy skirts and T-shirts beside the pond, Olivia massaging Cynara's neck . . . and Scott Nelson was walking down the trail from the parking area. Suddenly Margo felt *naked*—vulnerable, exposed—as she hadn't only a moment ago. She restrained the urge to scramble out; she'd just have to hustle bare-assed, searching for her towel. Better to remain at least partially covered by the water and hope that Scott was only passing by.

Olivia noticed Scott, too. She jumped up and stood in his path. ''What are you doing here?''

''I was invited,'' Scott replied.

''By whom?''

''Olivia, it's okay.'' Unself-consciously, Dylan waded out, his ponytail dripping down his bare back. He went to stand with her and Scott. ''I invited him.''

''Why, Dylan?'' Olivia's voice filled with anguish.

''Try to open your heart to him, Olivia. Scott wouldn't be here if he didn't feel some connection to us.''

It wasn't eloquent, but somehow it defused the situation. Olivia stalked away but said nothing more. Dylan pulled on some cutoffs and a pair of flipflops.

''Hey, people,'' he called back to the group at the pond.

"We're going to start in about an hour. I suggest that you spend that time alone, in silence." He turned to Scott and offered to help him unload his car.

"See, Scott does have a good heart, or he wouldn't be here," Paula whispered to Margo as they got out of the water. Following Dylan's advice, however, they stopped speaking as they toweled off, dressed, and drifted separately away from the pond into the woods.

Margo went back to her tent, drank more water, and prepared for the sweat lodge by changing into her cotton dress and getting her towel. For the time being, she pulled on a pair of sweatpants under her dress and donned a hooded sweatshirt—the late afternoon breeze was cool. She thought of taking a walk but instead found herself drawn back to the pond . . . and to a rock, still touched by the setting sun, that seemed a perfect place to sit. Someone else—a kindred soul—had sat on the rock before and left a wallet behind. Margo opened it to check for an ID. It belonged to Dylan. He might be famed for not driving, but the shaman had a license. And not too surprisingly, the license wasn't issued to Dylan Lightwing, but to Lewis Zeigler. Should Margo just hand him the wallet, or would he feel violated, knowing she'd learned the identity he had shed? She decided to leave the wallet on the rock; someone would find it eventually.

The sun disappeared into the trees. From the woods, she heard the slow, steady beat of a drum.

22 / Sweat and Tears

Following the drumbeat and the figures of the other participants, Margo took a path deeper into the trees. She hurried when she glimpsed Olivia ahead of her.

"Olivia!"

The young woman stopped, waited for her, and gave her a hug when she caught up. They moved over to the side of the path.

"Why did you come to this?" asked Margo.

"I've known Dylan a long time. He offered me a freebie."

"But I thought you hated white New Agers."

Olivia smiled. "I'm checking for cases of poison oak. Remember, my grandmother was found on a pyre of poison oak?"

Something stirred in Margo's memory, but she couldn't grasp it. "Would someone still have a rash, almost two weeks later?"

"I've had poison oak, it lasts a long time."

"So have you seen anyone with it?"

"Not yet, but I'm patient."

Olivia turned away, but Margo caught her arm.

"You don't really think one of these people killed Hannah? They all revered her." Except, of course, Scott Nelson. But judging from Olivia's reaction when he had walked up, she hadn't known Scott would be there. And Margo had the feeling Olivia wasn't telling her something. "Why did you really come?" she pressed.

Olivia continued down the path, as if she didn't want to face Margo. "Truth? I think Dylan has real power. He can summon spirits." She sounded abashed. Even for Olivia, it couldn't be easy to integrate premedical school and a respect for the occult.

The path emerged into a grove, where Dylan Lightwing— wearing shorts and a sweatshirt—stood beating the drum as people sat down in a circle around him. The circle of people surrounded a low circle of stones and inside that, a blazing, tent-shaped fire. Margo's eyes were drawn to the flames and then beyond them to a flattish dome, like a large turtle. "The sweat lodge?" she said to Olivia, sitting beside her.

"Yes," answered Olivia, as hands descended on Margo's shoulders, close to her neck. She yelped.

"Sorry, didn't mean to scare you." Art Smolin kneaded her neck muscles. "I just can't keep my hands to myself when I see a neck that cries out for adjusting. Has it been giving you trouble?"

"No!" She placed her hands firmly over the chiropractor's and added, "Don't try to crack my neck."

"Sounds like you've been to a lousy practitioner." Art removed his hands but continued, "Good chiropractic is very gentle. Call my office next week, I'll give you a free consultation. Oops . . ." He sounded like a kid caught with his hand in the cookie jar; Dylan was frowning at him. "Don't forget to call!" Art whispered, moving away.

Margo rubbed her neck. It did have a habit of going out, and she *had* been to an ungentle chiropractor. She'd also been subjected to the same sales pitch as Art's: *If you don't let me treat you (for a long time and a lot of money), you'll be crippled.* Was that the message Ted Costas III had received? Margo felt a surge of sympathy for Teddy's angry, litigious father.

She did a quick count around the circle. Sixteen people, in addition to Dylan. Paula was sitting across from her, an arm around Scott Nelson. Trust Paula to make a point of demonstrating her friendship with Scott.

Dylan stopped beating the drum. "We're all assembled," he said. "We'll start by calling in the four directions—east, south, west, north. Then, for those who haven't been to one of my sweats before, we'll take a few minutes, and I'll give you some idea of what to expect."

Resuming the drumbeat, Dylan faced east. Most of the group immediately stood and turned to the east as well. It was like being a new member of a dance class where everyone already knows the warm-up, thought Margo, mimicking the others.

Dylan chanted something in a language completely foreign to her—some American Indian tongue, she assumed. Several people raised their arms and waved them forward and back. Others drew their hands toward their hearts, as if gathering in energy. Margo imitated the energy gatherers, the dancer in her finding the movement lovely.

Dylan—and the group—turned to the south and repeated the ritual. Then to the west and the north.

He put the drum aside and gestured to them to gather in front of him. After introducing his assistant, James, Dylan said,

"The purpose of the sweat lodge is to purify yourself, so you can entreat the spirits. You might wonder, what spirits? Indians call on the spirits of animals, of the earth, of ancestors. These spirits can speak to you as well. Before we enter the sweat lodge, we're going to chant and to dance barefoot on the earth, to prepare ourselves. We want to be very grounded, very in touch with the earth before we begin the sweat.''

Dylan's voice was authoritative but warm. Maybe, thought Margo, his reputation as a shaman was deserved. Olivia believed in him and she was no New Age groupie.

"Then we'll enter the lodge, one at a time, the women first," he said. "Remember to bring your towel in with you and stay low. When you move inside the lodge, you should be on your knees. You'll spread out around the edge and sit on the ground. It won't be hot yet, so don't worry. You'll see a pit at the center of the sweat lodge. The pit is for the Stone People, which are heating out here." He pointed to the tent-shaped fire.

"What's he talking about?" Margo whispered to Olivia.

"There are rocks inside the fire. The lodge is heated by hot rocks."

"James is our fireman," Dylan said. "Once we're all inside the lodge, James will bring in the Stone People. It will get a little warm then, but at first we'll keep the lodge flap open. Eventually, we'll close the flap and pour water over the stones to make steam. At that point, it will be completely dark. It will get hot. Try to keep chanting, no matter how you feel. You can use your towel to cover any bare skin. We're going to do four rounds. That means that three times, I'll open the flap for a little while and let some cooler air in. I don't mean to scare you, but you should know that everybody who does a sweat the first time says there are moments when they think they can't stand it anymore and they have to get out. You can leave if you choose. But try to stick it out. That's an important element of the sweat, pressing through your fear. It will help if you keep chanting."

It probably also helped not to think of past instances of

claustrophobia. Margo's fractious mind, however, kept show-ing her an art installation in which she'd been trapped the previous spring, and the panic she'd experienced. Speaking of panic, she caught Paula's eye. Paula smiled. No doubt she found the prospect of being confined in a sweat lodge more comfortable than driving down the open highway. Margo pre-ferred the highway herself.

"When we come out, we'll have a closing ceremony," Dylan was saying, "and then we'll eat some light food to help replenish nutrients we've lost by sweating."

In response to several questions, Margo learned that the sweat lodge was constructed of willow branches covered by skins and a tarp, that Dylan drew on traditions from more than one Indian tribe, and that they would be inside the lodge for about an hour.

"No more questions?" said Dylan. "Okay."

He had them put their shoes and socks over to one side and re-form the circle. After teaching them a simple Navajo chant, he instructed them to stand and continue chanting, moving around the circle clockwise. "Keep your knees bent, so you're closer to the ground and really feel the earth every time your foot touches it."

The movement and chanting were hypnotic, and Margo melted into the dance—pressing her feet down, becoming warm in spite of the chill night air. She soon shed the sweat-shirt and pants she had put on in addition to her cotton dress. It was like the best times in dance class, when she felt herself truly descending into her body, reaching a level of "know-ing" that she inhabited too infrequently.

After perhaps half an hour (or perhaps ten minutes, since Margo had lost all sense of time), Dylan entered the sweat lodge and motioned for the group to follow, single file— "Women first," he reminded them. Margo picked up her towel and ducked inside. She crawled around the perimeter of the low lodge and sat cross-legged about a third of the way back. On her left was Cynara, on her right the graphic artist, Laura, both visible in the dim light.

Once everyone was inside, Dylan called to James. James brought in a pail of water and placed it beside the pit in the center of the lodge, then used a shovel to carry in the red-hot rocks and lower them into the pit; it took several trips. Margo was beginning to get warm but was still comfortable with the night air coming through the open flap.

Softening the drumbeat, Dylan invited each person to look inside themselves and speak their heart's desire—"what you wish to learn from the sweat lodge or what spirit you desire to call."

"I want to learn to be a more loving person," said a man. Margo, recognizing Art's voice, recalled that he was going through a divorce.

People spoke out, in no particular order, from around the lodge.

"I've been dreaming about bears for months. I want the spirit of bear to tell me what it has to teach me."

"I want to be healed from my cancer."

"I want a home." Cynara, beside her.

What did she, Margo, want? She hadn't come here as a spiritual seeker, yet she felt moved by the ritual before they entered the sweat lodge and by the longing she heard as people expressed their desires. And her skepticism wasn't because she disdained spiritual seeking, but because she had doubted it could happen, genuinely, in a primarily Anglo-European group appropriating Indian traditions. Now she asked herself what she could learn. She thought of her leisurely swim that afternoon, the awareness of how hard she'd become. But she didn't simply want to be softer—that implied losing an edge she valued.

Olivia's voice was ragged. "I call on the spirit of my

grandmother. I want to know who murdered her."

Without missing a beat, Dylan said, "I call on Hannah's spirit as well, and Leslie's. May both of these great healers be with us tonight. May we help them on their new journey."

For a moment no one else spoke. Then Margo heard Paula. "I want to stop resisting my fear. I want to find out what it has to teach me."

The chorus continued.

"I want to forgive my father."

"I call on the spirit of eagle."

Margo found her own words. "I want more of a connection between my mind and my body."

Several more people spoke, followed by a full minute of silence.

"Does anyone else wish to speak?" said Dylan.

There was no response. Dylan closed the lodge flap. Still not unbearable, thought Margo, relieved. Then, in the pitch dark, she heard the sizzle of water hitting the hot rocks. Steam poured over her. She had questioned the idea of covering herself with a towel, wouldn't that be hotter? Now she threw her towel over her like a shawl, shielding her head, face, and bare arms.

Dylan picked up the drumbeat and resumed chanting, occasionally pouring water over the rocks to create fresh steam. As he had warned, the heat intensified. What he hadn't said was that she'd feel like she couldn't take a breath, as if the air were too thick and wet to inhale.

"I can't do it!" a man cried out, somewhere across from her. Her sentiments exactly.

"Keep chanting," said Dylan gently. "Give it another minute and see what happens."

Another minute. Margo thought she could do that. Okay, she was able to breathe again, she had broken through the fear. It turned out that overcoming the fear once, however, didn't banish it. The choking feeling returned regularly. Every time Dylan opened the lodge flap, she sucked in the cooler air.

Earlier that evening, people who'd done sweats before had said the sense of "getting through it" gradually gave way to another, magical feeling, the physical discomfort pushing you to a more spiritual plane. "Your mind will give up control," they had promised. Margo waited, but her mind kept clicking away. She had loved the dancing before they entered the lodge, but dance had always been a kind of spiritual experience for her, ever since her first ballet class.

Humming along with Dylan, whose Navajo chants had no meaning for her, she kept having the same response as when friends in Santa Fe used to rave about Indian spirituality—that it was great for Indians, for whom it occupied a rich historical and social context, but it wasn't her religion. Not that Margo could walk into a synagogue and feel she had come home. Her family had been secular rather than religious Jews, and her own love for Judaism's emphasis on ethics coexisted uneasily with her dislike for the subordinate place of women in traditional Jewish culture. Nonetheless, tears had filled her eyes the first time she heard klezmer, the soulful clarinet- and fiddle-dominated music of Eastern European Jews; the music had stirred some deep connection that didn't happen in the sweat lodge. And her moral compass had always been her mother, who had regularly turned dinner table conversation into ethical debates. Alice Simon, at sixty-five, was currently studying for the Bat Mitzvah that custom had denied her at the age of thirteen.

Good grief! thought Margo, shielding under her towel from another shower of steam. Not only was she *not* letting go of her mind . . .

A wail ripped through the lodge. A woman, Margo guessed, although the cry was almost more animal than human. The chanting faltered for a moment, but resumed when Dylan pounded the drum harder. The woman kept wailing for a minute, then spoke. Olivia.

"I can see her," said Hannah's granddaughter. Dylan, alone, kept chanting. "I see her tied up in that canyon, with the fire getting closer. Oh! I feel the flames. Gram," she said through tears. "You always said that when Jesus came to take you, you'd be ready, you'd be full of joy. But you weren't. You were so afraid. And . . ."

Olivia fell from words into soft sobs, and Margo started planning her exit from the sweat lodge, so that she could catch up with Olivia as soon as possible. Had Olivia had an actual vision of her grandmother's death, or had she only imagined it, drawing on facts she already knew? And why did she abruptly stop speaking? Had she "seen" Hannah's killer? Was it someone present in the sweat lodge? If that were true, she shouldn't stay alone tonight. Margo would insist that Olivia share her tent.

Olivia was several people ahead of her when they crawled from the sweat lodge in single file. Margo had to restrain herself from pushing. But when she came out, Olivia was already gone. Not bothering to towel off, she pulled on her sweatshirt and tennies, grabbed her flashlight, and started to run.

"Hey!" she said, feeling a hand grasping her arm—Dylan's.

"Closing ceremony. It's bad medicine to break the circle." Dylan smiled and sounded mellow, but he was strong and there was something angry in his eyes.

"Olivia," she said.

"She'll be all right. She just needs to be alone."

"I'm worried about her," Margo insisted.

Breaking away from Dylan's grip took so much effort that she fell. Then she got up and ran.

After twenty minutes of stumbling around in the woods—
and no sign of Olivia—she returned to the grove. The final
ritual had apparently ended. People were now eating.

"Does anyone know where Olivia pitched her tent?"
Margo asked.

"She wants to be alone," said Cynara sharply.

Dylan put a comforting arm around Margo's shoulders; had
she imagined his anger earlier? "All kinds of things come up
in a sweat," he said. "Memories of childhood abuse, things
like that. Don't worry about Olivia; she can handle whatever
she has to. Have you eaten anything? You really should. And
drink, too." He poured her a large glass of water.

He had a point; she *was* hungry. She helped herself to fruit,
bread, and some kind of grain dish. She found she had no
desire to join an ebullient conversation about how fabulous
the sweat had been, however. Instead she took her plate of
food to her *spot,* the rock beside the pond. (Dylan's wallet
was gone. Someone else must have found it.) Once she had
eaten, she felt a great desire to slip out of her clothes—her
dress was still damp and clammy—and into the pond. She
did.

The water was warm, compared to the night air, and she
lingered, floating on her back. She had noticed no mystical
feelings in the sweat lodge but, gazing up at a radiant half-
moon and the Milky Way, she was aware of how deeply—
cleansed was the word that came to her—she felt now. *Something* had happened, between the sweat itself and her time in
this pond; something that was dispelled by a blinding flashlight beam directed straight at her.

"Hey!" She jerked herself vertical, treading water.

"How sweet, the Little Mermaid." Cynara's smile was visible in the moonlight, if that predatory look could be called
a smile. "Looking for love?"

"Turn off the flashlight, please?"

Cynara complied. "You're in the wrong place," she said. "Somebody else got lucky tonight."

"I can tell *you* got transformed by the sweat lodge." Two could play sarcastic.

"Oh, I did. Hmm, not bad," Cynara commented, eyeing Margo's body as she waded out of the pond. "How old are you?"

"Thirty-eight." Margo grabbed her towel and used it briskly.

"You know, I didn't do those things to Paula," said Cynara. "I suppose I might have made the phone calls, if I'd thought of it—she was being a pain in the ass. But I'd never use the Tarot like that, putting cards on someone's car."

"Because you wouldn't want to scare her?"

"Because I have too much respect for the cards. They're not toys." Having delivered her parting line, Cynara switched on her flashlight and left.

Margo put on her shoes and hastened toward the clearing where she and Paula had pitched their tents. Cynara's statement had had the ring of truth, which meant that someone else might have been harassing Paula, someone who might be at the sweat lodge. Scuffling sounds were coming from Paula's tent, and Margo ran to it.

"Paula, are you all right?" she called, starting to unzip the tent.

A hand stopped hers on the zipper, accompanied by Paula's giggle and then two murmuring voices, one of them a man's.

"I'm fine," sang out Paula. "Sweet dreams."

"Sweet dreams," replied Margo and went to her own tent, feeling a fool. *Somebody else got lucky,* Cynara had said. Cynara was sufficiently perverse to consider a night with Scott a stroke of luck. Margo was just dismayed that Paula would agree.

Margo always woke at first light when she camped. She lay in her sleeping bag, listening to the birds and observing the forest, soft as an Impressionist painting between her near-sightedness and her mesh tent flap. A man emerged naked from Paula's tent. *What's wrong with this picture?* thought Margo, reaching for her glasses. The man stretched languorously, as if the morning temperature were seventy instead of forty-five; as if he—Dylan Lightwing, not Scott Nelson—had had a *very* good night.

Well, why shouldn't he? Why shouldn't Paula? asked the tolerant self Margo had rediscovered the day before.

Because Paula looked up to him as a shaman. Because he abused that position by sleeping with someone after leading her through an intense spiritual experience.

Piffle, said her other self. *Paula was attracted to Dylan before any intense spiritual experiences occurred. And why not?* Margo added to herself, admiring the lanky, tanned body that turned and dove back inside Paula's tent.

Margo dressed quietly. Escaping the happy moans from next door, she took a walk.

Not until nine o'clock, half an hour after everyone else had gathered for breakfast, did people become concerned about Olivia's absence. Cynara, who'd seen Olivia pitching her tent, led the way to her campsite. No tent remained. And Olivia's car was gone.

23 / Smoldering

Nick coaxed on a pair of surgical gloves he had swiped from his father's office.

"What?" he said, turning at a sound—a whimper?—from the girl beside him.

"Nothing," Jenny whispered, but her eyes were enormous.

"You don't have to do this."

"I want to!" Jenny spoke so emphatically that she bounced on his bed.

He gave her a kiss. Another kiss. He started breathing harder, heard her do the same. This was the first time Jenny had been in his bedroom.

"Later!" she said, giggling.

What would his father think of his bedside manner? Just as Ted Costas always said, Nick had gotten the patient's mind off the procedure he was about to perform. Of course, Ted Costas was always confident of his ability. Nick was terrified he was going to make a mistake.

"Why the gloves?" said Jenny.

"To make sure everything is sterile," Nick lied.

Actually, the professional who'd done Nick's nose wore

gloves to prevent being infected by anyone he was piercing. Nick had no worries about Jenny infecting him with anything; but there was no telling what he might have in his bloodstream.

He had carefully noted every move the body piercer had made. Now he looked over the implements he'd lined up on a towel on his bedside table, praying he hadn't forgotten anything important. There was the Bactine with which he had cleaned the skin on Jenny's nose and the felt marker he'd used to put a tiny dot on the place where the ring would go—he had asked the piercer, wasn't there a risk of infection from the ink in the marker? but the piercer said no. In a Dixie cup holding about a half-inch of Bactine, the surgical stainless steel nose ring had been soaking for ten minutes, along with the bead that would hold the two ends of the ring together. There was a well-scrubbed, peeled carrot, antiseptic ointment . . . and, in sterile plastic wrapping, the two-inch-long 18-gauge needle he had taken from his dad's office along with the gloves.

"Ready?" he said.

"Sure."

"Put this inside your nostril and hold it there." He handed her the carrot, watched her insert it in her delicate nose. As long as he did it right, the needle would go into the carrot and not pierce the septum.

Carrot sticking out of her nose, Jenny looked at herself in the mirror and smiled. Nick knew he would die if he did anything that hurt her.

His hands were sweating inside the plastic gloves, but he managed to keep them steady as he unwrapped the needle, lubricated it with ointment, and positioned the point on the dot he'd made on Jenny's nose. Firmly but gently he pushed the needle through the cartilage and felt it go into the carrot.

"Oooh," Jenny gasped but quickly said, "I'm fine. I hardly felt a thing."

Very slowly, he tilted the needle down slightly and kept pushing, withdrawing the carrot from Jenny's nose, until only about a quarter-inch of needle remained outside her nostril.

"Okay, hold the carrot, but don't move it," he instructed her.

He took the ring from the cup of Bactine, separated the ends by twisting them sideways, and butted one end up against the end of the needle. He pushed with the ring and, thank God, the ring followed the needle into the hole he had made in Jenny's nose. He kept pushing, now taking the carrot and slowly withdrawing it, until the leading end of the ring was showing outside Jenny's nostril.

"Okay?" he asked her.

"Great," she said, although her face was white.

He put down the carrot and the needle, picked up the bead, and put it between the two ends of the ring to secure them.

"Done!" Nick sat back on the bed and breathed. He hadn't thought about it, but he had a feeling he'd stopped breathing for the past several minutes.

Jenny got up and looked in the mirror. "Nick, it's great! Thank you!"

She gave him a hug, which turned into kissing, which turned into lying together on his bed. Being very careful not to touch her nose where it was tender, he kissed her everywhere else on her face. His lips moved to her throat. She undid the top buttons of her blouse. Jesus, she had on a lacy pink bra that was the most beautiful thing he had ever seen.

He heard a car pull up right under his window, the car door slam. He and Jenny jumped up.

"Let's go for a walk," said Jenny, buttoning up her blouse.

"Yeah. Okay." He could barely think. But he was relieved to be going outside, away from the bed that seemed dangerous, though he felt like a total idiot. After what he'd done with the men in the canyon, why should he be so scared of a little petting with Jenny? But that was the point, wasn't it? Jenny. He wanted so badly for things to be okay with Jenny, for him not to ruin it.

"Want something to drink? We've got Snapple," he said as they passed through the kitchen. He heard his parents in the living room. With luck, he'd avoid them.

"Sure. Half a bottle."

He got a Snapple out of the refrigerator. They walked into the canyon, sharing the drink, talking, and occasionally kissing. But mostly talking. He had gotten kind of scared of kissing in the bedroom. Besides, now that Jenny had gotten past the actual nose piercing, she was pretty freaked about how her parents would react.

"Your mom went with you when you got your nose done, didn't she?" she said.

Nick nodded.

"I'm so amazed. She must really be cool."

"She's okay." How to tell Jenny that his mother was so doped she barely knew what was happening? "Want a cigarette?"

"Sure. Um, what about an ashtray?"

"We can just use the ground."

"Nick! Not with the fire danger. Here." She drained the Snapple. "We can use the bottle.

"Train!" she said with the excitement of a little kid. He felt the same way. They watched the train, a couple of football fields away, dash through the canyon.

Then he gave her a cigarette, took one for himself, and lit them.

"We're not going to start a fire with cigarette ash," he told her.

"They're always telling you you have to be careful with

cigarettes. You know, they have those ads where someone throws a cigarette out a car window and the next thing, the whole forest is burning.''

"Yeah, but that's from a lit cigarette, not from the ash. See?'' He ashed his cigarette onto a dry clump of sage.

"Nick, don't! Do you have some kind of thing about fire?''

"You never asked me about that before!''

"Don't shout at me!'' Jenny shouted.

"That was something I really liked about you, that you never asked me.''

"I wouldn't have said anything, except for the way you're acting now.''

"All I'm saying is you couldn't start a fire with cigarette ash. It's not a high enough temperature. You'd have to do something like actually holding the cigarette, like this.'' It was as if a devil had gotten inside him. He pressed the tip of his cigarette against a dried-up dead plant, and the plant started smoldering.

"Put it out!'' Jenny screamed. She hit his arm to make him drop the cigarette and ground her foot on the cigarette and the plant for at least a full minute. She was crying. Once she was sure the fire was out, she started running.

"Jenny!'' Nick yelled, running after her. "I'm sorry. I was an asshole.''

She didn't even half-turn, just kept running.

"Jenny!'' he tried one more time. But she was gone. Hating the world, hating himself most of all, he lit another cigarette.

24 / Wicked Stepmother

"I'm worried about Olivia," said Margo, as they drove down the mountain later that morning.

"I figure she just needed to get away and be by herself," remarked Dylan Lightwing, sitting in front of Margo in the passenger seat.

Paula was driving. Whether she had gained courage from the sweat lodge or Dylan's presence in the car (or his lovemaking), she was skillfully negotiating the twisting road; no panics this time.

"I bet Olivia is home by now," Dylan said.

He was probably right. But, "What if the killer was someone in the sweat lodge and she's in danger?" said Margo. No response. "What about Scott?" she added.

Not even that got Paula's—or Dylan's—attention. His hand was resting on her thigh, if *resting* could describe a gesture that, for all its stillness, appeared to electrify Paula.

Margo slouched down in her seat, feeling like a sulky kid . . . and detesting Dylan Lightwing. Not fair, she told herself. Did she resent him for intruding into her friendship with Paula? How petty. Though it *was* unquestionably annoying to

be in the presence of new lovers, who ought to go into se-
clusion for the first month. Dylan was now playing with Paula's hair. Soon, Margo was sure, he'd completely forget she
was in the back seat and go for a breast.

She ought to give Dylan a chance, she remonstrated with
herself. Not Dylan—Lewis Zeigler, she remembered from his
driver's license. Since Dylan surely lived a pure life, she
could do no harm by calling Donny Obayashi and telling him
Dylan's real name. She would do it right after she called to
make sure Olivia had gotten safely home.

She had figured Paula would dump her as fast as possible,
in order to race home and progress beyond the front-seat foreplay that had gone on for the past hour. Surprisingly, however, Dylan asked to be dropped off first, at a shabby stucco
apartment building in North Park, a working-class neighborhood slightly east of the area where both she and Paula lived.
After Paula gave him a two-minute good-bye kiss, Margo
moved up to the passenger seat.

"Not a word," warned Paula, as she drove away.

Was Margo's disapproval so evident? Whatever, she kept
mum the rest of the way to her house, except to say, "Talk
to you soon," before she hopped out of the car, grabbed her
gear . . . and walked through the doorway to hell.

"You!" Rae Parkman, the first Mrs. Barry Dawes, turned
toward Margo.

Rae stood in the living room. Her short, thick legs planted
like a boxer's, she was the center of a standing tableau that
included Barry and a weeping Jenny, whom Rae was grasping
hard by the arm. In the adjoining dining room, David stood
perfectly still, clearly dying not to be noticed and therefore
banished from the action.

Barry took a step toward Margo. Bad move, she thought,

but Barry had never learned not to push Rae's buttons, and vice versa.

"Of course, you'll side with her," Rae accused her ex-husband. "But this isn't her kid, it's ours. Yours . . . and mine. And I won't stand for *your* wife telling *my* daughter she can put holes in her body."

Sure enough, a ring decorated Jenny's nose. A wet ring at the moment. Jenny was crying so hard that she was shaking.

"Rae, I already told you, *I* was the one who told Jenny I'd consider it," Barry said. Margo considered clamping her hand over his mouth. His reasonable tone sometimes drove *her* wild. It made Rae go ballistic.

Releasing Jenny, Rae advanced on Margo. "*You* were the one who told her it was her body."

Christ, had she said something like that? It was possible. And was Rae about to hit her? Margo had to force herself *not* to take a step back. At least she had the advantage of four inches of height. She drew herself up to her full five-six.

"Whatever I said, Rae, the main thing was that she had to talk to you."

"Well, *whatever you said*," Rae repeated darkly, "you obviously lack the kind of parental authority a fifteen-year-old requires. Or a twelve-year-old. I'm leaving Jenny here now. I can't stand to look at what she's done to her beautiful face. But David, you're coming with me."

"Aw, Mom!" protested David, but he was no match for Rae, who kept going,

"I agreed to joint custody, even though I had doubts. But that was before *this woman* came into my children's lives!" No question which depraved stepmom that referred to. "I'm calling my attorney, first thing tomorrow."

The threat issued from Rae's lips at least twice each year and twice each year went nowhere. Still, Margo never heard it without feeling like throwing up. Nor, she suspected, did anyone else. She wanted to slap Rae, who was leading a white-faced David out of the house.

She heard the open and slam of Rae's car door. Jenny sank to the floor, sobbing, as her mother drove away.

Margo's own legs felt like spaghetti. She sat cross-legged beside Jenny. "Hey, let's see it," she said gently.

"Yeah, Jen." Barry joined them on the floor.

"No." Still shaking with sobs, Jenny held a hand over her nose and ran to her room.

Barry took a deep breath. "Leave her alone for awhile?"

"I think so."

"I'm sorry."

"Don't be." Margo planted several kisses on his face, then held him.

"Not just because of you, although I feel rotten that you ever have to go through this. But I worry what kind of example I'm setting for the kids when I let Rae control all of us with her rage. David and I had a chess match planned for tonight. What if I'd just blocked the door and said, 'David stays here?' "

"You want to take one arm while she takes the other and pull the kid in half? Rae doesn't get this mad very often, and it doesn't last. The kids know it's best if you don't fight her."

"Do they?"

"Yes." Margo wished she were certain.

Jenny, down the hall, was still sobbing so hard that the sound carried to where she and Barry sat. Margo had never seen her stepdaughter so upset. Jenny, in fact, usually *did* fight back; rather than being cowed by her mother's anger, Jenny used it to fuel her own. Had something besides Rae knocked the starch out of her? If so, Margo had a suspicion what it might be.

"Okay if I talk to her first?" she asked Barry.

"Hey, *I* don't question your ability to be a good mother to

Jenny and David. Maybe just give her another five minutes alone?''

''Yeah. I need a make a couple phone calls, anyway.''

The call to Olivia's house took longer than Margo had planned. Olivia hadn't arrived home nor at her boyfriend's, and her mother was frantic. Had Olivia been all right at that sweat lodge? her mother asked. She had been so upset since her gram died, and she'd wanted to contact her gram's spirit. Did anything happen?

''I'm sure she's fine.'' Margo was telling her share of—if not lies, then wishes—today. ''Could you ask her to call me when she comes in? Thanks.''

She wanted to call Donny Obayashi, but first she had her own family problems to contend with. She microwaved some popcorn, got two bottles of diet soda from the fridge, and knocked on Jenny's door.

''Go away!''

''No,'' said Margo, coming in.

Jenny, lying across the bed, eyed her from under wavy dark hair. Margo sat at the end of the bed and proffered a soda. Jenny hesitated, then accepted it. A moment later she was propped on an elbow, picking up one kernel of popcorn at a time and conveying it to her mouth. ''This is 'lite' popcorn, isn't it?'' she said.

''Yup.''

''Know one thing my mom always asks about you? She wants to know what you weigh.''

Margo had always suspected that one of her crimes against Rae-manity was her slenderness, but she and Barry had a rule not to disparage Rae to the kids. Besides, she had other things to discuss with Jenny.

''Can I see your ring?'' she said.

Jenny let her examine it, explaining, ''I'm going to get gold once it heals. But you have to start with surgical stainless steel.''

The surrounding skin was a bit red, but Margo saw no sign of infection, nothing to suggest that Jenny hadn't gone to a professional, as she had said she would. Except . . .

''Jen, I'm not going to set you up to lie. I called a professional body piercer last week. He said professionals won't do a minor unless the minor is accompanied by a parent or another responsible adult. Where did you get your nose pierced?''

The response was a fresh deluge of tears.

''I'm not going to get mad.'' Margo smoothed the girl's hair away from her damp face. ''I just want to know, are you so upset because of something that happened when you got it pierced?''

''No.'' Jenny sniffled. ''That was fine. A friend of mine did it, and he was great.''

Nick Costas, thought Margo, but refrained from asking.

''His father is a doctor,'' Jenny said. ''He was real careful about everything being sterile. And it hardly hurt at all.''

''But something upset you. Is this friend sort of a boyfriend?'' Had Nick pushed Jenny too far sexually? Damn, she'd kill him.

''Sort of. But you don't have to do the condom lecture again. We just kiss a little, you know? Mostly, when we're together, we talk. Or we take walks.'' The sentence dissolved into tears.

''More popcorn?''

Jenny ate another six kernels, again one at a time.

''Did you take a walk today, after he pierced your nose?'' said Margo, when Jenny seemed calmer.

''Yeah.'' Tears threatened again, but Jenny sniffed and continued, ''Promise you won't tell my mom? This is just between you and me?''

"Okay." Margo had probably just earned an F in stepparenting. But the alternative was not to be told at all.

"We went walking in Rose Canyon, right behind his house in University City—a couple blocks from where Mom lives. We shared a bottle of Snapple and then, um, Nick smoked a cigarette." She glanced up warily. Margo just took another handful of popcorn. She assumed Jenny had had a cigarette, too, but this was hardly the time for "the smoking lecture."

"Nick . . ." continued Jenny. "I don't know what happened, he's always so nice. But on purpose, he held his cigarette against a dead plant till it started to burn. I yelled at him to stop, but he didn't. So I hit him to make him drop the cigarette, and I stepped on it and the plant till I was sure they weren't on fire. Then I ran home. I don't know if I ever want to see him again," she ended miserably.

Margo put her arm around Jenny. "Sounds pretty scary. I'm glad you stomped out the fire."

"What if he starts another one? Margo, what's wrong with him?"

"I think he was just trying to act tough in front of you." Was this White Lie Number Three or Four? "Jenny?" Margo felt a spasm of anxiety, recalling a story Jenny had brought home from school the year before. "Is Nick the boy who started a fire in his locker?"

Jenny nodded but said defiantly, "That was the week after his older brother died of cancer. Nobody ever forgets that about Nick, that he started the fire, but they always forget his brother just died or that the school made him start seeing a psychiatrist and he's been going ever since." Jenny might be talking about ending things with Nick, but she certainly sounded like a loyal girlfriend. "And the rest of his family . . . We've talked in school about dysfunctional families, and sometimes I think I'm in one. But Nick's family is *really* screwed up."

"For instance?" Margo tried to stay calm despite the rapier of guilt that had just plunged into her heart. *Dysfunctional?* Did Jenny mean her and Barry, as well as Rae?

"Nick's talked about it with his shrink. His older sister always wanted their father's approval, and she thought she could get it by becoming a doctor. But the father just wanted the brother, the one who died, to be the doctor, even though he wasn't interested in medicine at all. And his mom—I guess she was totally devastated by the brother dying, but even though they're doctors, his father and his sister don't see that his mother needs help."

"What about Nick?"

Jenny teared up again. "I don't think his parents care very much what he does, but I thought he was okay. Sort of shy and unhappy, but . . ."

Margo reminded herself that she intended to talk to Jenny about independence and wounded birds. But not now.

"Thanks for telling me." She gave Jenny a hug, left the room, and curled up on her own bed, thinking.

She had intended to call Obayashi as soon as she'd talked with Jenny. Now, she had to consider how much could she say about the Costas family without violating her stepdaughter's confidence. Maybe she didn't need to say anything. The police must already be checking into the Costases, and Nick's locker fire would be in his school record, as would his whereabouts on the afternoon Hannah was killed. But what about Georgie . . . who was surely a lot more capable than her teenage brother of luring Leslie into a canyon late at night? How would the police know about Georgie's compulsion to please her father?

Then again, there was a huge gap between *dysfunctional* and *homicidal*. For God's sake, *Jenny* believed she lived in a dysfunctional family; and, given the scene that had occurred earlier that day, she was probably right.

Margo was still mulling things over when Donny Obayashi called her. Olivia's mother had reported her missing and had said Margo was present at the sweat lodge. Obayashi wanted to know about it.

"Not," he hastened to add, "that *I* believe Olivia could have talked to her grandmother's spirit. But I figure some of the people who were there believe that kind of thing. And if one of them killed her grandmother, Olivia could be in trouble."

Margo gave him a brief description of what had happened and the names of the people she knew who'd attended the sweat, as well as directions to the site.

"How did people react when Olivia said she could see her grandmother?" he said.

"It was impossible to tell. It was totally dark."

"What about afterward? You said you couldn't find Olivia. Did you see any of the other people, or did you just go straight to your tent?"

"I walked around for a while. I saw Cynara."

"Right, the daughter of the moon." It sounded as if Cynara had been no more diplomatic with Obayashi than she had with Margo.

"Paula was camping right by me. I talked to her for a minute when I came back," Margo continued. "And I talked to Dylan." Not precisely the truth, but far be it from Margo to inform the fuzz about Paula's love life. "By the way, his real name is Lewis Zeigler." She spelled it.

After all her soul-searching, she didn't say a word about the Costases. She was too caught up in thinking, fearfully, that Olivia had pitched her tent in a spot away from everyone else, that someone could have killed her during the night, hidden or buried her body in the woods, and abandoned her car down some side road. Had anyone acted markedly tired or jumpy this morning? Margo didn't remember and couldn't really know, since she had no idea what was usual for any of the people except Paula. And she knew how Paula had spent the night.

25 / Daughter of the Moon

You had to hand it to Dylan, thought Cynara, sitting in her room. The man really did tap into deep powers. All she had said, at the sweat lodge the night before, was that she wanted a home. (She hadn't said how desperately she needed one—how one of Leslie's kids had decided to move his family back to San Diego and wanted her and Art to leave the house within a month.) It didn't matter anymore, because by the end of the ceremony, Cynara had known how to get her heart's desire. She had made sense of the figure her nearsighted eyes had seen on the path to Leslie's house, the night that Leslie died.

And now, she decided, was the time to begin. She picked up the phone and called . . . Leslie's Lover, L. L., that was how she would think of the person. She didn't want even to form the name in her mind, as if the thought would then be released into the cosmos and do harm.

Even though it was one a.m., L. L., answering the phone, sounded fully awake.

Cynara didn't waste any time easing into her subject.

"I know you killed Leslie and Hannah. And I know part of why."

"That's insane," said L. L. but didn't hang up.

"You're going after the people who have the most power. I'm not sure why you're doing it, but I know it's true."

"Did the cards tell you that, Cynara?" So L. L. had recognized her voice. That was all right. If this went the way she intended, she'd be revealing her identity anyway.

"It doesn't sound like you think much of my abilities with the cards," she said.

A laugh.

"That's okay, I have no illusions about my abilities. I don't have power the way Hannah or Leslie did." Occasionally, as when that woman Margo came to see her, the cards were uncannily on the mark. But more often than not, they came up any which way, and she had to bullshit her way through the reading.

"If you really believe this ridiculous idea, aren't you afraid I'll kill you?"

She had thought of that, and answered, "No. For one thing, I don't have any real proof." That wasn't one hundred percent true, but what she did have—the memory of someone going down the path to Leslie's in the dark—was hardly ironclad. "For another thing, like I said, I'm not powerful. And I think you only want the powerful ones. That's why I'm calling. Because you've missed one."

Wasn't modern telephone technology wonderful? She could actually hear the intake of breath.

"Are you going to mention any names," said L. L., "or just let me guess?"

"You know who I mean. I can help you. The next time there's a Santa Ana."

"Why would you want this to happen?"

L. L. was no fool. Clearly fearing entrapment, L. L kept pressing until she revealed her and Richard's secret marriage and her desire to exercise her right to obtain some of his family fortune.

"So how are you going to help?" L. L said finally. "Bring the Bic lighter?"

"Of course not. You do whatever you want. Call him, say you want to talk with him. I'm sure he'll come. I don't want to know the details."

"As I said, what are you going to do?"

"I'll make sure the dog stays in the shop."

26 / The Shaman's Secrets

What a brutal day, thought Margo, sitting in her car waiting to cross the border from Tijuana back into the U.S. Because she had done a big story involving Mexico that summer, she had somehow become KSDR's Mexico expert (although she was hardly the most fluent in Spanish, some of the part-time staff being bilingual). She had just spent the entire afternoon chasing around Tijuana, first being assured by Mexican officials that they were aggressively tracking down stolen U.S. cars, then meeting a Mexican reporter who showed her cars driven by the Mexican Federal Police that were reputed to have come illegally from *el norte*. And for some reason—no doubt malign wishes directed at Margo personally—hundreds of people, most of them with nonexistent smog control devices, had decided to drive into the U.S. at exactly the same time she did. During the long wait at the crossing, she had one insight, a hunch related to Leslie's murder, but she doubted it would make any difference; nor did it make up for the toxic fumes doing unspeakable things to her lungs.

She returned to the station feeling gritty and grouchy, wanting a week back in the mountains just to breathe. At the least she wanted a shower. She considered ignoring her phone messages, until she saw that Donny Obayashi had called ten minutes ago.

"Have you heard anything about Olivia?" she asked, when she called him back.

The answer, as she had feared, was no. She went on to the thought she'd had at the border crossing.

"About Leslie's car. You haven't found it, right?"

"No." It didn't sound as if anyone had been looking, either.

"Where she died was really close to Tecate. Someone could have taken the car across the border there, driven it to Tijuana, and dumped it. Then all they had to do was walk back across and take the trolley into downtown San Diego the next day."

"Tell the sheriff's department; it's their case," grumbled Obayashi. Some turf battles must be going on. "By the way, thanks for the tip on Dylan Lightwing."

Margo felt a few brain synapses perk up. Obayashi had promised to tell her if he found out anything about Dylan.

"Turns out," he said, "that when this guy was Lew Zeigler, in the early seventies, he served three years in the federal prison in Phoenix for dealing."

"Marijuana?"

"Why do I get the feeling you don't consider that a serious crime?" His tone was light, but not so light that Margo delivered the first response that came to mind: *Come on, Donny, didn't you ever smoke?*

Instead she said, "It's not like he was an ax murderer."

"No. And it's not like he cared that we found out about his doing time."

"You questioned him? What would a decades-old drug charge have to do with these murders?"

"First of all, there's only one murder for sure," Obayashi

corrected her. "And the answer is, I don't know. I don't have a clue how these New Age people think."

Margo was regretting having ratted on Dylan. She liked Donny Obayashi, but the way he said "these New Age people" made *her* feel like lighting a smudge stick and singing a few chants to the goddess.

"What about people who are militantly opposed to the New Age?" she said. "Wouldn't they have more of a motive?"

"Like Dr. Theodore Costas and his people, for instance?"

"For instance. I suppose you've checked on where they all were when the Encanto fire started."

"I suppose so." Obayashi's tone clearly cut off further questions. "You mentioned Scott Nelson the other day. Sounds like he's your favorite suspect. Is there anything you're not telling me about him?"

"No," lied Margo.

As if he read her thoughts, Obayashi turned the conversation to Paula.

"Hey, your friend Chopin. Is she real into that New Age stuff?"

"Yes and no. Because of having agoraphobia, she's open to just about anything that might help."

"I asked one of the police psychiatrists about it. You know, the root problem isn't actually the agoraphobia, being afraid to go out. It's the panic attacks. Why doesn't Paula take medication for that?"

"It's primarily a psychological problem. She's gone to several psychotherapists." In addition to bodyworkers, an acupuncturist, an herbalist, a hypnotherapist, a nutritionist, and various psychic healers.

"That's what people used to think, that it was purely psychological," Obayashi persisted. "Lately there's been a lot of research indicating it's biochemical. There are medications to treat it.''

This conversation had certainly taken an intriguing turn. Margo doubted the lieutenant showed this much interest in most of his minor witnesses. ''Donny,'' she said, ''are you married?''

''Used to be. Gotta go,'' he mumbled, suddenly anxious to get off the phone.

Well, well, thought Margo, she'd have to tell Paula. Though not right away. She would wait until Paula's affair with Dylan had burned out. She definitely didn't expect it to last; Dylan, to indulge in a musical metaphor, seemed far too much a rolling stone.

Margo might not have been ready to talk to Paula, but Paula had plenty to say to her. She had already left one phone message, and she called again three minutes after Margo got home.

''You turned Dylan in to the police, didn't you?'' accused Paula, bypassing any preliminaries like *Hi, how are you?*

''Come on. I did exactly what you did. I found out Dylan's real name and let Obayashi know. I had no idea he had a record.''

''Do you know they brought him into the police station and made him sit there—just sit there, not knowing why he'd been brought in—for two hours, before they even got around to questioning him? Then they questioned him for an hour.''

Margo had a feeling Dylan Lightwing had survived the experience without any major wounds to his psyche . . . as she learned when Dylan, evidently hovering by Paula's side, got on the phone.

''Paula's mad at you, but I'm not,'' Dylan said. ''The cops talked to me earlier. They talked to a lot of us in the healing community. In fact, they virtually strip-searched me, who knows why. I guess that's how they get their jollies.''

Margo knew. They were looking for poison oak. Apparently they'd found no incriminating rashes on Dylan's exquisite body.

"You can understand," Dylan went on, "that under the circumstances, I didn't feel like opening up to them and telling them I did time. But it's no secret from any of my friends. In fact, it was one of the best things that ever happened to me. I didn't have a lot of direction then. In prison, I met some Navajo brothers, and they helped me start exploring that part of my heritage. When I got out, one of the guys sent me to his uncle, this incredible shaman. I studied with him intensively for several years, and I go back all the time. As I said, my prison time's no big secret. You can put it on the radio if you want to."

"Don't you dare put this on the radio!" Paula had grabbed the phone back. "Just a sec." Margo heard a murmur, Paula talking to Dylan, before she returned to the phone. "I wanted to talk to you with Dylan out of the room. Why are you so down on him, Margo?"

"I'm not."

"Bullshit."

"Okay. It's not that I have anything against him personally. I guess I'm uncomfortable with the fact that he slept with you for the first time right after leading the sweat lodge." Paula didn't respond, and Margo pushed on. "It's like a psychotherapist sleeping with a patient. He's in this position of power, and he's taking advantage of it."

"Funny, I don't feel like I'm being taken advantage of." Paula was virtually purring. "You're right, telling the police Dylan's name was the same thing I was doing, and you wouldn't have known he'd spent time in prison." Quick to anger, Paula was as quick to cool down.

"But hey, don't worry about me," Paula continued. "I know I don't have the best track record when it comes to picking men, but this thing with Dylan is just a case of major L.U.S.T. You don't remember what it's like out here in dating land. After a while, you'll take anyone who has a warm body with a working penis attached.

"Seriously, Margo, I've been getting to know Dylan, and he's not as powerful as you think. A lot of people see him as a shaman, but you'd be amazed how insecure he is about his abilities. He's gotten some awful criticism from Indians, both on the reservation where his teacher lives and outside. They refuse to accept him because he's only one-eighth Indian and he wasn't brought up among them. They call him a 'white wannabe,' even though he knows a lot more about the traditions and rituals than most of them do. And he gets flak because he charges people to attend his sweats. They don't do that on the reservation, but on the reservation a medicine man or woman could grow crops or something like that, and the tribe would help them out, too. Bringing the traditions out into the world, Dylan doesn't have the option of living that way. And there are people who don't understand it. Be there in a minute," Margo heard her say to Dylan.

"I've gotta go," said Paula. "But you do understand more, don't you?"

Margo said the only thing she felt Paula was willing to hear from her: "Yes."

She *did* feel she'd gotten a better picture of Dylan Lightwing, thought Margo, curled up next to Barry in bed, watching the eleven o'clock news. But that didn't erase her feeling that Dylan had exploited Paula's trust. In fact, the conversation with Paula had added to her uneasiness. In spite—maybe be-cause of—Paula's disclaimers, she sounded as if she had fallen hard. Was there anything Margo could say to her? Mulling over that question, she barely heard the weather report, that a new Santa Ana condition was predicted to start tomorrow.

27 / Rose Canyon

Lying on his side behind a clump of bushes in Rose Canyon, Nick Costas reached back and carefully ran a finger around his anus; his cutoffs and jockey shorts were bunched around his ankles. The wetness he felt could just be his own juices, but touching himself hurt and when he looked at his finger, he saw blood. Without shifting his body, he felt the ground behind him and found the discarded condom; it was bloody, too. This man had been rougher than most, shoving himself in hard without making Nick ready, and zipping up his pants and leaving seconds after he'd come. Had the guy even spoken? Well, that was what he wanted, wasn't it? Nick asked himself, angry at the tears forming in his eyes. Rough sex with unknown men. He must have fucked at least a dozen men here in the canyon in the past year. Or let the men fuck him, was more like it.

He ought to get up, at least to pull up his pants. In fact, he should get back to school in time for his next class; all he'd ditched so far was study hall, where he wouldn't be missed. But he felt so sore, like the man had injured something inside him. He decided to just lie still for another minute. The heat of the Santa Ana wasn't so bad in the shade.

What a dope he was to think he could get anything going with Jenny Dawes. At the thought of Jenny—of how he had totally ruined things with her two days before—the tears that had just been tickles in his eyes turned into sobs.

He stopped crying instantly, however, an animal sensing danger, when he heard someone walking in the canyon. Nick edged further under the cover of the bushes, the bone-dry grass scratching his bare side, and squeezed shut his eyes—not that closing his eyes was going to help him if this was his last fuck coming back for more.

Rapid, almost running, footsteps passed on the path below him. When he looked, the person had already rounded a bend and was no longer visible.

28 / Fire!

"Fire!" exclaimed Claire De Jong.

Anywhere else, the cry would send people scurrying for the nearest exit. In the KSDR newsroom, the adrenaline shot as high as in a crowded theater, but the response was, "Where?" "How big?"

"University City. Rose Canyon, west of Genesee," Claire read from the wire service printout. "It was spotted fifteen minutes ago, around three-thirty. The fire crews are just getting there, and they don't know how bad it is yet. But it sounds serious."

"I'll cover it," said Margo, her heart in her throat. Jenny's high school was just on the other side of Genesee Drive.

"Are you done with that story on the new policing policies in Mission Beach?" Claire asked her.

"Five minutes."

"Okay."

"I'm free!" offered a student intern.

"Thanks," said Claire, "but I want to go on this one. Why don't you go home and get some sleep—Howard, too—and both of you plan to show up around eleven, assuming the fire's still going? Margo, finish your story, and I'll round up equipment for us. Kev,'' she said to the chief engineer, ''will you be able to monitor us back here?''

''Sure thing.''

Claire already had her car started when Margo came out the door.

''How do I get there?'' asked Claire, still relatively new to San Diego.

''North on 5, then east on 52 through San Clemente Canyon.''

''That's not the canyon that's burning, is it?''

''No, that's Rose. San Clemente is south of University City and Rose is on the north.'' Between the two canyons were hundreds of pricey houses ... and Jenny and David. They should have gotten out of school half an hour before the fire was spotted, but maybe Jenny had had some after-school activity; or had she hung out with her boyfriend—her troubled boyfriend who thought it was a joke to light dead chaparral with a cigarette?

Faster! thought Margo, although Claire was already going seventy-five, maneuvering through the traffic like a racecar driver. The further north they drove, the darker and ashier the sky became, marked by the billowing darkness of the smoke to the northeast.

''Think they'll find another charred healer?'' said Claire.

Margo made herself remember that she liked Claire tremendously and that Claire's comment reflected the younger woman's instinct for a good story, rather than innate callousness. ''I hope not,'' she said.

Listening to KSDR in the car, they heard the latest fire department bulletin: The blaze had already consumed two homes on the south edge of the canyon and threatened at least another dozen. All Amtrak traffic had been halted. Residents who lived north of Governor Drive, the major east-west street through the area, were being evacuated, as were people north of the canyon. The latter were currently upwind of the fire, but the wind could shift. That was what made Santa Anas so dangerous.

Margo used the cellular phone to call Rae's house, two blocks south of the burning canyon, and got the answering machine. That was probably good news, meaning Rae and the kids had gotten out. Nevertheless, she called Barry, gave him her cellular phone number, and asked him to call if he heard from his former wife.

Claire turned onto the 52 freeway east . . . and into a massive traffic jam. Uniformed police officers were standing at the second exit, to Genesee, and directing people to keep going. Their car mired in the stop-and-crawl traffic, Margo got out and did a live broadcast of an angry exchange between a man insisting he had to get to his family and an officer telling him to go to a nearby evacuation center.

"Why aren't you letting people in?" she asked the officer, once he had won the argument and the man had driven on.

The cop looked disgusted. "You know why they had so much trouble fighting the L.A. fires? Because idiots trying to save their jewelry and their pet parrots blocked the emergency vehicles. If people are worried about family members, they should check the evacuation centers or contact a close friend or family member who lives in another part of town. We don't need more cars in the area. It's a real hazard."

"Can media get in?"

"Yeah." He didn't sound as if he liked the idea, but when Margo returned to the car, he waved her and Claire through.

The fire department command trailer was a quarter-mile north of the exit, at the corner of Genesee and Governor. Claire stopped the car and they ran in, along with several other reporters.

Ernie Velez, the department spokesman, was pointing out

on a map where the fire was thought to have started—just a few blocks from the Costas house, noted Margo—and how it was spreading. The flames were moving west, away from the high school. Margo didn't feel a great sense of relief.

"Has anyone investigated the source point?" she asked.

"There's still stuff burning there, because of the way the winds are moving," said Ernie. "We'll get in as soon as we can. Look, all of you can do us an important favor. The fire-fighters need every bit of water pressure they can get. Ask folks to stop watering down their roofs. It's not going to save their houses. If a thousand-degree fire comes roaring up that canyon, it'll get under the eaves, it'll blow out the windows. A few dozen gallons of water on the roof aren't going to make any difference, and people could be putting themselves and their families in danger. Tell them just to make sure their families are safe and leave the area."

"Fat chance," murmured a reporter.

Margo agreed. It was a rare Southern Californian who'd risk losing his or her own house to save the community.

"Can we get into the area?" asked Claire.

"Driving, only on Genesee or Governor, where emergency vehicles can pass you. Anywhere else, you've got to walk. And I shouldn't have to tell any of you this, but I will. Don't take any dumb chances."

Except for the newer, more upscale cars, and the primarily white faces in them, the scene along Governor Drive looked much the same as at the Encanto Hills fire: cars loaded with possessions, and frightened drivers—mainly women with children and pets—inching ahead in the thick traffic. Margo and Claire decided to split up and telephone each other or communicate through Kevin at the station. Claire would get as close as possible to the fire. Margo would interview people leaving; she could walk faster than the cars were moving. They each took a cellular phone and portable radios, putting the plugs in their ears to monitor KSDR.

"Remember," Margo said, feeling like a mother. "No dumb chances."

"Of course not!" Claire exclaimed, before running up the nearest side street, toward the fire.

Margo walked down the center of the four-lane road, feeling none too safe herself. The evacuating moms roughly divided into two types: Expressers, who gave vent to their fear and anger by laying on their horns, weeping, and so on, and Stiff-Upper-Lippers—even through the closed car windows, Margo could see them encouraging their kids to sing songs. She figured she'd be a Stiff-Upper-Lipper . . . and probably suffer nightmares for months. Maybe the Expressers had the right idea.

She phoned the station and in a minute was put on air, describing the scene.

"KSDR. Can I ask you a few questions?" she said, approaching a Stiff-Upper-Lipper with three kids and a terrier, whose window was open.

"All right."

"Are you okay?" she asked the woman.

"We're fine. I've got the kids and the dog, that's really all that counts."

"What else did you take? It looks like you packed a lot in the car."

"We'd already talked about what to take in case of fire. Photo albums, a few valuables, and some basic clothes."

"And you've got insurance?"

The Stiff-Upper-Lipper looked offended and rolled up her window.

Margo decided she might get more from an Expresser. She looked for a woman honking her horn or yelling . . . and saw

Rae, with David and Jenny in the car. She had never been happy to see Barry's ex before.

"That's all for now. Margo Simon for KSDR," she signed off, and ran to Rae's car.

"Rae, you're all right!"

"All right? The house Barry insisted on buying, and then insisted on giving me in the divorce settlement, is about to go up in flames. I . . ."

"Is the fire close to your house?" Margo interrupted.

"How am I supposed to know? I wanted to stay and water the roof, but some idiot cop made me leave." Margo fought the urge to strangle her—to think that Rae would have risked the kids' lives while she hosed the damn house. "The fire was a few blocks away when we left, but who knows where it's gotten to now?" Rae said. "And would you believe they told us we have to go to some kind of evacuation center, where we have to sleep on cots or probably the floor with dozens of strangers, all of them as traumatized as we are."

"Rae." Margo almost bit her tongue, but she got the words out. "Go to our house. The kids have keys. You can stay with us." She thought of asking Jenny in particular where she was when the fire started, but it wasn't a subject to bring up around Rae. "I've got to get back to work," she said . . . and did, as soon as she called Barry to tell him Rae and the kids were all right and that the whole happy family was going to be united under their roof. Barry didn't object, but she thought she heard a groan.

Margo kept walking down the center of Governor, occasionally calling the station and broadcasting live. Over her portable radio she heard Claire shouting questions at a fire-fighter. Eleven houses were now gone, and not just canyon homes—the fire had jumped a block south.

Several other reporters were roaming through the traffic,

just as she was. One of them started running back toward Genesee.

"What's up?" she yelled, running after him.

"They found a body!"

At the same time, she heard Claire broadcasting the news.

Olivia! The thought—the terror—hit Margo in the stomach, and she had to take several deep breaths before she could follow the pack of reporters running to the command center, knowing that Claire at the top of the hill was also running, to wherever the body had been found.

Margo crowded inside the trailer with a dozen of her colleagues, pushing forward to get the phone as close to Ernie Velez as possible.

"Everybody here?" Ernie looked around. "I don't want to have to repeat this eight times. Okay, the area we believe to be the source point of the fire cooled off enough for investigators to go in. They found a person. Deceased."

"Do you have an ID?" asked several reporters at once.

"Not yet."

"Male or female?" Margo heard herself speak but felt a sense of unreality. She took another deep breath.

"We don't know."

"Did the person burn to death or die of smoke inhalation?" asked someone else.

"The medical examiner will have the final say about the exact cause of death."

"Is it a homicide?"

"We probably won't be able to tell you anything else until tomorrow."

It didn't make sense for the victim to be Olivia, Margo tried to reassure herself. If anyone had killed Olivia, they'd have done it in the mountains two nights ago. Still, she couldn't control the sick feeling in her stomach as she continued, on automatic pilot, to work the fire. She and Claire stayed until eleven, when Dan Lewis and a student intern relieved them. Then they went back to the station and produced a brief story for *Morning Edition* on NPR; they'd supply a more detailed story later. The fire had now devoured thirty-two houses and remained out of control.

At one a.m., Margo finally went home, her fear for Olivia coexisting with creature needs for a shower and bed. It wasn't until she drove up to the house and saw Rae's car that she remembered her generous impulse that afternoon. She thought of Paula's bumper sticker—PRACTICE RANDOM KINDNESS— and wished she had invited some *random* family to say with them. And Jenny thought they were dysfunctional already.

Fortunately, Rae's new husband, Jeff Parkman, was a reasonable human being. He kept Rae from flying at Margo when she walked in, but no one could keep Rae's mouth shut.

"I took a sleeping pill, but a lot of good it's doing with the phone ringing!" complained Rae. "Some woman's been calling you every hour."

"Mo-om!" came a sleepy protest. Apparently David had been able to drop off in spite of the phone calls. He and Jenny lay in sleeping bags on the living room floor, Rae and Jeff evidently having been given the kids' beds.

"Who called?" asked Margo. "Did she leave her name?"

"Would she keep calling if she'd left her name and a phone number like a sensible person?"

"Rae, I'll stay up and get it on the first ring the next time. Why don't you go back to bed?"

"Come on, Rae." Jeff put his arm around her, and she let him lead her out of the room.

Margo did a double take when she saw them turn down the hallway toward her and Barry's bedroom. Damn! She could just see Barry letting Rae and Jeff use their bed, figuring they needed the comfort of sleeping together when they didn't even know if they still had a house.

She poured a large glass of orange juice—she hadn't realized how parched she was—and took the portable phone into the bathroom, where she removed her contact lenses, washed her face, and brushed her teeth. She still longed for a shower but didn't want to risk missing the phone call. Padding down the hall, she found the last empty bed (David's), peeled off her clothes, and got in, cradling the phone.

It took three rings to wake her, and then she fumbled with the receiver. When she picked up, Rae was already on the line, berating the caller.

"Rae, hang up." Margo's ash-seared voice sounded like a frog's and got more response from Rae than usual.

She heard the click of the other phone being replaced and then, "Margo, it's me. Olivia."

29 / Scratching an Itch

"Margo, are you okay?"

"Yeah," Margo got out between tears. She didn't turn on a light, as if it would protect Olivia to talk to her in the dark. "Where are you?"

"Safe. Are you sure you're all right?"

"I'm fine. I thought you were dead." She swallowed her tears, became a reporter again.

"In the fire? No, but Richard is. Jamal said they've got to do more tests, but they think the actual cause of death was smoke inhalation."

"Slow down. Richard?"

"Richard Del Vecchio, the crystal healer. Did you know him?"

"I met him." And Jamal, she remembered, was Olivia's boyfriend who worked for the medical examiner. "Okay, keep going."

"Someone cracked him over the head first, from behind, probably with a branch. Then they tied him to a pyre and lit the fire upwind, just like with my grandmother."

"Olivia, can they be sure it's Richard? I thought it took days to identify burn victims."

"Not one hundred percent sure," she admitted. "But there was a wallet in his back pocket with Richard's license and other ID that didn't get burned too badly. And his car was close to the fire area. Plus, the cops have tried to reach him and they haven't been able to. And Richard was the one, along with my grandma, who was being sued by Dr. Costas."

"Is that why you ran away after the sweat lodge? Did you have a vision of the killer and know it was Costas?"

Olivia expelled a tense breath. "I didn't see the killer. And I don't know about it being Dr. Costas. The main thing that happened in the sweat lodge was that I felt my grandmother's feelings at the time she died. She was scared, but that wasn't the only thing. Margo, she felt betrayed. It was like the killer was a person she knew and trusted. That's why I left. If it was someone my grandma trusted, it could be someone I trust, too."

"Someone who was at the sweat lodge?"

"Maybe. I don't know."

"What about Scott? Would your grandmother have trusted him?"

"Probably. She always believed the best of people. But I got the feeling it was someone she *really* knew. Besides, I looked real closely for poison oak on him, and I didn't see any." Someone spoke in the background. "I should go," said Olivia. "Maybe I'll call later this week."

"Wait! Does your mother know you're all right? Where are you?"

"My mom knows."

"Where are you?" said Margo again, but Olivia had hung up.

"You okay?" Barry was standing in the doorway.

"Yes. No."

He came over and held her, and she shed the tears she had

held back earlier. The two of them squeezed into the small single bed, and Barry fell asleep.

Margo lay awake beside her gently snoring husband.

Three healers, dead of fire. Three witch burnings? Except that Leslie's death was so different from the others. She hadn't been physically subdued, like Hannah and Richard, and there'd been no pyre. Nor was she being sued by Ted Costas. What if her death was a genuine accident, and it had given someone ideas? Not just *someone,* Margo corrected herself, but one of the Costas group? Any of them could have overpowered Hannah. And with a huge lawsuit pending against him, wouldn't Richard have gone if one of the Costases or their associates had called and said they wanted to talk?

She got up for a drink of water. Every pore in her body must have dried out from the fire. She went back to bed, tried to relax.

Olivia had said the murderer was someone Hannah trusted, which wouldn't apply to the Costases. But really—was Margo going to base her reasoning on a vision received in a sweat lodge? Something powerful had happened to Olivia during the sweat, she didn't question that. But didn't it make the most sense to look at who had real-life motives to kill Hannah and Richard? And the fact that the latest fire had started only a quarter-mile from the Costases' house?

Ted Costas blamed Hannah and Richard for his son's death. Georgie might do anything to gain her dad's approval—as would Scott Nelson, who had attached himself to Ted as if he had never had a father of his own. She made a note to ask Paula about that. Reluctantly, she added Anne and Nick Costas to the list of suspects as well. Anne was a cipher, but Margo suspected that she grieved more than anyone else did for her son, *and* she might be much less satisfied than her husband with the prospect of a legal victory over the people who'd "killed" him. Nick seemed too young to have planned the murders, but did Margo just think that because Nick was a white kid from a rich family? Kids younger than he committed murder every day. And Nick had shown a fondness for fire.

Another thing. Dylan claimed he'd been strip-searched. Even Paula had had to display her lower legs and arms. Had the police subjected the eminent Dr. Theodore Costas Jr. and his family to the same kind of examination in their hunt for signs of poison oak?

And damn, what kept nagging at Margo every time the subject of poison oak came up?

At four a.m., after little sleep, she figured it out. Within half an hour, she had showered, thrown on some clothes, and was driving to the radio station.

Checking with the overnight board operator, she learned that the Rose Canyon fire had destroyed fifty-six houses and wasn't yet under control. That answered any question as to where she was going to spend the day.

"Poison oak. Poison oak," she muttered, going to her office. Just thinking about it made her itch.

She kept the cassettes from current stories more or less neatly filed in a desk drawer. Old cassettes were another matter. Many she simply recorded over, but she had a hunch she had hung onto her original, unedited interview with Hannah, thinking it would make a good longer feature for NPR (if she ever got around to it, which she hadn't). She rummaged through a shoebox of cassettes under her desk—no luck there or in a file cabinet. She had changed offices since doing the Hannah story, thanks to her promotion. In her old office, she finally found the dusty tape on a shelf.

She played the cassette at double speed, the chattering Donald Duck voices clear to her from years of listening to tapes this way. Hannah was describing the healing properties of the various herbs they encountered as they walked through the canyon: "Horehound. As you can see, it's a small plant, close to the ground, with soft, fuzzy leaves. It's very bitter to bite into. You can make a tea from this, it's good for respiratory problems. . . . This is Southernwood, also known as Lad's Love and Maiden's Ruin, because it's considered an aphrodisiac. My boyfriend and I swear by it, ourselves. Of course, we're fond of fine bourbon, too." Hannah laughed. What a charming laugh she'd had, as light as a young girl's. The voice on the tape continued, "A tea made from California sage settles the stomach. . . . Plantain is always used in salves. It promotes cell growth. . . . Now, here's everybody's favorite—poison oak."

Eureka! Margo slowed the tape to regular speed.

"Does it have any medicinal uses?" She heard herself ask.

"As a matter of fact, you can grind it up and put it on a snakebite because it's an astringent. But the really interesting thing—now, don't put this on the radio," Hannah interrupted herself. "I don't want anyone out there getting sick on my account."

Margo heard her own, "Okay." As promised, she had edited the section out of her final piece, the one she'd reviewed when she did the story on Hannah's death.

"You can make yourself immune to poison oak," said Hannah. "The local Indians did. They used poison oak to make baskets, so they were touching it all the time. What you have to do is eat it, a little at a time."

There was a pause in the tape, and Margo remembered Hannah actually taking a leaf from the plant, chewing it, and swallowing.

"I used to tell this to my classes," Hannah said. "But then someone overdid it and had a bad reaction, so I don't teach it anymore. One day I'll tell my granddaughter, but right now she's only twenty. I can just see her and her friends making poison oak salad.'' That girlish laugh again.

Margo stopped the tape recorder.

Who might have known about the poison oak and also had a motive to kill Hannah, Richard, and Leslie?

All roads led to Scott Nelson. Whether or not Scott had taken Hannah's herb class, the poison oak story must have spread through the New Age community, a legend about a woman regarded as legendary. And Scott hadn't simply decided he *preferred* Western medicine to massage, he'd had a deep personal reason for renouncing his former life; he even seemed to blame the New Age movement for the dark place he had discovered inside himself.

"Now what?" Margo asked herself out loud. "Coffee," she answered.

She hoped to find some already brewed, courtesy of Ken Ayres, the local *Morning Edition* host, who had come on air an hour ago, at five. But Ken tended to stop for coffee at a convenience store on the way to work, and the pot in the tiny station kitchen contained yesterday's cold dregs; she briefly considered heating some up in the microwave, then resigned herself to washing out the pot, measuring fresh grounds, and starting a new one.

She could go after Scott herself, she thought as the coffee dripped, and take another reporter (preferably the six-foot-three student intern) for protection. The idea appealed to her, but common sense intervened. Why would Scott allow a reporter to question him? Margo had no authority even to make him listen to her questions, much less answer them. She really ought to pass her information about poison oak along to Lieutenant Obayashi; that plus the news that Scott had turned against the New Age after he had seriously injured a massage client and was horrified that he'd enjoyed it. Damn! That particular story was Paula's, who had refused to tell it to the police. But Richard was still alive then, nor had Margo figured out about the poison oak. Surely Paula would see things differently now. It was now six-fifteen. By seven—seven-thirty at the latest—Paula would be awake. Margo would call and convince her to contact Obayashi herself. Another hour wouldn't make a difference. Obayashi probably wasn't even at work now, but home asleep. Just thinking of sleep, she decided to forget the coffee and take a nap.

Returning to her office, she sat down and leaned her head on crossed arms on her desk—not the most comfortable position; in fact she didn't think she'd ever managed to drop off during rest time in grade school. She must have dozed, however, because she jumped when someone spoke her name. Lifting her head, she awoke instantly, adrenaline surging.

"Hi," she said to Scott Nelson, who stood in her office doorway.

30 / Mr. Bonebreak

How the hell did Scott get into the station this early? KSDR's security wasn't exactly tight, but only employees had keys to get in before business hours, and it was still only— she glanced at her watch—seven a.m. And where could he have come from except the fire, with his ash-smudged face and clothes and his bloodshot eyes?

"You look like you could use some coffee." Margo smiled and came around her desk. "Do you take it black or with sugar or cream?" If she could get past him into the hall, Ken Ayres was here; maybe Howard Biele, too, putting together his report after covering the fire last night.

"No coffee." Scott eyed her officemate's chair but apparently decided against wading through the piles of paper on that side of the office. Instead he stayed just inside the door, leaning against the wall.

Margo returned to her own chair, keeping the desk between them. She thought of Paula's latest remedy for anxiety. Would a little polka music help her take a deep breath?

"I want to go on the radio," said Scott. "They're crucifying Ted."

Inhale. Exhale.

"We need to go into one of the studios to get good sound quality." Preferably the one right next to master control, where Ken could see them through the glass wall.

"Sure. Okay."

Docilely, Scott got up and stood aside to let her lead him down the hall.

"Looks like you had a rough night." Margo stayed several steps ahead of him and walked sideways, keeping an eye on him. But if Scott had come here to do her harm, he showed no sign of it. Head hanging, he looked immensely weary, a small boy who might bring out the mother in a woman. Margo could see how he had appealed to Paula, though she didn't find herself affected by his charm.

She took him into the studio next to master control. Ken, visible through the glass, wasn't currently broadcasting, just playing the feed from National Public Radio.

"Why don't you sit here?" She directed Scott to the side of the table farther from the door. "I just need to get some things."

She went into master control and asked Ken to keep an eye on them, then fetched her cassette recorder and a fresh tape and returned to the studio. Studio interviews were usually recorded on reel-to-reel, but there was no one at work yet to operate the equipment.

"You're going to tape this?" said Scott as she set up the recorder. "I want to go on the radio live."

Margo had started to relax. Now she felt a fresh rush of fear. Scott might remind her of a small boy, but small boys could throw tantrums; and this small boy pumped iron.

"We're airing the national morning news now." She turned on the tape recorder and extended the microphone toward him. "Say again what you told me in my office."

"Actually . . ." He took a folded piece of paper from his pocket.

Margo disliked written statements but declined to quibble about this one. "Start by identifying yourself, okay?"

"I'm Scott Nelson. Um, I'm a premedical student at UCSD, volunteering with Physicians for Responsible Medicine." He spoke hesitantly, but adopted a pompous tone when he began to read: "Dr. Theodore Costas Jr., a respected ophthalmologist, recently started a bold campaign to place more controls on so-called alternative or New Age healers. As part of the campaign, Dr. Costas filed lawsuits against Hannah Jones and Richard Del Vecchio for practicing medicine without a license, because of their treatment of Dr. Costas's son, who tragically died of lymphatic cancer last year. Hannah Jones died in a canyon fire two weeks ago. Richard Del Vecchio was found dead in the Rose Canyon fire yesterday. I wish to state unequivocally that Dr. Theodore Costas had absolutely nothing to do with the unfortunate deaths of Ms. Jones or Mr. Del Vecchio. In fact, I am deeply concerned that someone is trying to discredit Dr. Costas and his campaign by attempting to implicate him in these two deaths. Theodore Costas is a *doctor*. He's dedicated to preserving life. Thank you."

Scott stood up.

"Wait! I need to ask a few questions for background."

"Uh. Okay." He took his seat again.

"Are you speaking on behalf of Physicians for Responsible Medicine?"

"I'm a premed student volunteering with Physicians for Responsible Medicine."

"I understand. But does Dr. Costas know that you're making this statement?"

"Oh, no. If that's what you mean, I'm acting on my own, because I know Theodore Costas is a great human being."

"Dr. Costas's house is right on the edge of Rose Canyon, isn't it, very close to where the fire started?"

"Yes. That's why I think someone is trying to implicate him. But why would he risk burning his own house? I helped the family evacuate. We don't know if their house survived." There was anguish on his face. Margo wondered if, when the Costas family said "we," they included Scott.

"You said Richard Del Vecchio was the man found dead in Rose Canyon," she said. "I talked to the police just an hour ago, and no definite ID of the Rose Canyon victim had been made. How do you know it's Del Vecchio?"

Scott looked confused. "Last night they kept questioning him about Richard. I just assumed . . ."

"Who was questioning whom?"

A savvy interviewee would have refused to answer or would start throwing around the phrase "off the record." Fortunately, Scott showed a deficiency of savvy.

"The police. They came around nine o'clock. The Costases had just gotten settled at their daughter's house in San Marcos. The police took Dr. Costas and his younger son, Nick, downtown for questioning. Someone brought Nick back at midnight, but they didn't let Dr. Costas go until two a.m., and he has to come back this morning. As if it's not enough that he lost his son and doesn't even know if his house is still standing."

"Why Nick?"

"Nick?" Scott sounded as if he had forgotten Nick Costas existed.

"Why did they question Nick as well as Dr. Costas?"

"Oh, yeah. Both he and Dr. Costas weren't where they were supposed to be yesterday afternoon. Dr. Costas left his office around one and went home. He had a terrible migraine, and he went straight to bed." So he was a short walk from where the fire started. No wonder the police had grilled him.

"You have to understand," said Scott, "he's under tremendous stress. All of this stuff with the lawsuit and his campaign to regulate the so-called healers, he's not doing it for fun. Every minute he's working on it, he's reminded that his son Teddy died."

"And Nick?" Margo had a feeling that a lot of people close to Nick forgot he existed.

"Just some dumb kid thing. He cut class, I guess."

"What were you doing when the fire started?"

"Studying at the UCSD library." About two miles from Rose Canyon. So why hadn't the police questioned Scott? Maybe because they didn't know what she did about his motive.

"Were you studying with anyone?"

"The point I came here to make is, Dr. Costas isn't guilty of anything."

"What about the day Hannah Jones was killed in the Encanto Hills fire? Did the police question Dr. Costas about that?"

"Yes. Except not until the next week, after he announced his lawsuit."

"Where was he that afternoon?"

"I didn't ask him. In his office seeing patients, I suppose. The point is, why would Dr. Costas kill Hannah Jones or Richard Del Vecchio? He was already going after them by legal means. That's why I say someone is trying to implicate him, since he's gone on record saying he held Hannah and Richard responsible for his son's death."

Scott had a point.

"I'm wondering," she said, "if there's anyone in your group—not Dr. Costas, but somebody else—who is so strongly opposed to alternative healers that they could be doing this?"

"We believe in healing people, not killing them!"

"But once a group starts, you can't control all the individuals who join. Think of some of the calls to our radio show last week, people saying New Age healers were satanists. Is there anyone in your group who believes that?"

"We're approaching this as medical people, scientists."

"You said you went to help the Costases move things out of the house. What time was that?"

"The second I heard about the fire. Three, three-thirty?"

"Didn't you have trouble getting there? They weren't letting people through."

"I didn't have far to go. Like I said, I was at UCSD, studying in the library. And I took surface streets, not the freeway."

"You're very committed to Dr. Costas's campaign, but you used to be involved with alternative healing yourself, weren't you? As a massage therapist?"

"Yes." Scott didn't seem to register the change in her line of questioning. Nonetheless, Margo sat back a few inches farther from him and stretched her arm across the table to keep the microphone in position.

"What made you change your mind about New Age healing?" she asked.

"Just gradually, over time, I saw that . . ."

"Was there any specific event? Some sort of 'aha!' experience?"

"Not really."

Margo glanced up, caught Ken's eye, before she said, "Didn't you do a massage where you hurt the person? You broke their shoulder?"

"No!" said Scott, but he was shaking.

"That must have been terrifying, to have the intention of helping someone and end up hurting them . . . maybe even enjoying the power of being able to do that? It must have been like seeing a part of yourself you didn't know existed, that you would have preferred never knowing about.''

''Who told you that?''

She said softly, confidingly, ''Did other New Age healers remind you of that part of yourself, the part you hated and wanted to destroy?''

''Who told you that?'' Scott repeated. ''About the woman I hurt? I only told one person in the world.'' *Oh, shit!* Scott ran out of the room. Margo had a feeling she knew where he was going . . . and he could get there in ten minutes.

She picked up the phone. Thank heaven Obayashi was at his desk. Barely explaining the situation, she urged him to send officers to protect Paula. He put her on hold for several minutes, then came back.

''The beat cops in the area will handle it,'' said Obayashi. ''Now, I want the whole story on Scott Nelson. You can tell me over the phone, or I'll have you brought in.''

Whoa! He sounded as if he'd been watching too many old cop shows. Resisting the temptation to remind him of the First Amendment, Margo told him about Scott and that Hannah used to teach people how to become immune to poison oak. Obayashi unleashed a few words she had never heard him use before. She got a feeling he was furious over more than the withheld information on Scott—or that she'd found out the police were looking for people with poison oak—but she didn't dare ask, nor did she get a chance. He slammed down the phone.

''You okay?'' said Claire, sticking her head in the door.

''Super. I just got chewed out by a cop.''

''Good for you,'' said Claire, who favored a more adversarial style of reporting than Margo; Claire figured she was doing her job when she made people mad. ''They got the Rose Canyon fire under control half an hour ago. Let's roll.''

Margo went to sign herself and Claire out on the board facing the receptionist's desk.

"Margo!" The receptionist half-whispered and held her hand over the mouthpiece of her phone. "Paula Chopin, for you. She sounds mad."

Margo grabbed the receiver. "Paula, I'm sorry. I can explain. . . . No, not now. How about coffee after dance class?" She hung up, wincing at the few words Paula had a chance to say to her, and turned to Claire. "Okay, let's roll."

31 / Nick in Love

It was insane to feel happy when his family's entire house had burned to the ground just last night, thought Nick, studying for a Spanish test at his sister's since school had been canceled for the day. Well, Nick felt totally insane, with what his Spanish teacher would call *alegría*—joy.

And to think it was because of being questioned by the police last night! The policewoman who'd talked to him had reminded him a little of his mom, his mom without the pills. She had a soft voice and the kind of face you wanted to fall into. She said to call her Jill.

Jill wasn't soft, though. She told him he could be in a lot of trouble, and it was important for him to say exactly where he'd been yesterday afternoon when he wasn't in class. But in spite of the tough words, it was the look on her face that got him, a look that said nothing he'd done was so bad. Before he knew it, he was telling her things he had never told Dr. Morgenthal—about going to the canyon, picking up men, and getting ass-fucked. He wanted to shock her, he guessed. Except Jill didn't act shocked. She just called in a doctor and left them alone while the doctor examined him.

Once the doctor said that Nick's story was true, Jill looked sad, but not angry or disgusted. She said something about him having to get an AIDS test and see a social worker. Nick was a little worried about that, especially the social worker. But mostly, it had just felt so good to tell her the secrets he'd had bottled up inside him and feel they weren't such terrible secrets after all. He had even talked about what happened with Jenny (well, he didn't say he had started a plant on fire, just that he'd been a jerk). Jill said, like it was the easiest thing in the world to do: "Sounds like you ought to apologize."

"How?" Nick had asked.

Jill had told him.

And he was going to. Not today, since no one was answering the phone at Jenny's house (but at least the phone was ringing, so her house must be all right). But tomorrow, as soon as he saw her at school. He could hardly wait.

32 / Re Visions

"Why are we driving down this street?" asked Claire, when Margo turned two blocks before the edge of the canyon. Here, the fire must have hiphopped, taking out one house and sparing the next, then taking another and skipping three.

"In the interest of my sanity." Margo explained about Rae staying with her and Barry. Thank heaven, Rae's house was fine. It might smell smoky for awhile, but Rae could move back immediately.

Margo headed next for the Costas home, hoping to get a statement from Ted Costas. On the way to the fire scene, she'd recapped her interview with Scott, and Claire had agreed with her that the material was of questionable use, since Scott wasn't speaking officially for the Costas group and much of what he said was hearsay. If Scott turned out to be the murderer, of course the interview was dynamite. In the meantime, Margo had to try to get something from Costas himself.

"Jee-sus," said Claire, when they got to the top of the hill. There was no longer a Costas home; there were no homes left standing on the entire block. Quite a few people were present, staring at their personal scenes of devastation. Margo learned which pile of rubble had belonged to the Costases and that Ted and Anne had been there earlier but had left. Claire went down the street to interview a family while Margo phoned Ted Costas's office. Not surprisingly, she was told that the doctor was out for the day, due to an emergency. She left a message to which she didn't expect a reply, though it must have given the office staff food for gossip: *I've talked to Scott. I want to hear your version of what happened Tuesday night.*

"Boy!" said Claire, rejoining her. "You live on a canyon, don't you? This must give you the willies."

"For the last year, we've been asking the landlords to clear the brush behind the house down to the property line. It's sure making me think that since they haven't done anything, we ought to have the brush cleared ourselves and send them the bill."

They split up, agreeing to meet back at the car and return to the station in an hour. They needed to have enough time to produce a story for NPR's *All Things Considered*, which started at two p.m. Pacific time.

As Margo talked to benumbed fire victims and relieved but guilty survivors, she kept thinking of Olivia's vision: that Hannah (and Richard and possibly Leslie?) had been murdered not by an enemy but by a friend. *Really, visions?* she asked herself, as she had in the middle of the night. Still, even though her sleep-deprived mind felt like the La Brea Tarpits, questions kept gurgling up from the ooze:

Who in the New Age community had Hannah trusted? By whom would she have felt betrayed?

Olivia herself? But she said she'd been in class when the fire started. And since she was one of Hannah's heirs, surely the police had checked her alibi first.

Margo thought of the other people who had been at the sweat lodge, at least those she knew.

Dylan Lightwing? According to Olivia, Dylan was an old friend. However, Margo remembered something Paula had said the day they met Dylan: that he'd just come to San Diego from Arizona. If the police had checked on Dylan—and they must have, given his prison record—they would have checked that.

Cynara seemed malicious enough to commit murder, but too lazy to carry it out. And Cynara had such an effective weapon in her tongue.

Art? Other than the fact that his hands around her neck had felt extremely strong, Margo didn't really know much about the chiropractor.

That was the problem. She knew very little about any of them. She hadn't met more than a few of the hundreds—perhaps thousands?—of local New Agers. As for knowing any of them well enough to have a clue as to someone's motive . . .

A fanatic who believed nontraditional healers were satanists might have seen the killings as sacrifices required by God. Within the New Age community, however, the motive had to be personal. Who would have had a personal motive to kill all three healers? Of the handful of people Margo knew, Cynara or Art might have had problems with Leslie as their landlady. And Cynara was doubly connected to Richard, as his former lover and his partner in Crystal Magic; surely both personal and business disputes had occurred. Two strikes against Cynara. But why would she kill Hannah?

What if someone were engaged in an illegal activity that Leslie, Hannah, and Richard all knew about? Or, say the murderer had only intended to kill Leslie, but Hannah and then Richard had found out?

Paula would know a lot more about individuals and possible motives. Margo called on the cellular phone, bracing herself for her friend's anger. But Paula, she learned, was unavailable. According to the receptionist, Paula had been asked to appear at the police station downtown.

Paula? Margo had considered every New Ager she knew, except Paula. It made her stomach churn, but she forced herself to think like a cop. Paula knew all three victims. She did accounting for a lot of people and groups in the New Age and nonprofit worlds, hardly high-end clients, yet she lived quite comfortably. She was right at the scene when the Encanto Hills fire started, and to a cop, her explanation of what she was doing—the Rambo exercise—must have sounded bizarre.

Margo sighed in relief. The more she considered why the police might suspect Paula, the less she believed it herself. She did a few shoulder rolls—she had tensed her shoulders up to her ears—and checked her watch. Time to reconnect with Claire.

Back at KSDR, she and Claire put together as much of a story as they could, lacking official confirmation that the fire was arson or the death a homicide. That confirmation came in the afternoon, at a news conference Margo covered at the police department. In addition to announcing the arson-homicide, the lieutenant commanding the team investigating the latest fire (not Obayashi, though he stood in the background), stated that the victim had been identified as Richard Del Vecchio.

Margo stayed silent during the ensuing flurry of questions. Her competitors tended to specialize, a luxury that a public radio station couldn't afford. Thus, none of the crime reporters had covered the Costas news conference the week before. Although they asked about Hannah and Leslie—as other healers recently killed in canyon fires, and was a serial killer targeting these people?—no one seemed to make the connection that both Richard and Hannah were being sued by Dr. Theodore Costas Jr. Margo didn't figure it was her duty to enlighten them.

She approached Obayashi afterward.

"Scott Nelson," she said.

"Yeah?" Obayashi looked at her as if he'd like to lock her in the nearest cell.

"Did you catch him this morning?"

"No. Did you or your buddy Paula tell him you were going to call us and give him a chance to get away?"

"Of course not." Margo knew the lieutenant was irked at her for not telling him about Scott sooner, but at the moment his anger seemed personal. She decided she'd just as soon keep the conversation on a professional footing. "What about Ted Costas? You had him in for questioning last night. Do you plan to make an arrest, now that both of the people he holds responsible for his son's death have died in arson-homicides?"

"Lady, what do you and Paula do?" Obayashi exploded. "Examine entrails? Look in a crystal ball? Hey, I'll tell you something. One thing, okay? We had to wait to release Richard Del Vecchio's name until we notified the next of kin. Guess who that was?"

Margo shrugged. She knew Obayashi was as tired as she was; but he ought to know she was just doing her job.

"Your friend Cyanide. Oops, I mean Cynara."

"Cynara? How come?"

"She was his wife."

Richard and Cynara, married? Margo almost picked up the phone and called Paula the moment she got back to her office. On second thought, she decided she'd better wait until she and Paula had their talk that evening.

*　　*　　*

"So you see, I fully intended to call you," Margo told Paula at a coffeehouse after their dance class. "I was sure you'd agree that the police had to be told about Scott." She had already explained how, early that morning, she had determined Scott was a prime suspect; and then he had shown up at KSDR.

Paula, staring into a cup of tea, didn't look mollified.

"You would have agreed, wouldn't you, to tell the police?" Margo went on. "Don't you think you told me the story about Scott breaking the woman's shoulder, even if you didn't want to believe he could do anything bad, because on some level you knew it was important? And when he ran out of the station this morning and I thought he was coming after you, I had to do something. Please, stop me any time. I'm babbling."

Paula finally looked up, but she didn't return Margo's smile. "I understand you felt the police needed to know about Scott. But Margo, you didn't tell the police first."

"Yes, I . . ."

"First, you told Scott. You were getting him on tape, and you'd established some rapport, right? And you thought, 'what a great opportunity to spring that incident on him and see how he reacts.'"

"You make me sound like a barracuda."

"I don't know. I'm not in your profession. Maybe if I were a reporter, I would have done exactly what you did."

"Sure, if you had the ethics of a toad."

Paula actually laughed. "Aren't you mixing your animal metaphors? Barracudas, toads? Look, I'm not saying you're a horrible person. I don't happen to think you're a horrible person. And you're probably right that I wouldn't have told you about Scott in the first place if I didn't, unconsciously, think there was something to it." She shook her head. "Consciously, I still can't believe it's him. In fact, I had to go to the police station this morning and look at a lineup, to see if I recognized someone from the Encanto Hills fire. They didn't look remotely like Scott. They were all older men, sort of distinguished, with gray hair."

Ted Costas, thought Margo. She also registered—and appreciated—that Paula had changed the focus away from Margo's behavior, horrible or not. Margo didn't feel finished with that subject herself, but she was relieved, for now, to be talking about something else.

"Did you recognize any of them?" she asked.

"No. Donny even had me look at them in a mirror, with my back to them. But I couldn't identify anybody." She frowned. "God, he was in a rotten mood. He acted so cold toward me, I felt like I was the criminal."

"Really? I think he likes you."

"Oops."

"What?"

"Maybe that's why he acted testy. He called me this morning, around seven-thirty, to say the police were on their way to protect me from Scott. Dylan answered the phone."

Margo echoed Paula's "Oops." That might explain why the lieutenant hadn't been a model of politeness that afternoon. Which reminded her . . .

"Did you know that Richard and Cynara were married?"

"No way!"

"She was next of kin."

"Everyone knew they used to be lovers, but married? Are you sure?"

Margo nodded.

"No wonder neither of them ever had me do their taxes. That and the fact that Richard was one of *the* Del Vecchios."

"Paula?" Margo stirred her tea slowly. She had a feeling she was about to rekindle her friend's anger.

"Yeah?"

"I want to ask you something. And I don't want you to tell anyone about this, not even Dylan. Not because it has anything to do with him," she said quickly, to forestall Paula's defense of her lover. "It's about Olivia. The less people who know, the safer she'll be."

"She's all right, then! Do you know where she is?"

"She wouldn't say, but she sounded okay. She called last night."

Margo recounted Olivia's story about feeling Hannah's sense of betrayal, as if the murderer was a trusted friend.

"I don't have any idea who Hannah felt close to," Margo said, "or who might have had a reason to kill her. Same thing with Leslie and Richard, especially if the same person killed all three of them."

"If Richard had been killed first," mused Paula, "I'd guess Cynara, since she must inherit lots of money. Then I'd figure she killed the others because they found out."

"What if that's how she was thinking? She must have known she'd be the obvious suspect if Richard got killed first. What if, even though he was her real victim, she got Leslie and Hannah first to make it look like some kind of serial killer was going after healers?"

"That's so devious. Not that Cynara isn't devious. Good grief, married to Richard!" Paula ran her hands through her black bob. "But I can't believe she would take anyone's life. Besides, the police must have thoroughly checked where she was when the Rose Canyon fire started. After all, what's the question they always ask in Latin? 'Who benefits?' "

"Look at it another way, then. What did the three of them—Leslie, Hannah, and Richard—have in common?"

Paula sat quietly for a moment, eyes closed. When she opened them, they shone with tears. "You know the obvious thing that comes to mind? They were all absolutely brilliant healers. Not just knowledgeable or skilled—there are dozens of people with knowledge and skill. But Leslie, Hannah, and Richard? Each of them had a genuine gift.''

Margo thought of the crystal Richard had helped her choose and how peaceful she felt when she held it. And Hannah, in their interview last spring, had impressed her as a true wise woman.

''There's going to be a memorial out in the mountains Friday night for them,'' Paula added. ''Do you want to go?''

''No, thanks. Barry's taking the kids on a research ship, and I'll have the house to myself Friday night. All I want to do is read. And drink.''

''The more I think about it, the more I think the killer has to be someone who hated the New Age. I'm not disputing Olivia's vision. But you shouldn't take things like that too literally. What if Hannah felt betrayed not because the killer was a friend of hers, but because what happened betrayed her faith in humanity? Margo, I really think these were witch burnings. Someone found out who the best healers were and went after them. Oh, God.'' Paula jumped up, wild-eyed.

''What is it?''

''Dylan. He's the one other person I can think of who has that kind of gift.''

She ran out of the coffeehouse.

33 / The Shaman at Home

El Mirador. The viewpoint. There was nothing to see in the dark bedroom, where Margo lay awake in spite of bone-deep exhaustion. In her mind, however, she was seventy miles south, standing on a cliff in Mexico watching the sun set into the ocean. Seventy miles away and two months ago . . . and wondering then, as she wondered now, how she had changed and what the change had cost her.

Barracuda. It was her own word, not Paula's, but if the animal fit . . . Margo had always prided herself on lacking the instincts that characterize a born reporter, but she had regretted the lack as well, fearing it held her back in her job; and who'd ever said reporters were born, not made?

Had she really needed to break Paula's confidence when she'd talked to Scott that morning?

Everything would be easy if the answer were a clear no. Then at least she'd have no doubt that she had become a despicable human being, and she'd know she had to try to change back to whatever she'd been before.

But every time she asked herself the question, she thought, "Maybe." *Maybe* she had connected with Scott in a way that, if he were the murderer, at that moment he would have confessed. *Maybe,* if the subject had been raised even an hour later—in the police station, by someone else—by that time Scott would have raised the drawbridge forever. True, Margo had gotten no confession; but *maybe* it was worth the attempt.

She listened for her conscience, which invariably spoke with her mother's voice. All she heard was, "Accepting ambiguity is one of the major tasks of adulthood." Thanks, Mom. Margo felt as if she were swimming in ambiguity, as if she were drowning in it, the cliff in Mexico high above her.

And while she was keeping herself awake with questions, how about the question of who else Ted Costas III had gone to for alternative health care? His family was only suing Hannah and Richard, but hadn't he consulted half a dozen different healers?

The next morning—after four hours of less than refreshing sleep—Margo called Paula and asked whether Teddy Costas had gotten bodywork from Leslie. Paula didn't know.

She thought of trying Ted Costas Jr. But the doctor hadn't returned her call yesterday and she doubted, in light of the police attention on him, that he'd talk to her today. Of course, Ted wasn't the only articulate member of the Costas family. Margo called Georgie's office, telling the receptionist she had some questions about Physicians for Responsible Medicine. She had to wait for ten minutes while Georgie finished seeing a patient, somewhat eased by the fact that the office used a chamber music tape for people on hold.

"This had better be about the organization," said Georgie when she came on the line. She sounded as if she'd been getting as little sleep as Margo. But she switched to a calm, friendly tone when Margo started taping.

"Regarding your father's lawsuit against Hannah Jones and

Richard Del Vecchio,'' said Margo, ''I believe you said they weren't the only alternative practitioners your brother saw?''

''That's right. But as I said on your call-in show, they were the people Teddy placed the most trust in. And, in my opinion as a physician, they were the ones whose areas of so-called knowledge have the least basis in any kind of science.''

''Who else did he see?''

''Heavens, who didn't he see? That's why we want more regulations placed on these so-called healers. People who really need good medical care will go from one of them to another and spend a fortune.''

''Art Smolin, a chiropractor?''

''You're asking if Teddy got treatment from him? Teddy saw at least two chiropractors.''

''Did he ever go to a sweat lodge? Say, with Dylan Lightwing?''

''*I* even went to a sweat lodge with Teddy, and a few other things. He was so enthusiastic, and he was my brother. He was always trying to convince me to go to one thing or another. I didn't object to giving it a try, as long as I didn't feel I was endangering my health. I want to make it clear, I—we—have nothing against spiritual exploration or whatever you might call it. The thing we're concerned about is helping sick people get proper medical care.'' Georgie was good. If her father had any sense, he'd make her the spokesperson for their organization.

''Any massage therapists? Leslie Getz?''

Georgie hesitated. Margo was sure she recognized Leslie's name, but was that because Teddy had been treated by her or because Leslie had recently been identified as the victim of the Deerhorn Valley fire?

''As I said,'' Georgie stated, ''we chose the two people Teddy seemed to trust the most and who had the most dubious credentials. Excuse me, I have to go. I have a patient waiting.''

Margo felt too tired and dispirited to make another call. Nevertheless, she forced herself to phone Donny Obayashi to say that Teddy Costas might have seen Leslie, as well as Hannah and Richard, for treatment.

Obayashi sounded as if he'd gotten more sleep last night than she had. He actually thanked her for the information, and volunteered his own, off the record, of course: that Scott had been picked up at his apartment the night before and was being held for questioning.

"Did he try to go to Paula's yesterday?"

"Not as far as I know. He says he spent the day wandering around on the beach. Whether he did or not, he must have spent quite a long time outdoors—he's got a hell of a sunburn.''

Once she'd hung up, Margo realized she had neglected to ask how long the police would keep Scott in custody. She found she didn't much care. Somehow the fact that Scott had neither rushed to Paula's nor, apparently, made any effort to go into hiding made him seem less of a threat; or maybe she was just too tired to give a damn. She had a raging headache, too.

Alone in her office, she took two aspirin, then held her amethyst crystal and closed her eyes. She thought of what Paula had said the night before: that Dylan was the only other person locally who had the kind of gift for healing that Leslie, Hannah, and Richard had possessed. Margo didn't know Dylan's phone number, but she thought she could find the apartment in North Park where Paula had dropped him off after the sweat lodge. She needed to do an interview that afternoon, about yet another public art project vetoed by the port district. But she had time to stop by Dylan's first, as long as she could force her eyes open and her body into motion.

*   *   *

Spartan was the word Dylan's lodgings brought to mind. Or maybe *spartan* implied more comfort than Dylan Lightwing permitted himself. The one-room apartment smelled of mold, and the only furniture was a rolled-up single futon bed, where Margo settled in a half-squat while Dylan fixed herbal tea, boiling the water on a hot plate. Some half-dozen articles of clothing hung on hooks on one wall, along with the drum he had used at the sweat lodge. There was a rotary dial telephone on the floor, and a few books were stacked neatly against a wall.

"I don't believe in possessions," he said, noting her scrutiny of the room as he brought over two mugs of tea and sat on the floor. At least he owned mugs. "The cop who came by earlier today thought it was weird, too."

"What cop?" she said, knowing he'd baited her but willing to be hooked.

"The one who took me into the station and grilled me about where I was when Leslie, Hannah, and Richard died. They didn't say, but I think it had something to do with hearing I might be in the habit of eating poison oak."

"Do you?"

Dylan's smile looked genuine. "You don't understand, and the cops sure don't understand. I wouldn't presume to call myself a shaman. It takes decades to develop that kind of wisdom. But I try to follow the discipline involved in shamanism. For example, I ingest a variety of things that others might consider poisons."

"Including poison oak."

"Including poison oak."

"You don't sound angry," observed Margo. "I assume you know I was the one who told the police about how someone could become immune to poison oak."

"Part of the initiation as a shaman is to undergo various

trials. People used to be buried in the earth, with only their heads exposed, for a full day, and members of the tribe would spit on them. It helped them give up their egos. Mind if I sit here?'' he added, moving onto the narrow rolled futon beside her.

Margo instantly became aware his physical closeness. *Admit it,* she told herself, *you're turned on.* If she believed it were possible, she would have said Dylan was deliberately secreting pheromones. Maybe it was a shamanic technique.

''The police didn't charge you,'' she said.

''They came up against a small problem. Lack of motive. Actually, two problems. When Hannah died, I was leading a retreat in Sedona, Arizona. Have you been to Sedona? It's one of the incredible power spots in the world.''

She shook her head. Was it her imagination, or had he inched closer? Was Paula's lover really making a move on her? Worse, was Margo turning to liquid inside? The answer to the last question was easy and humiliating: Yes. She knew she wasn't going to do anything—out of loyalty to Barry and to Paula, not to mention her distrust of Dylan. But her body had no such scruples. *Ambiguity,* she heard her internal mother saying again. She could do with a little certainty.

Margo stood abruptly, saying, ''Sedona. Isn't that close to where you were in prison?''

''Not far geographically, but Phoenix is no power spot, believe me.''

She left without asking what she had meant to—whether he could think of anyone who would have targeted the best healers in town and if he himself had received any invitations to intimate meetings in canyons. She had little question, however, that Dylan could take care of himself. He had laughed when she got up, as if he'd known exactly how he had affected her . . . and also knew that she would never dream of telling Paula. What was there to tell? That Paula's lover had gotten her thirty-eight-year-old hormones racing?

What about *his* hormones? she wondered. Maybe he had genuinely felt attracted to her. But Margo had a feeling that Dylan's lust had less to do with sex than with power.

Why would Dylan Lightwing want to have power over her, however? Just because he enjoyed manipulating people? Or was he trying to influence her in some specific way, for instance to divert her attention from the questions she was asking because he had something to hide? Dylan had an alibi for the time of Hannah's death; there were people who must have seen him at the retreat he was leading in Arizona—unless his shamanic practice was so advanced that he had learned to be in two places at one time. Maybe his secret had to do with something he knew about somebody else? Something he had found out the same way Olivia did, through a vision? Whatever she thought of visions, however, Margo trusted Olivia and she didn't trust Dylan Lightwing. *He has an alibi*, she reminded herself. Maybe, she admitted, she was only reluctant to drop Dylan as a suspect because she didn't like him as Paula's boyfriend. But being a lousy boyfriend didn't make someone a murderer; prisons would be overflowing if it did.

Whatever Dylan's reason for coming on to her, she had a feeling he had a lot more work to do if he wanted to abandon his ego.

34 / Widow's Mite

Cynara had dressed up this morning—a conservative silk dress, high-heeled pumps, even pantyhose—and the *click click click* of her heels as she walked through the underground parking downtown suited her mood. If she could drive one of those heels through Richard Del Vecchio's heart, right now, she'd do it.

She got into her car, squealed over the concrete . . . and had to pay four dollars to get out. That smirking lawyer—Raleigh of Witherspoon, Peake, Raleigh, and Keel—hadn't even validated her parking. She'd just bet Richard had chosen the lawyer because of the smirk. He'd probably imagined her coming here one day, hearing Raleigh say in his upper-class Boston accent, "Actually, I'm afraid there's no money" . . . and then having to see that *gotcha* smirk.

"What do you mean, there's no money?" she had questioned him. "Richard inherited several million dollars."

"He set up a foundation. He's been donating to various nonprofit organizations for years."

"Sure. He's been donating the interest."

Raleigh looked a little surprised that she was acquainted

with the difference between principal and interest—score one for her, but it was an empty victory.

"No, the principal as well," he said. He looked about Cynara's age chronologically. It pleased her to think that he was an extremely young soul who had years of suffering awaiting him in future lives.

"There must be something left," she said. "You can't make me believe he squandered his entire inheritance."

"Mr. Del Vecchio transferred the bulk of his money to the foundation. As you can see—" Raleigh tapped a manicured nail against a page of Richard's will—"from his personal assets, he left you a bequest of thirty thousand dollars, as well as full title to your, um, business, Crystal Magic."

"I was his wife, goddammit! Don't I have any say over what goes into foundations and what gets left to me?"

The lawyer steepled his fingers, a gesture that made Cynara want to slap him. "There was no pre-nup, of course," he said. "Still, it's a bit sticky, legally. You see, our office never knew that Mr. Del Vecchio was married. I gather you and he kept your marriage a secret?"

"But we were legally married." She picked up the license, which she had already shown him. "And how can you say you didn't know about me? There's his will, with me in it."

"I'm sorry."

"No, you're not!"

He arched a blond eyebrow. He looked like the kind of man who had grown up hanging out at "the club" every summer. Hell, with his name, he probably traced his ancestors to Sir Walter.

"I was going to say," he remarked, "that although you're named in the will, there is no mention of your being his wife. I understand that you and Mr. Del Vecchio hadn't lived together for . . . nine years? ten years? Now, the law gives you every right to contest. But I do feel compelled to caution you that, the way Mr. Del Vecchio, um, your husband, set things up, you may end up with attorney's fees greater than anything you might gain. Obviously, you couldn't be represented by this firm; it would constitute a conflict of interest. But I'd be happy to give you the names of some of my colleagues who are specialists in probate.''

Cynara leaned across the desk and spat at him. The spit landed on target, the smirking face.

That, she reflected, driving home at considerably over the speed limit, had been the one satisfying moment of the appointment——seeing her gob of spittle glistening on Raleigh's pale cheek and his instinctive moue of disgust, before he glued the smirk back on, removed an immaculate pressed white handkerchief from his breast pocket, and dabbed. (She'd bet he had raced to the men's room the second she left and was still scrubbing his face with soap and steaming water!) She wished she had a disease she could have transmitted to him, something that would cover that WASPy face with sores oozing pus. Hannah might have been able to do it. But such talents had been denied Cynara. And now the one thing to which she was truly entitled, Richard's money, was denied her as well. Was it worth consulting a lawyer? She had a feeling Raleigh's resources outweighed any she could call on. She could promise a lawyer a healthy percentage of anything she got, of course; but it infuriated her to think of any of *her* money going to one of Raleigh's buddies.

She got home and would have stormed inside but nearly tripped over the damn dog, lying in the doorway. She had kept Frodo ever since Tuesday, when she'd insisted she felt nervous alone in the shop and sent Richard off to his meeting alone.

She closed her door to keep the dog out while she took off her banker-impersonator outfit and changed into real clothes: an orange tunic, an Indian print skirt, and sandals. ''Let's go,

Frodo,'' she called. The dog followed her to the car, tail wagging, and jumped into the back seat. She regretted having brought him with her, however, when they got to Crystal Magic, and the mutt started to whine and pace. He could smell his master, thought Cynara. So could she. Richard had never placed a premium on bathing. She would hire a couple of teenagers and clean up the whole place, maybe this weekend. In fact, maybe she'd just sell the business and move . . . up the coast, for instance.

''Get real, Cynara,'' she said out loud. ''No one's going to want to buy this business if they look at the balance sheets.'' She and Richard had never been able to keep the store going on its own. It was always his monthly infusion of cash that allowed them to stay open. Was he being generous or malicious in giving her full ownership of the shop? How far did he think his thirty goddamn thousand dollars would take her?

A customer came in looking for a crystal, and she did her best to sell him one. She had watched Richard do it often enough. ''Emerald aids the eyes, memory, and speech. Some people say it also has a beneficial effect on cancer. Malachite is good for emotional distress and general health.'' But she couldn't make the sale.

''What are you laughing at?'' she asked the dog after the customer left; she'd swear it was grinning.

She looked into Frodo's brown eyes . . . and Richard stared back at her.

''Nuh uh.'' It occurred to her that she was talking to herself again. No, actually she was addressing Frodo. ''I am not going to get spooked,'' she told the dog. ''I am not going to start thinking Richard's spirit has gotten into your mangy body.''

She said that and variations to the dog several times that day. It didn't help that a police officer barged in and questioned her for an hour, the identical questions she'd answered the day before.

Was Richard in the shop early Tuesday afternoon? Yes.

What time did he leave? Around two-thirty.

Did he say where he was going? No.

Didn't you ask? No.

But you were husband and wife, right? Legally, but we hadn't been a couple for years.

Did anything happen right before he left? Did he get a phone call? Not that I remember, but we had some customers.

You're sure he didn't say anything about where he was going? I already said no.

What about an appointment calendar? I gave it to the other detective. (In a candle flame, she'd burned the scrap of paper where Richard had jotted down the meeting time and place.)

Where were you when he was gone? In the shop, of course.

You didn't leave at all? Not until six o'clock, when I closed up.

Were there customers? Sure, people always wander in.

Have you got the sales receipts for that afternoon? I gave a copy to someone.

I'd like to see them, too . . . Hmm. Your cash register doesn't mark the time of sale on the receipt. No, it's an old one.

What about the customers? Anyone you remember? Anyone who paid by credit card? I don't know.

By the time she was closing the store at six, Cynara was frantic. She locked up, then made a telephone call.

"What's up?" said Leslie's Lover, lightly.

"It's the dog. Every time I look at him, I see Richard's eyes."

"You're mourning. It's natural."

"Come over tonight?"

"I'm sorry. I've got plans."

"You think the phone is bugged or something?" Cynara said. "Why are you acting like this? You know that I know what you did."

"Um . . ."

"Except I bet the police haven't questioned *you* for two days in a row!"

"I don't think you should call me like this," remarked L.L. "Don't you have a friend who could come stay with you?"

"Fuck that. I'm getting questions like, 'Why doesn't your cash register print the time of sale?' I want to know, are we safe?"

"Sounds like the question is, are *you* safe? I don't see why not, since you really were in the store all afternoon."

"No, the question is, are *we* safe? And don't kid yourself. I'm not going to meet you in any canyon to discuss it."

A laugh. "We're fine. Well, there's one person I'm a bit concerned about. That radio reporter, Margo Simon. You know her, don't you?"

"We're not exactly bosom pals."

"But you know her. Why don't you call her, just girl-talk?"

"Girl-talk."

"Get some feeling for what she knows. Find out a little more about her."

"Like what?"

"Like, you're so upset about your husband's death, and does she know anything she hasn't been able to say on the radio? Or, what's she doing this weekend? Is there any time she's going to be alone? Use your imagination, Cynara."

"What about Frodo?"

"Who?"

"The dog. I can't stand being around him."

"Take him to the pound. Say he's a stray."

"All right," she said. The dog pushed its nose into her free hand. She couldn't help it. She looked at him . . . and saw Richard's eyes again. She felt like she was going to throw up.

35 / Girl-Talk

Margo had forgotten that the amethyst crystal was supposed to cure insomnia. But after holding it several times during the day, she came home from work early, went straight to bed, and fell into a delicious sleep.

She didn't even hear the phone ring three hours later. Barry had to wake her. It was Olivia.

"Olivia!" Margo still felt half-asleep.

Olivia's voice was taut, as if she'd been getting little sleep herself. "Have you found out anything?"

"The police questioned Ted Costas, but they haven't charged him. And Scott's in custody."

"It's not Ted Costas!"

"Olivia, how do you know that?"

"I told you. My grandmother was killed by someone she knew and trusted."

"What about Scott?"

"Maybe. I don't know."

"Olivia." Starting to feel awake, Margo repeated what Paula had said last night. "About your sense of your grandmother feeling betrayed—maybe it wasn't because she knew the person who killed her, but because they betrayed her faith in humanity?"

"It was someone she knew," insisted Olivia. "You don't believe me, do you?"

"I'm a reporter. I'm trained to base my judgments on facts." Margo heard a beep, her call waiting.

"Go ahead and get it."

"Don't hang up!" Margo begged, then pressed the switch-hook to connect with the other line.

"Margo! Hi! It's Cynara." The Tarot reader made it sound as if she called often.

"Cynara, can I call you back? I'm on the other line."

"Sure. I'm up till midnight." Cynara gave her the number, and Margo pressed the switch-hook again.

"Olivia? Are you there?"

"No, Margo, it's still Cynara."

She tried again, but Olivia had hung up. Damn!

"Hi," she said, returning to Cynara. "I'm sorry about Richard."

"What for?" Even acting friendly, Cynara hadn't lost her edge.

"You knew each other for years. You were in business together."

"Not to mention being married," added Cynara archly. "I heard it was getting around. Hey, I didn't know you and Olivia were friends. Is she okay?"

"She's fine." Margo had gone to bed without dinner and was becoming aware that she was ravenous.

"I've been thinking," said Cynara. "There've been a bunch of stories in the news about Richard since he died. They dug up some old picture of him with his hair down to his ass, and they're making him sound like some kind of mental case. You know, heir to family fortune drops out and starts weird hippie store. I'd like to talk about the real Richard, on the radio.''

''You mean you want me to interview you?''

''Well, yeah.''

''You know,'' she told Cynara, ''if we do an interview, I have to be able to ask you all kinds of questions. Like, did Richard have any enemies? Or, do you know if he was planning to talk to Ted Costas about some kind of out-of-court settlement of that lawsuit?''

''Yeah. Sure.''

''Or, how much money do you inherit?''

Cynara gave a bark of laughter.

''You do inherit, don't you?'' said Margo.

''Actually, very little. Richard set up a foundation and gave most of his money to various nonprofit organizations. We both thought that was the only moral thing to do.''

Margo questioned whether Cynara had ever had a moral impulse in her life, but decided to save her skepticism until she had the widow behind a microphone. She doubted Cynara had really called to request an interview, anyway, especially when Cynara continued:

''Margo, mind if I ask you a few questions?''

''Shoot.''

''Do the police have any idea who killed Richard?''

''Nothing they're telling me.''

''I just thought sometimes they start to narrow in on someone but they can't say anything until they have enough evidence to really make a case. Like, you mentioned Ted Costas earlier. Do they suspect him?''

''Who knows?'' Margo felt as if giving any snippet of information to Cynara was like having a little power drained out of her. She regretted that Cynara had found out she was in touch with Olivia. And she *had* to get off the phone and eat something. She said, "Why don't you come into the station sometime tomorrow?"

"I'm sorry?"

"For the interview."

"Oh. Well, I'm covering the store by myself, until I find someone to help out. Could you come there? No, that's a bad idea, I'd have to stop every time a customer came in. Well, I guess I don't really need to do an interview. I just wanted to talk to someone. How's your, uh, your stepdaughter doing? She wanted to . . . remember, you talked about her when you came into the shop."

"She wanted to pierce her nose, and she did it. Sorry, I've got to go. Bye."

Margo hung up without giving Cynara a chance to say anything else. She wanted to fumigate the phone to remove the taint of the woman's voice. She'd probably feel better once she ate. She wandered into the kitchen in the long T-shirt she wore as a nightgown and a pair of wool socks. Nick Costas was sitting at the big wooden kitchen table, eating a sandwich.

"Hi," said Margo with what she considered admirable calm, despite the adrenaline coursing through her. Yesterday Scott had surprised her at her office. Now Nick was making himself at home in her kitchen. Would Anne Costas show up next? And where?

"Hi." Nick scrambled to his feet, an exemplar of good if awkward manners.

"Margo, this is Nick." Jenny came in. "His house burned down and Dad said he could stay here for a few nights—sleeping on the couch," she added quickly. "He's coming on the research ship with us tomorrow."

"Well, hi, Nick," said Margo, reaching to shake his hand. "I'm sorry about your house. What kind of sandwich are you eating? It looks good." In fact, Margo was salivating just looking at it.

"Turkey and avocado."

"Want me to make you one?" offered Jenny.

"Sure. Thanks." Might as well take advantage of Jenny's stellar behavior, whether it was intended to impress Nick or to overcome any resistance Margo might have to his staying overnight.

Margo went back to bed shortly after she'd eaten and slept for nine hours. Barry, however, looked haggard the next morning. Margo had a feeling he'd kept peeking into the hall all night, guarding his daughter's bedroom door.

36 / Human Torch

Sitting in her car in a Burger King parking lot in El Cajon, Cynara lifted the cheeseburger she'd just bought to her lips. The smell of the cooked meat hit her nostrils, and she nearly gagged. She lowered the burger to her lap without biting into it.

"Richard, I won't let you do this to me," she said out loud. "You screwed me over for fifteen years in life. You aren't going to have any hold on me in death. And not that stupid animal, either," she said, as the image of Frodo came into her mind. The dog hadn't whined, he had just stared at her when she'd left him at the pound that morning. Stared at her with Richard's eyes.

Cynara, you fool! she chided herself. Richard did not inhabit Frodo's body, nor was he exerting any other effect on her from the afterlife. All that was happening was that she was feeling a surge of guilt, a ridiculous quality she didn't happen to believe in. Of course, she countered, if anyone could communicate from the beyond, Richard probably could. But why pay any more attention to him dead than she had given the live man for years? Defiantly, she took a big bite of cheeseburger. Bile came up in her throat.

"Shit!"

She threw the damn thing out the window, peripherally aware that three or four kids in a neighboring car were staring at her. She made a face at them. She wished she *did* have power. She'd like to turn them into toads.

At least she could eat her fries. She wanted to eat something before she went to the ceremony in the mountains, something substantial, since the only food at the ceremony was sure to be crap like bulgur casseroles. Not just vegetarian but vegan, no eggs or cheese. She pushed a couple of fries into her mouth . . . and got a hit of nausea so intense that sweat broke out on her forehead. She spat out the fries and tossed the bag out the window. A one-woman littering squad. A pimply adolescent in a goofy uniform was coming toward her, probably alerted by the mom in the next car. Cynara started her car and backed up fast, smiling as she made the pimply kid jump. She zoomed out of the parking lot and back to the 8 freeway.

Who the fuck had thought it was a swell idea to hold this thing in the Cuyamaca Mountains? Didn't she have some say, as Richard's widow? Not that anyone had consulted her. To get to the damn site, you had to take 8 east and then go north on Sunrise Highway, which was some demented engineer's idea of a roller-coaster for adults—constant twists and turns and a constant need to keep her eyes on the road because every five seconds it changed direction. In a nice car, like that silver Miata she'd seen Margo Simon driving, this might be fun. But Cynara had never had a really nice car.

Richard had always given her just enough that she'd hesitated to break with him completely (afraid, too, of what his lawyers would make of their secret marriage when it came to a divorce settlement). But it was *just enough* to pay her rent; *just enough* for a car that ran, not one that she might actually enjoy driving; *just enough* to keep her clothed like a hippie, more and more of an anachronism as she got older. Not that she wanted to dress the way she had when she'd gone to see Richard's lawyer—prim, tailored, and boring. But suddenly she had a ferocious desire for a closetful of silk. Blouses, skirts, dresses, underwear. And every kind of silk—slinky camisoles that would drive a lover wild; a jacket, maybe bright red, in raw silk that she could run her hand over, sensually feeling the slubs.

Thirty thousand dollars could buy a lot of silk. The only minor problem was continuing to eat and maintain a roof over her head for the coming thirty or forty years; and her family was long-lived. Damn Richard! With her anger, her appetite returned. She wished she had kept the food in the car. Fuck. At the ceremony, she'd get nothing but grains or maybe lentils disguised (poorly) to resemble something else—she'd once been served lentil chopped liver. And they probably wouldn't even get to eat until the ceremony was over.

If she ever got there. This road felt like it would never end. She pulled over, checked her map. Okay, she was close.

Waiting before the thing started, Cynara thought she'd scream every time someone came over and gave her a sympathetic hug. And no one in this crowd settled for unobtrusive little cheek pecks. She kept being pulled into two-minute bear hugs. Finally, a young woman with that sallow, unhealthy vegan complexion and a garland of autumn leaves in her hair (*how swe-eet*) announced that it was half an hour before sunset. She led the group, which numbered about fifty, down a path. At the end of the path, they had to pass, one by one, through an archway made of branches. Just inside the archway, two more pale young people, a man and a woman, were waving smudge sticks—smoking bundles of dried sage about the size and shape of a large cigar—around each person's body to purify them.

"Cynara," someone said.

She turned to see Paula Chopin in line behind her. She looked past Paula, who was mumbling the usual condolences about Richard.

"Isn't your friend with you?" asked Cynara.

"Dylan? He really wanted to be here, but he got a call from his teacher in Arizona and he had to go. I took him to the bus this afternoon."

"Not Dylan! Margo, the radio reporter." Bile rose in her throat again.

"No, she's got the house to herself tonight, and she really wanted some time alone."

Cynara reached out blindly, feeling faint.

"Are you okay?" said Paula, putting a hand on her shoulder.

"Yeah." She couldn't bear to look at Paula for another minute . . . and definitely not to be touched by her. She shook off the hand. Couldn't this line hurry up? The young smudgers were really getting into it, however. Even though there were two of them, they only did one person at a time, waving the smoking sage around the person's head infinitely slowly and then gradually moving down the body as if they were performing a dance. Sheesh!

When Cynara got to the archway, she tried moving fast, but the man grabbed her arm; he was stronger than he looked. The acrid scent of burning sage hit her as the two smudge sticks came at her head from either side. Shit! They'd gotten too close. Sparks had landed in her hair. Her hands flew to her head, pressing her hair to extinguish the fire. She yelled at the kids, who just looked scared and stepped back. Jesus, why weren't they helping her put out the fire?

"I'm burning," she cried. She felt her hair flaring up and igniting her clothes. "Water!"

"Cynara, you're okay. Nothing's on fire," said someone behind her.

She didn't register the words, just the presence. She turned, saw Paula, and screamed.

"It's okay," Paula said again. "You're not burning."

Cynara felt like a torch. Everything was so hot, she could feel her skin blistering.

"Water!" she cried. Someone brought water, but just a cup of it, the cretin. Cynara poured it over her hair. "More!"

Her clothes were flaming. She rolled on the ground. Why wasn't anyone helping her?

37 / Sunrise Highway

"Cynara! Cynara!" Paula knelt beside her, trying to stop her from rolling around. "You're not on fire. Is it something about Margo?" she said, thinking of how Cynara had reacted when she'd said Margo was spending the night alone.

"More water!" screamed Cynara.

"Someone bring water," Paula yelled; Cynara really seemed to believe she was burning. "You've got to tell me about Margo." Paula tried to force the Tarot reader to look at her, but Cynara was too far gone.

Yelling, she started tearing her clothes off. She was half-undressed when someone brought a bucket of water. She poured the whole bucketful over herself. Several healers had come to her and were trying to calm her down.

"Is there a phone here?" called out Paula, pushing her way back through the line. "Does anyone have a car phone?" This was the wrong crowd to ask. At a professional gathering, half the accountants would have replied yes. Here, Paula got nothing but blank stares.

She didn't even try to find the friend who had come with her. She just jumped into her car and started driving. Paula believed in ESP, but she'd never thought she had any personal gifts in that area. Still, she couldn't stop feeling that Margo was in some kind of danger. Couldn't stop thinking, her heart in her throat, *Margo lives on a canyon.*

What bliss! thought Margo, sipping an excellent Chardonnay while she sat on the patio and admired the sunset. Barry and the kids, including Nick Costas, had left on the research vessel after school, so she'd come home from work to a gloriously empty house. She had opened the wine and poured a glass, put scented oil in the bath, and soaked for so long, savoring the first glass of wine and then another, that her fingers metamorphosed into fragrant pink prunes; and she had a lovely buzz on. Finally she'd risen from the tub, feeling like a pampered, slightly tipsy goddess, and put on her softest clothes, well-worn jeans and a twenty-year-old University of Wisconsin sweatshirt; the sweatshirt had a few holes in it, but who was going to see? She'd poured more wine, started the coals for the barbecue, and proceeded to enjoy the sunset.

After the last rays touched the canyon, she checked the coals. The environmentally responsible metal chimney (that eliminated the need for charcoal lighter) had done its job. The coals were perfect. She spread them in the barbecue, put a fresh salmon steak, lightly brushed with olive oil, on the grill, and went inside to make salad. She had treated herself to gourmet salad ingredients, arugula and radicchio, that she sampled as she washed them, loving the bitter, almost peppery taste.

Georgie Costas? she wondered, measuring olive oil and raspberry vinegar for the salad dressing. Unlike her father, Georgie had been open to Teddy's forays into New Age spirituality, had maybe met some of his healers . . .

Forget it, Margo commanded herself. She had been through

a rotten couple of weeks. She intended to have one lovely evening.

She set a place at the dining room table, lit three candles, and put on a Villa-Lobos CD that included the composer's haunting "Bachianas Brasilieras." Back to the grill: The fish looked divine. Margo lingered over her meal, then went back outside carrying a tray with her dessert—Viennese roast decaf and her all-time favorite, citrus sour cream cake from the bakery whose owner had studied at the Cordon Bleu in Paris. The tray also held a plate of cooled salmon for Grimalkin.

"Grimalkin! Here, kitty!"

The cat didn't respond. Funny, now that she thought about it, that Grimalkin hadn't been hanging out on the patio, rubbing greedily against her leg, every second the fish cooked.

"Grimalkin!"

She took a few seconds to put on the sneakers she kept on the patio, clay-grimed since she wore them for doing pottery, and started down the path into the canyon that the kids, and kids before them, had worn through the chaparral.

Paula didn't give a damn how scared she was, driving the twisting mountain road. She had made it up the road just fine—so what if it was in the daylight instead of shadowy dusk and with a friend in the passenger seat? She had to stop crying, or she wouldn't be able to see to drive. A therapist she used to go to had taught her to be an observer, to identify her symptoms and rank them from one to ten, ten being a full-blown, take-no-prisoners panic attack. She was feeling tightness in her chest, that was about a six. Heart pounding, a seven. A sense of doom, that got her up to an eight . . . but was that a panic symptom or just her real fear about Margo?

Curve. Curve. Sharp curve, she had to slow to twenty, no, fifteen, miles an hour. Around the curve, she stepped on the gas, back up to thirty-five. Wasn't there anyplace along this road that would have a telephone—a market or a bar? Dirt roads led off the highway, and she thought of trying one, to see if anyone was at their weekend place. But what if she took a side road and found no one, just lost twenty minutes? Better keep going until she reached the bottom of Sunrise Highway. There had to be a phone along Highway 8.

The sun had set, and now everything looked fuzzy. Or was that a number nine, blurred vision?

Keep going, Paula, she commanded herself. *Faster!*

38 / Sacred Fire

"Here, kitty!" Margo moved further along the path, holding the plate of salmon. "Dinner!"

She thought she heard a familiar meow, but Grimalkin didn't come. She hastened down the path. It occurred to her to go back to the house for a flashlight, but the meow hadn't sounded far away, and she didn't want to take the time. Most likely Grimalkin had done nothing worse than getting stuck in a bush, but in the canyons, cats were prey to hawks and occasional coyotes; she hoped he hadn't had a run-in with anything that saw him as dinner.

"Here, kitty!" she kept calling.

She must have misjudged the cat's position, she realized, descending deeper into the canyon and still hearing mewing ahead of her. Damn! She should have brought the flashlight after all. She'd come too far to bother with it now. She kept going, the chaparral not just rustling but clattering in the wind. Santa Anas, she'd learned from a meteorologist last week, could blow up to a hundred miles per hour.

"Grimalkin? Are you there?"

This time the meow was close.

"I'm coming!" She bent down as she walked, figuring the cat had wandered into an interesting-smelling patch of flora and been unable to wander out. Her nostrils filled with a bouquet of scents, predominantly sage.

Meow!

The path had gotten steep, and in the dark Margo half-fell into the man holding Grimalkin, squeezing the cat to make him mew. She instantly recognized the man, whether by silhouette or by some more primitive sense than vision, and she stepped back, poised to flee. But she could identify the silhouette of the other thing the man held, besides Grimalkin: a gun, pointed straight at her.

"Dylan?" she said.

Her mind felt like three radios playing at once, all of them jabbering questions at her: Wasn't Dylan supposed to be at the ceremony in the mountains tonight? What about his alibi for Hannah's murder? And if he had killed his fellow healers, then *why?*

Out of the static—the fear—she managed to get out one sentence. "What's going on?"

"Don't move. And don't yell." Definitely Dylan's voice. He gently dropped Grimalkin, who ran to her.

Yelling was exactly what she ought to do, screaming like a banshee while she raced up the path. He wouldn't really shoot her, would he? Okay, maybe he'd shoot, but how good were his chances of hitting her in the dark? Margo half-turned but stumbled over the cat, which had twined itself around her ankle.

"I said don't move!" Dylan took a step closer, and she heard a sound she recognized from movies. He had removed the gun's safety.

"Okay." Until she thought of a better plan, she would follow his instructions. At the moment, her knees felt so wobbly that she was amazed she could still stand up.

"I'm going to step aside," said Dylan. "I want you to get ahead of me." He stepped into the bushes, keeping the gun on her. His voice had the same authority as in the sweat lodge . . . as if he had done this before.

"I just want to put down this food for Grimalkin, okay?" she said, realizing that she was still holding the plate of salmon.

"Just drop it."

She did. Nevertheless, Grimalkin ignored the fish and continued to cleave to her ankle as she walked past Dylan.

"Keep going," he said, now walking behind her.

Margo considered her alternatives. She could still try running. But they were moving deeper into the canyon, and she wanted to go up. She couldn't run back past him on the narrow path, and it would be foolish to climb into the dense chaparral—too easy to get stuck. She'd have to keep her eyes open for another path. Or what if she dashed ahead of him and hid? But how long would it take him to find her? She had a feeling Dylan was far more experienced at getting around in the dark than she.

Meanwhile, she thought, *keep him talking. And start small.* "Were you Paula's breather?"

"Yeah. When I saw her at Hannah's church that day, I recognized her car and the bumper sticker. She *gave* me her phone number." As if Paula had invited him to terrorize her.

"Did you leave the Tarot cards under her windshield wiper, too? Death and the Queen of Pentacles?"

"I wanted to shake her up a little, you know, keep her off balance. After I got to know her, I realized she didn't have any idea she had seen me . . . and there were a lot more pleasant ways to control her."

You shit! Margo wanted to say. But she didn't want to antagonize him. She wanted him to keep talking. Especially now that they'd gotten to the piece of the puzzle that had made her drop her suspicion of Dylan Lightwing—his alibi.

"How could Paula have seen you? I thought you were in Arizona when Hannah was killed." She raised her voice. Maybe some of her neighbors were sitting on their decks.

"Not so loud." Dylan poked her with the gun again. "I *was* leading a retreat in Arizona, outside Sedona, when Hannah left her physical body. At the retreat, we did a vision quest—one day and one night where we all went into the mountains alone. Everyone saw me go into the mountains, and everyone saw me come back down the next morning."

He paused, and Margo supplied the expected, "But?"

"I had my motorcycle in a cave."

She had to remind herself to keep looking for escape paths. Listening to Dylan, she felt mesmerized, not just drawn in by her own curiosity but as if his presence behind her were the only thing keeping her moving, and it kept her moving where he wanted her to go. They were heading not merely downhill but to the west, the wind at their backs.

"But why?" she said.

"Why did I keep my motorcycle in the cave?" He didn't sound ironic. Margo felt like throwing up.

"Why did you kill Hannah?"

"It was my spiritual path. With Leslie, it started out as an accident. We went into the canyon, smoked a joint, drank some brandy, and made love. Making love, we must have kicked over the abalone shell we were ashing the joint into— Les was *real* active, especially outdoors. I guess the shell still had something hot in it, a roach we hadn't put out all the way. Anyway, the canyon was real dry, and some of the stuff started smoldering."

"But you got out."

"Yeah. I was awake when the fire flared up. And I wasn't as drunk or stoned as Leslie."

"Couldn't you get her out?"

"She didn't want me to."

"What do you mean? Did Leslie tell you she wanted you to leave her in the fire?"

"I tried to wake her. But she'd passed out completely. I was going to carry her. Then I saw!" He paused, but only for effect. "It was Leslie's path to leave her body that night. And my path was to open my spirit fully, more than I ever had before, so her spirit could merge with mine. See, the body, the physical shell, wasn't important. It could have been my physical body burning and Leslie's body that was going to carry both out souls."

But it wasn't.

"Helping her make the transition from the physical plane to the purely spiritual was incredible," Dylan said. "I could feel her soul; it was ecstatic. When I'd incorporated her soul, I left." He sounded as if he'd been longing to share this marvelous experience.

"Did you take her car to Mexico?"

"Very sharp."

"What about Hannah and Richard? Why did you kill them?" she said, looking up. Although they weren't yet in the deepest part of the canyon, the nearest house—with no lights on—perched high above them.

"It was so beautiful with Leslie. I knew I could make it even more sacred if I planned it. I built beautiful pyres for them. This way."

The gun in Margo's back prodded her off the path into the brush, Grimalkin still padding beside her. Tears flooded her eyes. She forced them back. She had to remain rational. And she had to try to get away!

Now!

Crouching to make herself a smaller target, she took off into the brush.

Dylan didn't shoot at her. In fact, she could swear he was

laughing. Margo heard him laugh again, seconds later, when she crashed into something big—a pile, perhaps three feet high and four across, of dry branches that scraped her arms and face when she fell on them. A pyre. Even though she'd known this was what he must have planned for her, she had denied it until now. Every sense heightened by fear, she picked herself up, grabbing a thick branch with both hands. But as she had figured, Dylan's night vision was keen.

"Put the branch down," he said, casually walking to catch up with her, and aiming the gun as if he knew exactly how to use it.

She dropped the branch. A line from a folk song came into her mind: *She knelt down before him, pleading for her life.* Pleading hadn't done the trick for Pretty Polly, however, and it didn't come naturally to Margo.

"I don't understand," she said. "You have such gifts yourself. Why would you need anyone else's gift?" When she spoke, however, she remembered what Paula had said about Dylan's insecurity.

He was silent a moment, as if pondering his answer. "You're right, you don't understand. It isn't that I, Dylan, wanted what Leslie or Hannah or Richard had. It's that *we* wanted to merge our abilities. Like I said, it didn't really matter which of our physical bodies carried them . . . except for Hannah, I suppose, since she was so old."

Margo only half-listened. He would have to tie her up, she thought; that meant he'd have to put the gun down. She could make a break then. Nor had she exhausted her verbal arsenal.

"My husband should be home now," she said. "He was working late. He'll see my car and come looking for me."

"Nice try. He's on a boat."

"Aren't you supposed to be at that ceremony tonight?" Margo persisted. "Won't they miss you?"

"I had an urgent call from my teacher in Arizona. I had to leave this afternoon."

"A phone call?"

"That's not how we communicate. Turn around."

"Leslie, Hannah, and Richard were gifted healers. I don't have the ability to heal anyone. How is it part of your spiritual path to kill me?" She wasn't kneeling, but she heard the plea in her voice.

"Ah, you have gifts you're not aware of. Knowing the right questions to ask is an essential part of the shaman's path. You knew to talk to Hannah about poison oak. You gained Olivia's confidence. You figured out what I did with Leslie's car. And yesterday you asked me an important question, about the prison I was in."

"I did?" Margo vaguely recalled bringing up Dylan's time in prison. She had done it to short-circuit the sexual tension between them. Jesus, what had she said?

"You helped the cops find out I did time, but all they cared about was what I was in for. I figured you were going to start asking what I did there. See, I used to volunteer for the work crews that fought fires."

"And that's how you know how to start a fire?"

"I told you, you have the gift of knowing the right questions. Turn around."

When she did, he knocked her out with the gun.

Awareness returned by degrees. Margo's head hurt like hell, not just an ache in the back of her head that made her keep her eyes closed, but something pulling tightly across her mouth and cheeks—a gag, she realized. Her arms were pulled uncomfortably behind her and sharp things stuck into her back. Oh God, the pyre. There was a funny weight on her chest, too—what in the world? Margo opened her eyes, saw

Grimalkin sitting on her chest and, beyond the cat, the orange of flames.

A medium-sized bonfire, it was some hundred yards down the canyon—close to her house, although that was the least of her immediate worries. She tried to scream, but Dylan had gagged her efficiently; all she got out was a croak. He had bound her well, too, not just tying her wrists behind her back, but securing her legs to thick, heavy branches. Struggling in an attempt to roll off the pyre only brought fresh pain from the thorny wood beneath her. She struggled nonetheless, hoping at least to push Grimalkin away.

The cat dug his claws into her chest, and Margo gave in to terror. Every orifice of her body opened. Tears erupted from her eyes. Her bladder and bowels released, and she felt piss and shit dampening her jeans.

"That's it, let go of the body," said a voice near her.

She turned her head to the left. Dylan was standing beside her.

"I'll help you make the transition from the physical plane," he said. "I'll stay with you as long as I can."

"No!" she tried to yell but only grunted. She pushed up her chest, hoping to make him notice the cat. Creature of instinct, Grimalkin would take off when the fire got closer, but it might be too late by then for him to find an escape route. There was no reason to fry Grimalkin; Dylan could save him. But Dylan didn't understand or didn't want to. She looked down the canyon again. The bonfire had gotten larger. Wouldn't someone notice?

"It takes a little longer at night." Dylan followed her gaze. "But this brush is bone-dry, and the wind's strong. It'll catch. She-it!" he exclaimed, hearing the scream of a siren. "I'd better go speed things up." He ran toward the fire.

A minute later the fire flared up. Then Dylan was running

back, carrying a blazing branch aloft like an athlete sprinting to ignite the Olympic flame. If Margo's body had had anything left to release, she would have done it. He meant to torch the pyre.

39 / Death-Fires Dance

Bright lights flooded the canyon, coming from the side Margo lived on. Blinded by the lights, she couldn't make out what was happening, but she had a sense of noise and activity. Oh God, would they spot her, with the smoke thickening around her? And if they did see her, would they get to her before Dylan did?

She squirmed in her bonds, hoping the movement would catch someone's eye, expecting that any second Dylan would return and light the pyre. But he didn't come. Margo lifted her head and saw flashes of flame through the smoke. When the lights had come on, he must have started using his torch to ignite the dry brush around him.

She heard a roar. Fire now filled the canyon, not more than seventy yards away. Grimalkin, thank heaven, fled.

She was hearing something else now—men's voices. "Get that fool out of there!" They must be talking about Dylan, highly visible as he torched the brush. Please, didn't they see her? She kept moving, a frantic shimmy on the branches that ripped into her back. She would have wept, but her eyes felt sucked dry. Thinking of an exercise they'd done in dance class two nights ago, she alternately arched her back and did her best to jackknife her upper body and legs together, pouring all her strength into raising her legs in spite of the heavy wood tied to them. With an internal *sproing!*, her back went out.

"Forget it, the guy's toast," one of the firefighters said . . . and then called her name. "Margo, where are you? Margo!"

Could they possibly see her through the smoke? She kept arching and contracting, in spite of the pain spasming her lower back . . . and finally rolled off the pyre. Now to stand up.

"Margo, we see you. We're coming!"

Through the haze, she saw two firefighters running toward her. One, aiming a hose, watered down the vegetation around them. The other cut her legs free and released her gag. She had forced herself to her feet a moment ago; now she couldn't stand. The man slung her over his shoulder.

"We're going to get you out of here," he told her.

"Oh, Christ!" his partner yelled. "A blowout!"

Her rescuer flung her to the ground face down and flung himself on top of her. Her back cried out and her arms, still tied, felt as if they were pulling out of her shoulders. "Don't move," he said. "And keep your eyes closed." As if it mattered. In the second before he'd thrown her down, she'd glimpsed a wall of flame that had to be thirty feet high.

Now the other fireman hit the ground, the two of them covering her body with theirs in their protective gear. For some bizarre reason, she was getting drenched. Had it started to rain?

Then came the heat and roar. Margo opened her eyes despite the firefighter's order, sure she was about to see her last sight on earth. Everything was brilliant orange and so painful that she squeezed her eyes shut against it. Her lungs hurt, too.

She tried not to breathe. But her body fought her and gasped the searing air.

"I love you, Barry," she said in her mind. "I love you, Jenny. I love you, David. I love you, Mom. I love you, Barry. I love you, Jenny. I love you, David. I . . ."

"Hey! Hey! Are you all right?" It was one of the firefighters. She was amazed she could hear him over the roar of the fire.

Then she realized the roar had diminished. Opening her eyes, she saw that the fire had passed through that part of the canyon, devouring everything except herself and the two firemen.

"Are you okay?" repeated the fireman, cutting her arms free.

She nodded, unable to speak. Her lungs and throat felt as if they'd been blowtorched. How the hell, she thought—astonished at her mind's ability to leap from the jaws of death into the mouse-teeth of the mundane—was she going to produce this story if she couldn't utter a word?

* * *

"A blowout," Margo half-whispered to Barry and the kids from her hospital bed two days later, "happens when a spark suddenly ignites a whole area."

She had suffered smoke inhalation but only minor burns, having been well protected by Phil and Hernando; the two firefighters had occupied a room down the hall for a day, burned themselves, but not badly. In fact, Margo had been less injured by the fire than by her struggles on the pyre. She'd had to have several deep cuts stitched up, and she was lying in traction for her sprained lower back. The torn muscles in her shoulders would, the doctors assured her, heal in their own time, which she suspected meant agonizingly slowly. She didn't know when she'd be able even to reach up and brush her own hair, a task Jenny was now performing gently. Grimalkin was the one party who'd survived unscathed; the cat had made it to the street and been scooped into the car of an evacuating neighbor.

"When they saw the blowout, what did Phil and Hernando do?" asked David. He already knew the answer; actually, he knew the whole story, Margo having managed to croak it out to Claire the day before, for national as well as local broadcast. But David—all of them—seemed to want to hear it directly from her.

Pausing frequently for sips of water, she said, "They got me face down on the ground, where there's the most oxygen, and they covered me with their bodies, since they had on protective suits. Then they both pointed their hoses up and put them on 'full fog.' That made a fountain of water all around us. So even though everything else burned up, we were okay."

The hoses had partially melted, but she left out that part of the story. Nor did she have much memory of the trip back up the hill, Phil carrying her as she drifted in and out of consciousness.

"Were you scared?" asked Jenny gravely.

"Yes."

"What did you think about?" Jenny must have given Margo's hair two hundred strokes, but she kept brushing.

"I thought how much I love you all." A tear formed in Margo's eye. Tears all around, in fact.

The door to her room opened—more visitors. Had Paula and Donny Obayashi come together, or simply arrived at the same time?

"Have Paula and Donny tell you what they did," she said, too drained to continue.

Those stories, too, had been on KSDR. Still, Margo welcomed the respite from talking as Paula told about Cynara's hallucination that she was on fire and Paula's own presentiment that Margo was in danger. After her wild drive down the Sunrise Highway, she'd stopped at the first gas station and insisted on making a call even though they had no public telephone. Reaching Obayashi, she had persuaded him that Margo might be in serious trouble. He had taken it from there. It was thanks to them that the fire crews had arrived so quickly and that they'd been looking for Margo.

Obayashi had then contacted the sheriff's department to pick up Cynara. Medicated out of her delusions, she'd simply said she was suffering from grief over Richard. But her phone records showed calls to Dylan shortly before, as well as after, Richard's death. Cynara now had a new home, the city jail.

"Off the record," said Obayashi, sternly catching Margo's eye, "she thought Richard's spirit had entered his dog. She got to where she couldn't stand to see the dog. She had to take it to the pound."

Paula placed a hand on his arm. "Can I talk to Margo alone?" she said.

Barry took the kids out, promising to return in a few minutes, and Obayashi told Paula he'd wait for her outside.

I'm sorry about Dylan, Margo thought of saying, but she could muster no sympathy for Paula's dead lover. Paula, in fact, said it.

"I'm sorry about Dylan. I told him you were going to be alone on Friday night."

"You didn't know," replied Margo.

"I still don't understand how he could have been a murderer. You'll laugh, but the best way I can say it is, he was highly evolved in so many ways."

"One of the major tasks of adult life."

"To become highly evolved?"

"To accept ambiguity." She'd have to discuss this with

her mother, who was flying out from Connecticut that afternoon. "Hey, what's with you and Donny?"

"We had brunch together this morning and then came over here. That's all."

"What did you talk about? Your ex? His ex? Or are you both past that?" Hard to have a good gossip when one's voice was a croak.

"Mostly we talked about drug treatment for panic disorder. He's really studied it."

"Are you gonna try?"

"Maybe. But you know, even though Dylan was a rotten apple, I think the New Age people are right to be wary of Western medicine."

"Hmm." At the moment, Margo had nothing but gratitude for Western medicine, especially painkillers.

"You call if you want anything." Paula kissed Margo's cheek and left.

Margo had expected the family, but Barry re-entered the room alone. The expression on his face immediately made her ask, "What?"

He sat down.

"What is it?" she said again. Had they lied to her about Grimalkin escaping the fire?

"The house," he said. "It was badly damaged. Our renter's insurance will cover some of the cost. But a lot of things are gone."

For a moment, Margo felt a biting sense of loss that focused, ridiculously, on her hat collection. Vividly she pictured the dozen or so berets, fedoras, and so on, gathered over the years, hanging on their pegs on the bedroom wall. Then she started to laugh.

"It's all right," she assured Barry, who looked as if he were about to summon a nurse to deal with her hysteria. "I just thought of something. Where are you staying now?"

"The kids are with Rae. I'm bunking with Sam and Trish," he said, naming fellow oceanographers. "They're about to spend six months in Australia studying the Great Barrier Reef. We could sublet their house while the landlord repairs ours . . . or while we decide if we just want to rent somewhere else."

She was laughing again. "Really, I'm fine. Would Sam and Trish mind if we had a dog?"

Barry didn't even do a double take. "Probably not. Do you think Grimalkin would adjust?"

"Yeah, this is a mellow old dog. He won't threaten Grimalkin. But you have to call the pound right away!" She gestured to the bedside phone. "His name is Frodo."